MOON & SUN

II

HOLLY LISLE

MOON
& SUN

THE SILVER DOOR

RIVER FOREST PUBLIC LIBRARY

ORCHARD BOOKS
NEW YORK
An Imprint of Scholastic Inc.

Library of Congress Cataloging-in-Publication Data
Lisle, Holly.
The silver door / Holly Lisle. — 1st ed.
p. cm. — (Moon & sun ; bk. 2)
Summary: When Genna is chosen as the Sunrider of prophecy,
her destiny is to unite the magic of the sun and the moon for the
good of both nightlings and humans.

ISBN-13: 978-0-545-00014-7; ISBN-10: 0-545-00014-9

[1. War — Fiction.   2. Fantasy.]   I. Title.
PZ7.L69116Si 2009
[Fic] — dc22
2008040153

10 9 8 7 6 5 4 3 2 1   09 10 11 12 13

Printed in the U.S.A.
Reinforced Binding for Library Use
First edition, April 2009
Book design by Phil Falco

FOR MATT, BECKY,
MARK, AND JOE, WITH
ALL MY LOVE

MOON & SUN II

CHAPTER 1
MASTER NAVAN

I had thought learning the magic of the sun wizards would be the most fascinating subject in the world. I was wrong.

"Again, repeat after me," Master Navan said. "I am. *Be sha.*"

I sighed and repeated what he'd said.

"He is. *Noen sha.* She is. *Haen sha.*"

Beside me, my best friend, Catri, shifted in her seat. Next to her, Yarri, with her dandelion-fluff hair and green-to-the-edges nightling eyes, yawned and hid the yawn behind her hand. Doyati, black-haired and blue-eyed, looked sidelong at me and his left cheek — the one I could see — dimpled. He'd not had dimples as a hundred-year-old man, but as a boy of perhaps fifteen or sixteen, he had them. I blushed.

"It is." Master Navan's nasal voice grew sharper as he noticed our attention was not on him. *"Ruen sha."*

We studied in the library of Doyati's magnificent suite on the Kai — or royal — level of the underground nightling city of Arrienda. We had the comfort of well-padded chairs, beautiful surroundings, and sturdy tables set with fresh fruit, nuts, and hard bread. We should have been comfortable, curious, and fascinated by our studies.

Instead, my brother Danrith, visiting for the day, gave me a look of bored desperation. All I could do was shrug while I repeated the Tagasuko phrases. These awful classes with Master Navan, and the tasks he set us afterward, had been my life, and Catri's, and Doyati's, and Yarri's, for nearly three months.

Danrith had sat in on classes with us when my family visited before, and afterward he could only talk about how grateful he was to be training with Papa to become Hillrush's next headman. I envied him his teacher. I missed Mama, who had been mine before everything changed.

"We are. *Beni shan.*"

Three months of learning Tagasuko, the language of the sun wizards, and I could barely read it, could speak only a few pitiful phrases, and could not grasp at all how speaking the sun wizard tongue would be useful in wielding magic, which for me worked just fine in Osji, the language of my own people.

Prior to everyone around me coming to the conclusion that I was the long-awaited Sunrider, my mother had been training me to become a yihanni — a village wisewoman — like her. She had been a wonderful teacher. She demonstrated what I needed to know, I did what she did until I got it right, and I learned.

But Master Navan insisted that to command sun wizard magic, we had to be fluent in sun wizard words. Doing things Master Navan's way, if I lived to be as old as Doyati, I thought I might know Tagasuko. I'd be too old by then to do anyone any good, though.

"They are. *Rueni shan.*"

The cat, draped across the thick, overstuffed back of my chair and feigning sleep, spoke directly into my thoughts. *I could rip out his eyes and then he would stop this torture.*

I forced myself to swallow the laugh that almost burst from me. Master Navan had no tolerance for laughter, and I suspected had never laughed in his life. *You keep offering,* I replied, *but you never actually do it.*

"You are . . . for one person. *Su sha.*"

The cat thought to me, *Well, he did say he'd finally found documents that explained what you and Doyati are*

3

supposed to do as Sunrider and Moonspinner. And he did at least suggest that he'd tell you what he found out today. I thought maybe I could rip his eyes out afterward.

Master Navan droned, "You are . . . for many people. *Suni shan.*" All of us except the cat repeated after him.

The cat is not a cat. This much he has admitted. What he is, I have no clue. I don't even know his name, for he won't tell it. He answers to "cat" if he answers at all. He knows magic, he says he's not quite as old as Doyati, and he walks the moonroads and fears them. Beyond that, I know he hunts mice and bugs and chases the occasional bird when he gets the chance, because I have seen him do it — but he's embarrassed by this.

"Everyone is," said Master Navan. *"Benini shan."*

If I knew the sun wizard word for "bored," I could say the sentence "Everyone is bored," loudly in Tagasuko, and my fellow sufferers would laugh, and Master Navan would get red in the face and assign us extra studies.

So I suppose it was lucky I didn't know the word for "bored."

Master Navan cleared his throat. "I do not believe I have your full attention."

We all looked at him, our expressions variations on

boredom and weariness and desperate longing to be somewhere — *any*where — else.

Anywhere.

Some of our desperation seemed to break through the blanket of self-importance he wrapped around himself, for he coughed once, cleared his throat, and said, "Well, perhaps you have had enough of language studies for a bit. We could move on to what I've discovered about the roles of the Moonspinner and Sunrider, I suppose."

In my mind, the cat's voice said, *Oh, could we? And how will you make* that *dull enough to kill us, old man?*

That time, the laugh got away from me, and Master Navan turned on me as a snake turns on a mouse. "You don't take this seriously," he snarled at me. "You're a child, a *girl*, and why all these fools think you're the Sunrider I shall never understand."

"They think it because she is," Doyati said, coming out of his chair and to his feet in one smooth, threatening movement. "The audiomaerist says it. The nightling scholars say it. Even the human scholars say it."

"And according to them, you're supposed to be the Moonspinner, the other half of the equation that will free the nightling slaves, bring humanity back to power, and close the moonroads . . . and to hear some people talk, unspoil curdled milk, change rocks to bread, and make sand into gold. I have the intelligence to question what others say.

"You're older than I, Lord Doyati, at least by a bit. You're half nightling, and you have lived on the moonroads, whereas I cannot even see them. And yet you, supposed to be half the salvation of a mob of slaves and the last remaining humans, gave over your position and your *power* as kai-lord of this vast kaidom so you could . . . could . . . so you could *chase moonbeams* with this ridiculous child!" His screech sounded like a piglet trapped in brambles, and the noise scratched under my skin and made me want to bury my head in the chair cushions until he stopped.

Doyati's voice was quiet in response. "I do not have to justify my decision to relinquish the throne, Master Navan. But you know that those who pursue power do it at risk of their souls. My soul is tattered enough already without the might of the kaidom waiting at my whim to shred it further."

"And yet as kai-lord, you might have done something good with that power. Now, some child and his mother have a tenuous hold on the throne, and you . . . what of you, *Lord* Doyati? You don't like me. Would you have my job? If you know so much, *Lord* Doyati, why aren't you teaching all of these scatterbrained children?"

"I do not teach, *Master* Navan," Doyati said, and the nightling magic in his blood touched his voice for a moment, so that his words came out bells and choirs in harmony, "because I do not know. You have admitted more than once recently that you do not know, either. Those humans who study sun wizardry, who are in turn recommended by Genna's father, vouched for you as a tireless scholar, as one who would be able to discover the truth from many sources and tell us" — and here he looked at me, and I felt my cheeks growing hot again — "what path we are to take to fulfill this destiny we did not seek, but which has been thrust upon us."

"I have been vouched for. I have been recommended. I am teaching you. Yet you treat me with disrespect." I did not like the mocking tone of Master Navan's voice as he told Doyati that.

"I wait for you to present us with information we can actually use," Doyati said. "Telling you this is not being disrespectful. Do you plan to continue to waste our time with pointless grammar recitals in a dead language and the scribbling of essays about long-dead sun wizards, or will we, sometime soon, get to the point of this?"

Navan started to sputter, but Doyati held up a hand. "Gennadara is the Sunrider. From all I've heard, she is to free the nightling slaves and lead freed slaves and the surviving humans to a new future of allied harmony and peace. I am to help her. Of that, *Master* Navan, and how we are to accomplish it, you have told us nothing."

"I have been searching the records. Nightling records. Human records, too. I have been seeking out people, asking questions, doing what I am paid to do. You know that."

"I do," he said.

"Why, then, do you abuse me about the manner in which I present what I find?"

Yarri and Catri and I all sat in our seats, still as trapped mice before two fighting cats, hoping Master Navan would not turn his temper on us. Dan, on the other hand, was clearly cheering Doyati on. "Tell him," he was whispering. "You tell him, Doyati."

Dan's few experiences with Master Navan had left him with no love for the man.

The cat had finally opened his eyes, and he crouched on the back of my chair, his tail lashing, his ears halfway back.

Doyati shook his head. "Whispers that have reached me suggest we have little time. The candles of opportunity burn quickly in our fingers, and if we do not act quickly and decisively, they will gutter out and our chance — this moment when we might do good, when we might free those thinking creatures of your kind and mine who die at the whim of their owners, when we might create better lives for many — runs short. I believe my impatience is justified."

And Master Navan all but screamed, "Then why did you wait so long before coming back to Arrienda?"

Doyati's eyebrows rose, and his hand swung around and pointed to me, though his gaze never veered from Navan's. "She is only fourteen. Do you think she might have chanced the moonroads and the monsters she has already faced ten years earlier, dragging her rag dolly along for comfort? Have you any idea what she has already faced, old man? Ten years might have given *us* time, but she came when she could."

Right. It wasn't as if I had any say in when I was born. I glared at Navan.

"Sit," Navan told Doyati, speaking to him as if he were one of us — another child.

Doyati did not sit. "Just tell us what you have learned, Master Navan. And do not think to overstep your place and command me."

Navan burrowed through his papers while his face grew redder and redder. His lips, never full, became thin lines surrounded by a web of wrinkles. His eyes narrowed into slits.

"I have identified seven tasks that the Sunrider and the Moonspinner are to accomplish if the future the seers whisper about and the slaves dream about is to come to pass." He leaned forward and glared at me. "And I'll tell you right now, child, you have no way to accomplish any of these tasks. Not one. The Sunrider and the Moonspinner together must save humanity from pending extinction; restore sun wizardry and the old human knowledge; win allies for humanity from among the nightlings; conquer the Thirteen Twisted Kings of Sky, Forest, and Stone; master and then destroy the moonroads; put humans and nightlings on an equal footing; and lead an army made up of all the peoples of the world to slaughter the Green Sorceress."

He glared at all of us. "Seven enormous tasks, tossed into the hands of children."

I sat back in my seat, bewildered and a little sick. I looked to my brother Dan, whose eyes had gone as wide as mine. Catri reached out and took my hand, Yarri made a little noise in the back of her throat and drew her legs under her and wrapped her arms around her chest, and even Doyati looked taken aback.

The cat still on the seat behind me stretched and yawned and in my head said, *That did not go well.*

Master Navan stood tall before us, and his glare twisted into a cruel smile. "There is your future, children. Whatever will you do with it?"

Doyati recovered first. Still standing, but now with arms crossed, looking very much like someone who would be only too happy to fight, he said, "Master Navan, it is your duty not to simply list the tasks we must carry out, but to help us find out how to fulfill our duties. Who, for example, are the Thirteen Twisted Kings? I have never heard of them before. Have you? And the Green Sorceress? In all my years — and I have lived a few and traveled widely during them — no mention of her has passed my ears."

I stood up. "Doyati's right. Where do we start in saving humanity from extinction? Where do we start in restoring the sun wizardry? To whom do we present our cause for the alliance of humans and nightlings? And how does one close a moonroad? You must tell us how to do these things."

Master Navan's smile was the smile of the wolf with a pack behind him and a lamb before. I realized suddenly that he disliked me as much as I disliked him. "Thank you for telling me my duties. You'll be pleased to discover that I have addressed them. I have tasks for each of you and will expect full reports tomorrow."

He looked at Doyati and said, "Lord Doyati, the Mafeeth Lyring's collection of ancient documents is rumored to hold within it information on the Moonspinner, but I am human and without rank in this accursed city, and no matter that I come in the name of the Sunrider. The Mafeeth will not even meet with me. *You* he cannot refuse. See if you can get the records titled 'Moonspinner Prophecies of Seer Hanji' from him. There are supposed to be an even dozen of them. Either borrow the lot or copy what you can."

Doyati's eyes were cold and hard, narrowed with suspicion — but he nodded and said nothing.

"Yarri, you know Arrienda well. Find out where a Flower named Dashee resides."

The Flowers are nightlings who drank a drop or two of the elixir of night taandu essence, and who, because their spirits and wills were pure and focused on goodness, changed into creatures of great beauty and magic. Nightling Flowers are rare and renowned among the nightlings for their wisdom, their gentleness, and their skills in such arts as music, healing, storycrafting, and philosophy.

For every Flower — I've heard it said — night taandu essence gives birth to a thousand monsters. Doyati introduced me to one Flower not long after he passed the throne to his cousin. I've already crossed paths with hundreds of taandu monsters, so I find this saying easy to believe.

Master Navan told Yarri, "Dashee is supposed to have solid information about the Green Sorceress, but again, as I am human, no one will tell me how to find her. Locate her, win her over to come speak with me, or if nothing else, wheedle out of her what she knows about the Green Sorceress."

Yarri frowned. "By tomorrow? I am a freed slave. And a child. How am I to gain audience with a Flower?"

"You are a companion of the Sunrider, are you not? Do what you can; bring me what you find out tomorrow morning. As *Lord* Doyati has so ably pointed out, our candles burn quickly, and we have but little time."

He turned to my brother. "Even for you, Danrith, I have a task. Speak with your father, ask him if he has heard of the *Agbak Codex*, and if he has, find out if he knows where one might find it. Or a decent copy, if such might be had. Some of my sources point to the *Agbak Codex* as the definitive source of information on the Twisted Kings, and also to ghosts who have been bound to humans. Information on how the ghost of the mercenary was bound to your lineage, and how it moved from your father's father to him and from your father to you, would be most helpful. I have reason to believe these things are related to the Sunrider, the Moonspinner, and their futures."

Danrith chewed on his bottom lip and said, "I'll ask him."

"Catri," Master Navan said, "you will take these three books and sift through them for anything you can find on the origins of the moonroads. Simply mark each page that refers to moonroads — I do not expect you to understand what you read. Have them finished when you come in tomorrow."

They were not thick books, but as Catri turned the pages of one, I could see the handwriting within was small and crabbed. I did not envy her the work that awaited her.

Master Navan turned last to me. He said, "You will read *this* book. All of it. By tomorrow. And you will do your best to understand it, for it is the only account I have been able to find of the one man who was thought to be the only previous Sunrider. This man lived and died before the beginning of the Long War. The manuscript was translated long ago, and the language is difficult. Do not be bothered that this man is not called Sunrider in the book. Earlier generations referred to the Sunrider as the Avatar, I believe." He glowered at Doyati. "I have been able to find no historical mentions of a Moonspinner."

Then he took his pack and papers and notes in hand and said, "Go, all of you. You have much to accomplish and little time in which to accomplish it. I expect your best effort on this, since you and I agree it is of the utmost importance."

And he stalked out of Doyati's library and Doyati's suite, slamming the huge door behind him.

CHAPTER 2
PASSING NOTES

We all looked after him, and then Doyati said, "I would as soon be an old man in a mud hut again as go chasing after Master Navan's errands for him." He looked to me. "But if any of these errands of his might lead us to something useful, they'll be worth it."

"I don't mind," I told him. "Reading a book will be less of a bother than listening to him talk." I glanced through the book, which was thick and written in Old Hand Osji, which is much fancier and harder to read than New Hand Osji. "Reading a dull, difficult book," I amended.

My brother nodded. "I don't mind helping, either. Asking Papa a question is no problem." He grinned a little. "Getting him to *stop* answering is the only real problem."

I laughed. Dan was right. Papa *loved* to answer questions.

Yarri shrugged. "I do not know that Flower Dashee will meet with one as unimportant as I, but there can be no danger in asking. It is not as if Master Navan asked me to meet with a monster."

Catri, who had already begun reading through the first of her books, looked up when she realized we were all looking to her. "I've read worse," she said. "I'll finish as much as I can in the time he's given us."

Doyati smiled at all of us in turn. "Then let us begin. We'll meet back here in the morning if we do not see one another before then, and we'll compare results before Master Navan arrives, yes?"

I was almost excited. Master Navan had managed to turn finding out about being the Sunrider into a chore, but in the end, I would still know more about being Sunrider than I had known before. "Yes," I agreed.

The cat yawned. "Since that old crank didn't give me anything to do, I'm going to go hunting. Perhaps aboveground. I tire of constant twilight — I want to stretch myself in a puddle of sun and enjoy spring. And all the tasty little animals it brings out."

Doyati leaned in and whispered to me, "We're all with you in this, Genna. Don't worry. We'll come back with good information, if there's any to be had."

They scattered then, all save Catri and me. We sat curled in our chairs, reading. According to her, her books were not bad. Mine was terrible, though — about a man who had been a hero to both humans and nightlings before the start of the Long War, but who did not travel moonroads, who did not use any sort of magic, and who, as I worked my way into the book, seemed to have nothing at all to do with being a Sunrider, no matter if people were calling him the Avatar back then, and no matter what Master Navan had said. I wondered if Master Navan had accidentally given me the wrong book.

Catri and I had moved into Arrienda as winter was coming to an end. Aboveground, spring had come, and the new lambs were already born and wobbling about in the pastures, and trees were in flower, and the snow had melted away from all but the highest and coldest places. Days were growing longer, the sun was getting brighter and warmer, and the air would smell green with new growth.

Reading a dull book in a room lit by the nightlings' magic, held deep beneath the surface of the earth, I found it hard not to think about spring and all I had missed and was missing.

In the nightling world, nothing changed, and I could only keep track of how long I had been away from my village and my family by making marks in my daybook and writing faithfully every day of what I had done. I had not missed a day.

Three months.

Three months of Master Navan and his shrill voice. Three months of going in circles on language and history and doing things that seemed meaningless, and learning nothing that seemed to me to apply to what I needed to know or what I was supposed to do.

The longer I read, the more this latest chore of Master Navan's felt like more of the same. Work to keep me busy. I began to resent it.

I leaned my head on the cushioned back of my chair and stared at the ceiling. "By Spirit and little gods, Catri," I groaned, "I want to see the sun again."

"I do, too. I miss my family. I want to go home." She looked at me. "I want you to be able to go home, too. I know you cannot — I know Banris said he would kill you if you went back to Hillrush." Words poured out of her as if a dam had burst. "But I could go, just for a few days, and then come back. And I could tell you about the new lambs and maybe bring you some of Mama's cooking. . . ." She looked at me, her eyes full of hope.

I did not want to consider the possibility of her going.

But my family had come to visit me, and hers had not been able to leave crops and livestock to visit her.

"That sounds wonderful," I told her. It was a lie, but she looked so happy I tried to be happy for her. I yearned for the sunshine, and to play with the spring lambs, and to run through the village with her and sit under the trees and listen to the water gurgling through our brook. As comfortable as the huge bed in my wonderful apartment within the royal complex of Arrienda was, I missed my little bed under the rafters, and I missed knowing that my brothers and sisters were down the stairs, and that my parents were only a shout away.

Catri at least would get to experience those things again. So long as she was away from me, Banris was no threat to her.

We looked around the enormous library, and at the foods Doyati's servants had set out for us, and at the pens and paper waiting on the long table for our use.

"We ought to work," I said.

"I know. How much longer could this take?" Catri asked.

I looked down at my book. "Long."

She said, "I wish you could do one of these. They don't seem to have anything to do with moonroads so far, but at least the man who wrote them is interesting."

"Be grateful. Mine doesn't seem to have anything to do with being the Sunrider yet, but the man who wrote it seems to think the harder something is to read, the more important it is."

"Idiot," Catri said.

"He is. And boring, too."

We read for a while, and then Catri said, "This could be something. Would you say 'I wandered through the wilderness at twilight along a dreary road, lost in shadow, and nothing my eyes fell upon reminded me of home,' would be about the moonroads?"

I considered the question for a moment. The moonroads seemed anything but dreary to me. But the worlds they led to were definitely shadowy, and full of twilight, and none of them so far had led me to places anything like home. "How did he get there?"

"He rode his horse."

"Probably not, then." I closed my eyes, remembering the moonroads — the sparkling lights, the feeling of falling, the sounds and smells and tastes and shapes that marked each one as different for me. I remembered the sheer breathtaking magic of them. Not everyone experienced the moonroads the way I did. The cat, for example, said he only saw the initial lights and didn't get sounds or smells or other things while on them.

"I think," I told her, "if that man had been on a moon-road, he would have mentioned *something* besides the horse."

"I didn't know."

"Moonroads are not much like roads at all," I told her. The cat and Yarri and Danrith and Doyati and I had been on them, but Catri had not. "The cat says they're different for everyone. For Yarri, they're just being someplace and then suddenly being someplace else. She can't feel them at all. Dan was like that to begin with, but he started being able to feel them, and maybe even see them a little bit, toward the end of our search for Doyati. The cat says he just sees lights — but he can see intersections and passageways that connect them to one another, too, and I can't. For me ... they're ... they're wonderful. Each road looks and tastes and smells and sounds and feels different. And it sounds silly when I try to explain it, but falling through one isn't silly at all."

"I wish I could go on them," Catri said.

"When we get out of Arrienda and back aboveground again, I'll take you. I need a good moon and not much cloud cover to call them, but it isn't hard."

"Could you teach me how to do it?"

"I don't know," I told her. "I could try."

The door to the apartment slammed again.

"Do you think Master Navan came back?" Catri whispered. "Perhaps to tell us how lazy and foolish we have been, or to give us more books to read by tomorrow?"

But the footsteps on the stone floor scurried toward us, light and fast, and Master Navan had never been light of step, nor had he ever moved quickly.

A nightling child, with skin the pale blue of a robin's egg and eyes the green of spring leaves, poked his head through the library doors, looked around, and saw just us. He ran to me and pressed something white and square and small into my hand. I noticed that he was breathing hard. "Note from Yarri," he said. "She says it's urgent."

With not another word, he fled back the way he had come, slamming the door as he exited. I stared at the folded parchment in my hand, afraid to open it. Urgent? Was Yarri in trouble?

"Hurry up and see what it says." Catri came over and leaned over my shoulder.

I unfolded the note. It read, *Meet me in Fallowhalls level, Friends' Gathering. Look for these marks when you come up, and hurry! You have to know about this before we tell anyone else!* And then a few additional, illegible scrawls that might have been additional instructions, or might have been her scribbling the extra ink off her pen nib, followed by her name.

Catri and I exchanged glances.

"It looks like she wrote it with her feet," Catri observed.

"She sounds like she was in a hurry. Is she in danger? In trouble?"

We both stared at the note, willing it to say more, to explain itself. But it did not, of course.

"Something we need to know before we tell anyone else?" Catri asked.

"I cannot imagine what that might be," I told her. "But Fallowhalls level is the very top level of the city. The oldest one. Doyati said it was run-down and crumbling in places, and most people stayed away from it. Why would one of the Flowers go there?"

"Maybe Yarri found out something that doesn't have to do with the Flower."

"Maybe." I ran my fingers along the slender chain around my neck, the one that held the little light crystal Yarri had made for me. "We have to go."

Catri said, "We have never been permitted to go up into the old city — not even accompanied by someone else."

"It sounds like Yarri could be in trouble." I looked at the note, wishing it said more, and wondering how much trouble she was in that she could not have written a longer note.

"We have to go, of course," she said after a moment. "But maybe we should tell someone."

"Would *someone* let us go?"

"No."

"Right."

We looked at each other. "You have your dagger?" Catri asked me.

It was a silly question. Like every other child in Hillrush, I'd carried a small dagger since I was eight and a larger one since I was twelve. I just raised an eyebrow.

"I sometimes think about not carrying mine," she said.

"So do I. But do you ever leave it?"

"No. Of course not."

"Exactly." We studied the marks Yarri had drawn beside the word *Fallowhalls*. They were the nightling words for Fallowhalls, and they would be carved into the stone arch that was the gateway into that level.

"Shouldn't be too hard to find," I said. "We just go to a back passage and run upward. If we hurry, we can be there and back before anyone realizes we've gone."

"What about Master Navan's books? Will we have time to finish them?"

I looked at the books he'd given us. "Will it matter? If we don't, we'll tell him what we *could* learn. If they stay true to form, that will be nothing."

"True," Catri said.

We slipped out the front door of Doyati's suite, nodded to the nightlings we passed in the twilit corridors, pretended to be enchanted by the lightning bugs that swarmed next to one of the hundreds of public fountains on the Kai level of the city, and, without drawing attention to ourselves, sought out the nearest spiraling walkway that led up, into the older parts of the underground city, nearer the sun, nearer our homes, nearer the world where we belonged and where we fit.

And nearer Yarri, who certainly had found something important, and who might have found trouble.

CHAPTER 3
FALLOWHALLS

The stone arch well behind us had borne the nightling marks for Fallowhalls. But this part of the city must have been truly ancient — and inhabited by those least loved by the nightlings who ruled. Most of that level of the city was carved out of stone, but in places the stone had cracked, and the roots of trees pushed through. There were none of the delicate magical lights that kept the lower parts of Arrienda in a perpetual state of twilight. Instead, torches burned in brackets along the passageways, and lanterns hung from the arched ceilings every so often. The place smelled of wood smoke and oil smoke and cooking meat and old fish and things better left unmentioned.

"I don't know where we are," I told Catri. I held out Yarri's note, squinting at it in light even dimmer than what I'd become accustomed to, and she leaned over it with me.

She said, "This is the Fallowhalls level. The marks carved into all the arches match Yarri's mark. But I don't see a Friends' Gathering here."

Neither did I. We had become familiar with the Friends' Gatherings. They were nightling meeting halls that served food and drink, and that used a little bit of magic to keep the atmosphere within calm and friendly. It wasn't that fights and arguments weren't permitted. They simply weren't possible. Catri, Yarri, and I met in the one in Kai level because they were, the nightlings insisted, the safest places in Arrienda. Safe enough for three girls to meet unsupervised.

But Catri and I couldn't find the one in Fallowhalls.

Catri frowned into the dim cavern that was the central open space in the Fallowhalls level, watching the strangers milling and wandering with seeming aimlessness. "I don't like this place," she added.

I did not like it, either. Arrienda, vast and layered, had seemed warm and welcoming to us — at least after the death of the kai-lord who'd tried to kill me and everyone in my village.

But Fallowhalls was different. I couldn't put my finger on how, exactly. But something felt wrong.

I saw taandu monsters — nightlings and other creatures twisted by their own inner evil and the magic of the taandu trees — talking with well-dressed nightling men. And creatures I would have sworn were from the nightworlds watched us as we passed. In the lower levels, we saw more Flowers. Not all taandu monsters were ugly, not all Flowers were beautiful, but it was possible to look at them and sense the terrifying hungers or the true beauty they held inside.

In Fallowhalls, I did not see any Flowers, or any children, or many women.

"Yarri will be at the Friends' Gathering, if we can just find it," I told Catri, trying to reassure myself as much as her.

One of the few nightling women we'd seen in the level evidently heard us, for she stopped and studied us. And smiled. "Lost?"

"This is Fallowhalls, isn't it?" I asked.

"Yes. But you were looking at your paper. And you *look* lost."

"We're trying to find the Fallowhalls Friends' Gathering."

She leaned over our little paper, and laughed softly, and said, "I can see why you haven't found it yet. It's very simple. You are not so far from it. From here, take that first passage to your right." She pointed, and I saw the tall, narrow archway slightly behind Catri and me, off to our right. "Follow it. It doesn't branch. You just walk along it until you reach the Friends' Gathering. It has the same blue sign as all of them, with the same stars. You know what they look like?"

Catri and I nodded.

I stared down at the paper again and at the bits of Yarri's handwriting at the end that neither Catri nor I had been able to decipher. "I suppose this could say 'turn right,'" I said, though I could have made as good a case that it said "cow rebels." Staring at the scribbles, trying to make them form something that made sense, I said, "Thank you."

The woman said nothing, and I looked up. She was gone.

Catri looked startled, too. "Where did she go?"

We both looked around for her. We were brought up by parents who would never have tolerated children who did not thank their elders for help given. "She should be easy enough to spot," I said. "She was one of the pale yellow ones . . . like Yarri. . . ." I faltered to a stop. Had she been? I had looked at her, had seen her face, had seen her hair and her eyes and her clothing. But I found myself struggling to remember even the simplest detail about her.

"She was light green and had green hair the same color as summer grass," Catri said. "I'm almost . . . certain?"

"We need to pay more attention," I muttered.

"But she did say, 'Go right.'" Catri gestured to the same arch I'd seen the woman point out.

"Yes. Right. That arch. At least we both paid attention to that."

We hurried to the arch the woman had shown us and entered. The passageway was narrower than what either of us was used to in Arrienda, and it crowded everyone close. We found ourselves squeezed against the stone wall, hurrying past closed door after closed door. The air, thick with smoke and animal stinks, did not move the way air in the lower levels did. There was no freshness to it. And the deeper we traveled, the dimmer the light got, the farther apart the torches burned, and the smaller the circles of light the oil lamps seemed to cast.

There were fewer and fewer nightlings around us, too, and more taandu monsters, and more nightworlders. Eyes watched us as we passed, teeth bared, and claws flexed.

"The Friends' Gathering better be close by," Catri whispered.

I was uneasy. "I'm not sure it's going to be here at all." The woman who had sent us this way had seemed kind. But the more I thought about her, the less I could remember. I was no longer even certain that she had been a nightling, though at the time I would have sworn she was.

Something dripped down my neck. I jumped and turned and looked up. Above me one of the multitude of tree roots that had pushed its tangled way through cracks in Arrienda's beautiful stonework had been cut, and it was dripping sap. Sticky sap, I discovered, when I tried to wipe it away. And sweet-smelling. Familiar. Raw taandu sap, I realized.

An ugly, squat, heavily muscled creature the colors of fungus under rocks waddled up to me and glared at me with fangs bared and eyes narrowed. "You want that, you have to pay for it," it growled.

"The . . . the sap? I don't want it." I started backing away. But its rasp of a tongue whipped out and licked the remainder of the sap from my neck.

"Don't get in the way, then," it said. "People who do want it pay good money to stand there. *Human.*"

Heads turned, and everyone stared at us. The word *human* rippled among the well dressed and the unsavory, through the talkers and the doers and the leaners-on-walls. Catri whispered into my ear, "I think we need to be going."

We did, so very much.

But the creatures of this level were moving toward us slowly. Menacingly. "Humans," they muttered. "Humans. What are they doing here? Humans." I did not sense a parade in the making — this felt more like the start of an execution.

I took Catri's hand and pulled her away from them, toward a clear space in the crowd. We walked backward, but they kept moving in our direction, muttering, growling, and I whispered, "Run."

We ran down the darkening passage, with them behind us, and they began to run, too. The corridor grew darker yet, and Arrienda went from rough around the edges to raw. Living rock replaced worked stone; the ever-glowing moon lights gave way to intermittent, smoking torches; and smoothly graded and polished marble ceded its place to rough, uneven sandstone.

Faint light gave way to true darkness, and the corridor became an unshaped passage in a true cave, a place where things dwelled that never saw the light and never needed to. Blind and groping things. Creatures that could hear the faintest breath, the beating of a heart, the rush of blood through veins.

The sounds of pursuit faded. When we realized this, we pressed ourselves against damp sandstone and did not move. I could hear the trickle of water, but I could not begin to guess whether it was far away or nearby. I could not hear any footsteps, any voices, anything other than the two of us breathing. We had left nightlings and taandu monsters and nightworlders behind us. Where we had come, they had not followed.

Pursuing that thought, of course, I tripped over a second and more worrisome one. Perhaps we had moved into a danger so great it frightened them away. This is the sort of thing I think when I am in the dark and lost. I'm never much of a comfort to myself.

"Genna?" Catri whispered. "Something's dripping on my head. And my shoulder."

We couldn't see anything. I had the light crystal around my neck — and if I tapped it, clear pale light would illuminate the area around us.

If I tapped it, anything that still searched for us would find us.

And if I tapped it, we might discover that the liquid dripping down Catri's back was not another cut tree root, but drool from a monster crouching on a ledge above us.

I am *no* comfort to myself.

I pulled the light from beneath my sweater and whispered, "Get ready to run." I tapped the light.

Water trickled down the rock wall against which Catri leaned. No monster. No taandu root. No one ran screaming at us, brandishing a club or a sword. The darkness beyond our circle of light stayed dark, the silence around us stayed silent, and there we were. Two girls alone beyond the Arrienda Old City, alone in the dark, alone in a maze of caves. Alone. Where no breeze blew, where nothing skittered or whispered or moved, where I could see only stones and bones on the ground around us.

I winced when I realized they were bones and looked away.

Catri's eyes were huge. "Where are we?"

I gave her the look everyone reserves for people who ask stupid questions.

"I was just hoping you might have some idea," she said.

I did not say a word because I did not trust my voice not to squeak. I was terrified, but I was also supposed to be an adult — or so my village had made me — and I was responsible for seeing that Catri was safe. Her parents had entrusted her to my guardianship. So I started back the way we had come, trudging, listening for the sounds of pursuers.

"Why wouldn't they have followed us here?" Catri asked. She walked at my side so she could stay within the half-circle of light my crystal cast. This created terrifying shadows that ran along the rough stone beside her.

I shrugged. "Because it's dark?"

"There were torches in the walls. They could have brought them. They would have caught us easily."

"Because they didn't really want us?"

She shook her head.

No, I thought. They had wanted us.

Behind us, a growling voice said, "I suspect it was because *they* have the sense to be afraid of me."

Something big and fast leapt over our heads, so that I felt the wind of its passing and heard the flapping of what sounded like enormous wings. It, whatever it was, landed on the ground in front of us, outside my pathetic little circle of light, amid a shower of pebbles knocked loose from the stone passageway through which we moved.

Catri screamed, I screamed, and we both drew the daggers we wore tucked within the folds of our skirts.

In front of us, the creature in the darkness chuckled. "The kittens have claws. How delightful."

A different voice said, "Eat them now and be done with them. Don't play with your food."

And a third said, "Filthy humans. How did they end up in our quiet cave?"

The voices all seemed to be coming from the same place.

The creature moved a step closer to us, for suddenly the light from my crystal reflected in its eyes. Enormous eyes, very high off the ground, reflecting orange. Eyes the size of big summer cantaloupes. Very far apart.

Running would not save us. I did not think flying would have saved us, had we been able to sprout wings. I wished that I had a walking stick with me, or a sword, or an army. Especially an army. One of those would have made me feel much better.

Beside me, Catri shivered. She had never stood against anything terrible before. I'd killed a dire-worm once, but while it had been toothy, it had been smaller than this . . . this . . .

"What are you?" I asked. "And what do you want with us?"

And the creatures chuckled again. "Shall I move into your tiny light, so that you may see me in my glory?"

"Just kill them and be done with it."

"No, don't kill them yet."

"Quiet!"

All different voices. Whispered, thin, creaking voices, except for the one that was so deep it shook the floor. The one that had chuckled.

That one asked again, "Do you want to see me, little kitten?"

No, said my stomach. "Yes," said my mouth.

"Brave child." I heard shuffling, and it sounded to me as if the whole passageway ahead of us shifted forward. An enormous triangular head, scaled and horned, with a mouth wide as a draft horse's back and teeth twice as long as my hand, slid into the circle of light. My people do not have many stories of dragons, and to me they always seemed silly. Some great beast flying off with a cow in his jaws, indeed. Seeing the creature, I could only wonder why it would take just one.

Those huge, glowing eyes looked very small set in that head.

Without knowing how I got there, I was on my knees, and so scared I couldn't breathe. Beside me, Catri had lost her legs, too. She slumped against the rock passageway, mouth open, eyes blank.

"Nice to see I haven't lost my touch with little girls," the dragon said.

I heard my throat making whimpering noises without any help from me. I seemed to be someplace other than in my own body. Someplace the dragon couldn't touch.

And the dragon said, "They haven't tossed me children in a very long time. (They should have tossed you children. You're a god. They should treat you like a god,)" he whispered in another voice. And in a different voice — in a voice that sounded like a clamor of other voices, he hissed, "(Give us meat. Give us living flesh.)" But he did not even seem to be aware of those other voices talking through his mouth. He said, "But you aren't even nightling children. You're human children. How intriguing. Human sacrifices. I wonder what I've done to deserve that particular honor. (Give us human flesh! We hunger. We hunger!)"

My skin crawled. I was wordless, terrified of the enormous mad beast with his terrible gleaming teeth and his orange-glowing eyes and his many voices.

Then I heard Catri speak, and I could only be amazed.

"We're not sacrifices for you," she said. She had found her legs, and she walked right up to the dragon, a mere hand's breadth from his enormous maw, and almost shouted at him, "It's a mistake. We were to meet a nightling girl at a Friends' Gathering in the Arrienda Old City. In Fallowhalls. We got lost, and nightlings and monsters chased us, and we ran in here to hide. But we're not supposed to be here. It's just a mistake." And then Catri added, "She's the Sunrider, and I'm her best friend," and my stomach knotted.

I thought she shouldn't have told him that. Should not have said a word about the Sunrider.

The corners of the dragon's wide mouth curled back and

up in an enormous grin. "No one comes here by accident. If nightlings chased you here instead of throwing themselves before the dark doorway that leads to my domain, they did it because they meant you to come to me. (The nightlings have not sent us gifts in a long time.) But, oh, my. The *Sunrider*, you say. (The Sunrider? The *Sunrider*! Kill it now, and end our hope and suffering. Kill it now, and let the world die!)"

He blinked at us slowly. "So, Sunrider, you're the mighty warrior who is going to toss down the nightling kai-lords and free the nightling slaves across the whole of the world, and bring a new age of humans ascendant, of sun magic revitalized? (It's trouble. Kill it, before it stirs them up against us, before it reminds them of what was before.) Going to change things that a lot of nightlings don't want changed, the Sunrider, going to break a lot of treaties rich men in high places don't want to have broken. Going to fix a lot of things the poor and the dispossessed and the weak want to have fixed. *That* Sunrider?"

From the corner of my eye, I'd been watching Catri nodding. Yes, yes, yes . . . but ever more slowly, as the expression on her face changed. As realization dawned.

Realization was visiting me, too. I thought of rich and powerful nightling men who had no reason to love me or to want me to succeed. Of the poor — the nightling slaves, the human villagers — who smiled at the mention of my name, or at the story of Doyati, the lost son returned to Arrienda and to power and favor, and of the royal child Oerin returned to life from a hundred years of death and placed on the Arriendan throne, and of his human mother, Oesari, standing over him as his regent.

I had in a distant way known there were men who did not love me or what I and those who had stood with me had done when we overthrew the murderous Kai-Lord Letrin.

"We had a note," I said. "From our friend Yarri, who was on an errand. She asked us to meet her." I pulled out the map and with trembling fingers held it before the dragon.

The dragon sniffed at the paper in my hand with surprising delicacy.

"It's scrawls and scribbles. You know them to belong to your friend?"

In truth, I didn't. Usually, her writing was better than mine. I'd made allowances because the child had said it was urgent, that it was from Yarri, but I did not ask him if he'd taken the note from her hand or from someone else's who claimed to speak for her. I had not questioned him at all. I had simply guessed that she'd written it in a hurry.

"I do not know it was from her hand," I whispered, "for when we went to Fallowhalls, we got lost and did not find her."

"Fancy that," the dragon said and chuckled. "Instead of meeting your friend, you two and your note that smells of nothing so much as human wizardry and moonroads find your way to me. (Moonroads!)" A hiss. "(Say nothing more of moonroads!) And in a tragic accident that no one could have foreseen, two foolish little human girls wander into a dragon's lair and are eaten. (Yes, eaten. Oh, eat them now. Now. We hunger.) (I hate little girls.) (Quiet! They will be fresh meat. Sweet meat.)"

The dragon and his many voices fell silent, and I looked at the note in my hand. "Human wizardry?" I whispered.

The dragon said, "Someone clever and powerful wants you dead. Because no one who walks into my lair walks back out. The bones of my victims line the passages, and the screams of the sacrifices that have been thrown to me echo still through all these chambers. (Bones? Even bones would be delicious.)"

"But," I said. "But. You know the truth. We are not supposed to be here. Surely you'll let us live. . . ."

Many voices laughed — soft, wicked, hungry laughs. "Surely I won't," the dragon said. "If any lived who had walked into my domain, do you think humans or nightlings would still fear me? (No one would fear you. They would hunt you down and kill you.) My head would hang above some hunter's dining table, and he would make tents of my wings."

His head lowered until it lay almost on the floor, and he growled, *"None who walk into my lair walk back out. None."*

His great jaws gaped wide, and he roared to deafen us both. We screamed. Oh, Spirit and little gods preserve me, but I screamed until I was sure my throat would tear itself apart. I was in his mouth, his teeth a cage around me, and Catri was with me. His tongue pushed at me, at her, and I toppled into a great bag of skin I thought must be his stomach, and Catri was gone. I kept screaming. Screaming and flailing. I had my dagger yet, and I tried to stab anything, anything.

I did not even scratch him. Catri was gone, though I could hear her screaming, too. And beyond the gaps between the dragon's teeth, which the light around my neck still showed me, I heard cheering from a distance.

The cheering of men and monsters.

CHAPTER 4
TO NEVER WALK AWAY

My voice gave out and I stopped screaming. I'd thought my death would be quick, that the dragon's razor teeth would have ripped me to shreds in mere instants. But instead I lay in a wet pouch of flesh with rows of teeth above me. The little light at my throat cast shadows behind me and to my sides, and made the teeth look bigger, and the black, snaking tongue that flicked the air seem bigger. I wondered where Catri was. I could not hear her, and she was not with me. I did not want to call out, for fear the dragon would discover that he had not swallowed me and correct his error.

He was moving at great speed, and his movements threw me backward and forward. But not downward. In fact, as I had the chance to realize more fully that I was not dead, I also discovered there was no place downward where I might go.

I would have expected his stomach to be wetter. Full of acids that would burn. To have an opening above and one below. When my father and the other men of the village butchered hogs in the fall, they caught the stomachs and entrails in buckets and rinsed them to get out the acids and the filth. Hog stomachs are edible once they've been cleaned, and along with my mother, I'd tied shut the hole at the bottom in order to stuff in greens and roots before tying off the top and boiling the whole thing for evening meal. Sheep stomachs are the same. Rabbit stomachs. Deer stomachs. A hole at the top, a hole at the bottom, acid and wetness and a lot of muscle in between.

And that's not what I was in.

I was in a tough, slick sort of a bag. I was getting damp, but the liquid in it didn't burn my skin. There wasn't exactly a hole at the top — I could see teeth, top and bottom, on one side of the dragon's mouth. While it wasn't a pretty sight, it was . . . well . . . there's always a long tube that lies above a hog's stomach. Or a sheep's. Or even a rabbit's. And I would think you'd know if you went down that tube, and once the hole closed above you, you wouldn't have a view of teeth.

So, once I'd calmed down a little, I had to admit I was not in the dragon's stomach.

Still someplace in his mouth. That didn't seem much better.

And going someplace awfully quickly. He was running, his claws scrabbling over rock, his body thundering forward. And suddenly there was light that didn't come from my amulet. I touched the crystal, and it went dark, and there was still light. Light between the dragon's teeth, coming from outside. Bright light, unlike anything my eyes had seen in the three months I had been beneath the earth in Arrienda. It shone through his partly opened mouth and through the skin that wrapped around me.

Sharp, fresh air blew in, and the dragon stink abated a little, and I could breathe.

I heard flapping, the sound of huge leathery wings beating the air, and the sensation of movement ceased for a moment. The bouncing stopped. And then, for an instant, I weighed nothing and floated upward in the dragon's mouth, and an instant after that I was thrown into the flesh below. I weighed so much that I could barely draw air into my lungs to breathe.

I heard Catri scream again, and I rejoiced for just an instant that she was still alive. Then, however, I was tossed back into the air, and came crashing down, and I was certain I was going to throw up. It was a mercy my stomach was empty, I thought, and then felt acid burning at the back of my throat. I closed my eyes and stretched my arms and legs wide, fighting for purchase in the dragon's slippery cheek, where none might be had. Up again. Down again. Up again. Down again. In rhythm with the beating of his enormous wings, up and down. It's like riding a horse, I thought. Move with the rhythm. This is no different. Move up. Move down.

Then it was just all floating up, and up, and up, weighing nothing, spinning and slamming into the bone of his upper jaw, and all my best efforts came to nothing, and I was sick.

Followed by slamming downward. Down into stillness. Into darkness.

And the dragon saying, "Really? You could not have held on just a bit longer? You had to do that? (We told you to eat them. Nasty, filthy creatures.)"

He spit me out onto dirt. Catri landed beside me. It looked like the middle of the day somewhere, but we were under the shadow of a large rock overhang, and sheltered enough that my eyes, unused to daylight, were not completely blinded.

The dragon was still spitting, though away from Catri and me, not on us. It gave me a chance to truly see him. All of him. He was . . . huge. His wings would have covered houses; his tail would have wrapped around them with some left over. He was black, but only the way some beetles are black, so that when the light shines on them, they contain rainbows. I hated him, and feared him, and in the same instant was in awe of his beauty.

I lay on dirt and smelled fresh air — better than any smell in a dragon's mouth. Too weak to move, too sick to fight, I lay watching him, and felt Catri's hand wrap around mine, and heard her crying softly.

Now, I thought. Now he would eat us, and it would hurt, and then we would be dead.

The dragon said, "So. When you are dead, little Sunrider, you and your weeping friend, what will change?" And then one of those other voices of his hissed, "(That's right. Show them no mercy. No mercy. They are poison.)"

Tucked back into its sheath, belted at my waist, and hidden in the folds of my skirt, my dagger. Close to my hand, tipped sideways to look at me closely, his enormous golden eye. And to my left, away from where he crouched, a cliff that, if I rolled over the lip of it, dragging Catri with me, fell away, I knew not how far.

Better to be shredded by his teeth? Or to stab that

enormous eye and in the resulting pandemonium leap to our freedom? Or fall to our death?

My fingers wrapped around the blade.

Something stung me. In my right arm, high up. It *hurt*. I swatted at it, and in front of me, the dragon jumped a bit at my sudden movement, and just like that, his eye slipped out of reach, and my moment — when I might have hurt him and freed the two of us to whatever fate lay below — was gone.

"My question," the dragon said. "I would have an answer from you. (Yes, answer us, meat. We want to talk to our food.) When you and your little friend are dead, Sunrider, what changes?" He was watching me with curiosity. Interest. Almost . . . expectancy.

I did not want to play his game. I did not want to speak again. But perhaps I could buy us time, buy another opportunity for that eye to dip within my reach.

I kept my hand in the folds of my skirt, and my fingers wrapped around the dagger I held there. I said, "The kai-lords and the corrupt old men of power celebrate."

"Yes . . . ?" The dragon waited.

I thought it through a little deeper.

"The slaves in far-off places never hear that some of their kind have won freedom."

"... Perhaps ... but perhaps ... not. Think closer to home. What will surely happen?"

"My parents will mourn me."

"Not just your parents."

"Well, my sibs. But aside from Danrith, they're too young to understand."

"Oh, not your sibs."

"They'll mourn me!" I was hurt.

"Who would you be *happy* to have mourn your death? (She's a stupid chit. Stupid. Be done with her.)"

Who would I be happy to have mourn my death? Larrota Yervisdattar, who was the prettiest girl in our village, and who hated me as much as I hated her? I might *wish* to have her mourn me, but if she heard I was dead, I had no doubt she would dance in front of my parents' house wearing orange socks.

Who might actually mourn —

Oh. Banris the taandu monster, Banris seeker of immortality, Banris the betrayer of my father, Banris who had sought marriage with my then-dying mother and the deaths of all my sibs and me so that he might complete a spell he had bought from the Kai-Lord Letrin at the price of every life in the village. Banris would mourn, for when I was dead, not only could he not kill me to make his immortality spell work, but he could not threaten my family anymore, either.

"I see realization on your face." The dragon sounded almost as if he were proud of me.

"Banris would mourn me, for I — alone or with my sibs — am the key to his immortality. If I die, he loses the key to his spell."

I paused, thinking. "And my family could sleep nights, knowing that he no longer seeks my mother or my sibs. Without me, they would be useless to him."

The dragon nodded. "Your sibs could walk through the village without your parents fearing some neighbor had taken the gold Banris offers to snatch one away to sell him as a hostage, so that he might lure you to him."

"He's offering gold . . . ?" I sat up and nearly stabbed myself in the thigh with the knife still in my hand. I'd forgotten I held it. "He's offering gold to my parents' neighbors? To their friends? To steal my brothers and sisters?"

"He's offering enough gold that one of them will, sooner or later, accept it."

"Mama and Papa never said anything. In their visits, they never even mentioned . . ."

"What would you have done if they had? (What would

she have done? We don't care.) (I say enough.) (You're listening to that one, aren't you, and not to us?)"

The voices distracted me. Whom did he think he was talking with? Talking about? But I did my best to answer his question. "I would have . . . gone after Banris. With friends. Allies. Nightlings. We could have raised an army; we could have walked the moonroads."

"You could have died, squeaking kitten," the dragon said. "And your people would have lost their Sunrider. (All to the good. There is no hope for us. Let there be no hope for any daylight creature.)"

"Which they have lost now anyway," I said slowly. "But I'm not so important. I got Doyati to Arrienda, and I helped destroy Letrin. Now I'm simply something no one knows what to do with anymore."

I thought of my parents and my brothers and sisters safe. I thought of Banris stripped of any hope of immortality. I thought my family might never know how much I loved them, but I would know. I stood up, weak and wobbly, but as my father had taught me, I looked the dragon in the eye. "If you devour me, will you promise to let Catri go? To take her home?"

Catri said, "I'm not leaving you here!" And she stood, too, and held on to my arm.

I turned to her. "You don't need to die. It won't fix anything, and you can take a message to my family that . . . that this is for the best. That I do this for them. But . . . but . . ." I closed my eyes and took a deep breath. "Be quick about it, dragon. Try to make it not hurt too much. And just me. Not Catri. You understand?"

"I do." The dragon grinned, and my knees went weak, and the ground beneath my feet started spinning. "But I don't think you do."

He was going to eat both of us. I knew it.

But he said, "Did you *walk* away from my lair? Did the cowardly criminals lurking on my doorstep laugh at a monster gone soft enough to spare the lives of little girls?"

". . . No-o-o . . ."

"The ones who were hired to see you dead have witnessed your death. The ones who hired them will pay. The gears of the world turn; the word already spreads. To all the world save me and you, child, you are already dead. None now living has eyes to see where I brought you. None has the magic to penetrate the secrets of this hiding place. You are somewhere special," the dragon said. "You stand on sacred ground. This is one of my places, claimed by me after the Fall of men, when the last of the sun wizards died. I've kept it safe, waiting, I think, for just this day. (No, they cannot have this place. This is our place. We won it. We kept it!)"

The dragon shook his head like a dog bothered by fleas, and the voices fell silent.

"This is not a place nightlings dare come. Nor taandu monsters, nor moonroaders. The magic that still lives here will kill the Moonkind if they dare cross into the shielded space that surrounds it. I have made this place mine. But situations change. Perhaps, perhaps not all hope is dead."

"(Never hope!)" the other voices wailed. "(Never hope, never hope. Hope is lies and lies are death!)"

"You're not going to eat us?"

The dragon studied us. "I have done an owed favor," he said softly. "I have repaid one unasked-for kindness. I speak these things to the wind and to the roads, that I have served as I was bidden, and now my debt is paid." He stared up at the sky and roared, "That debt is paid!"

He jumped then, and shivered so hard his scales rattled, and he snarled in some other voice, "(She wants more. She always wants more.)"

It was not a heartwarming moment. I got the feeling that he was telling me if we met again, he might consider me an acceptable tidbit.

But it was . . . enough. Catri and I looked at each

other — really looked — for the first time since the men chased us into the darkness. We were wrecked, both of us. Her hair was plastered to her head and face and stuck out at odd angles, her clothes were stained by dragon spit and puke, her eyes were red from crying, and I knew from the expression on her face that I had fared no better. Travel in a dragon's mouth is not for the fastidious. Or the weak-stomached. Or even, truth to tell, for the strong-stomached.

Filthy, disgusting, we still hugged each other, grinning madly.

"We're going to live," I whispered.

Catri hooked her thumb through mine and we both whispered, "Sisters not blood, not bone, not born, but sisters still by choice."

I turned and got my first real look over the edge of the cliff where we stood — the cliff over which I would have thrown us to escape the dragon — and my knees turned watery. The ground lay so far beneath us, the trees of the forest looked like a soft green blanket of moss. In that moment, I knew where I was. Even above the taandu forests, even from Hillrush, we could see the pinnacle of this place. The Spire.

My father refused to talk about it. He did not even like to name it. He said it was a bad place — a place of death —

and for anyone whose life the dragon had not decided to spare, I have no doubt it was.

The dragon nodded at me. "Go. Walk on ahead. You'll find your way to where you need to go. Before you leave my presence, I have been given three things to tell you. (Don't tell them. They'll make a mess of everything.) *Three things,*" the dragon continued doggedly. "Sleep behind a blue door, eat behind a green, learn behind a silver door. . . . (Well, go on, you've given them that much, give them the rest.) (He doesn't remember the rest.) (She didn't push him hard enough.) (He never gets any quiet with all of you *screaming in his head all the time*!)" The dragon fell silent and closed his eyes. He was very still, though his mouth moved.

"Sleep behind a blue door," he repeated after a moment, slowly and carefully, and this time was not interrupted by other voices. "Eat behind a green. Learn behind a silver door the truth that has been . . . hidden. Yes. She didn't make it rhyme very well." He opened his eyes.

"You want to be going now. Up, up. You'll find your way. But I have not eaten in a very long time, and I need food. Go, before I . . . forget . . . my promise." When we were not quick enough, he added, in a terrifying roar, *"Run!"*

Hanging on to Catri's hand and carefully not looking anywhere near the edge of the cliff, I fled in the direction the dragon had pointed us. Up, up, we charged at as much of a run as we could manage. Just out of sight from where we'd landed, the ledge turned into a tunnel of black glass, illuminated by tiny carved windows pierced through in hundreds of places by careful hands long gone. It was far too narrow for the dragon to follow us, and once we were well inside, we stopped and collapsed on the steps and clutched our aching sides and caught our breath.

The windows let brilliant sunlight brighten the filtered light of the tunnel itself, for sunlight found its way through the black glass, too, though at greatly reduced strength.

Those same long-gone hands that had carved the windows had cut steps beneath our feet. Countless steps, all of them seemingly new, crisp, as unworn as the steps in Hillrush must have been hundreds of years earlier, when the village and its houses were new. These steps seemed never to have known a footfall before ours.

We climbed, stopping two or three times to catch our breath, and once to stare at the perfect circle where the taandu trees came close to the base of the spire, then stopped. That circle seemed to both of us a creation of art, not nature, and I wondered aloud if the dragon had made it.

We came out of the tunnel at last, onto a broad, flat expanse of granite. Before us stood what I can only call, for a lack of better words, a castle made of hundreds of soaring towers, carved out of the top portion of the Spire's living rock. From far away, the Spire looks like a giant, unbroken column of black stone with black threads laced all around it. No sign exists that it is anything but a strange rock, though.

Up close, the hands of its long-dead creators still spoke poetry. Pinnacles rose up, tight-clustered, uncountable, curved like the horns of great beasts, interlocking, twisting around and through one another, and all of them reaching so high I had to lean my head back as far as my neck would bend to see what I thought might be the tops of them.

I could not believe my eyes. People spoke of the Spire — if they spoke of it at all — as a bad and dangerous place, somewhere people never went.

But men had been here. Men had *made* this place. Their statues still stood along the broad balconies, their carved faces looked out from stone facings, their beautiful artwork lingered in testament to their presence. This place had been human once. It had been ours.

"Oh," Catri whispered.

I could not even manage that syllable. Right in front of us, granite flowers bloomed on black glass walls, carved as roses, as fuchsias, as irises, as sunflowers, so delicate they might have been real. Doorways were arches, grand and broad and peaked at the tops, and the doors were of black glass set on central spindles, so that with a push they would swivel to open on either side from the center. An army could have marched through them, but I discovered I could open or close one with a single finger.

There should have been screaming winds, for high places are almost always windy, but only gentle breezes brushed my cheek, scented with flowers and faint, enchanting perfumes. This was magic, I knew — the nightlings in Arrienda had the same sort of magic. But *this* was human magic, and to me it seemed all of a sudden cleaner and crisper and infinitely better.

I imagined living in this city back when it was full of life, when people called to one another in that courtyard or sat talking on the many benches. I imagined waking each day to see those graceful spires through a window, and to see the world spread out beneath me from the balconies that marked many of the spires.

Life then would have been full of people like me. All of them were gone. All gone, with this ghost of what they had been to taunt those of us who had lost the sky and who lived on the ground, on dirt and grass, not far removed from our herd beasts. What had the world been like when it was ours? How had we lost so much and fallen so far?

Catri and I pushed open the closest door and found ourselves in an enormous hall, ringed around with carved
balconies stacked one atop another up to a far distant
ceiling.

No sound echoed in the place. No creature moved. It
was perfect: spotlessly clean, new-looking, unbroken. It was
as huge inside as Arrienda, I thought, but it was different.
And not just because it was empty. Because it was human. I
looked up and around, and I understood it. I understood
the design. I understood the placement of windows, the
shape of doors. Nothing seemed wrong or out of place.
The Spire was a human place, and it fit me and how I saw
and felt the world in a way the nightling city of Arrienda
never could.

Catri pointed to the middle of the entry hall, where the
sun wizard's blazon — the sun with curling rays — had
been inlaid in different-colored stones in the center of the
floor. I had seen that symbol before, on the uniform Danrith
had put on when he appeared before the Kai-Lord Letrin. I
had seen it again in books by sun wizards about their magic.
That symbol had frightened a kai-lord, and when I saw what
the people who had worn it had been capable of creating, I
understood why.

Sun wizards had built the Spire.

"What do we do now?" Catri whispered.

I understood the whispering. Even that faint sound echoed into the vast space around us and came back at us in shivery echoes. "Now, now, now, now?"

"The dragon said we would sleep behind a blue door and eat behind a green, and learn behind a silver door. . . ." And I couldn't remember the rest, either.

"The truth that has been hidden," Catri finished.

Right. It didn't rhyme, which made it hard to get right.

A hundred, two hundred corridors opened out from that vast central hall, running like spokes deep into the interior of the single pinnacle in which we stood.

In the one nearest us, I could see both blue doors and green doors. I pointed.

Catri saw them and said, "Well, that seems simple enough." She paused. "Do you suppose it's safe?" she whispered.

"Safer than being in a dragon's mouth," I said.

"Well, there is that," she agreed.

We picked the closest corridor, and stepped into it.

CHAPTER 5
LIGHTS AND ECHOES

As we crossed the threshhold, the entire corridor lit up, in the same fashion as empty passageways in the lower levels of Arrienda lit up when entered, but much, much brighter.

I jumped, Catri jumped, and we squeezed back to back, watching both directions down the corridor, our hands wrapped tight around dagger grips.

"I wish Danrith were here," I said.

Catri said, "I wish he were, too. Him and his sword. He was so brave when he stood against the kai-lord."

Dan was two years younger than Catri and me, but he liked her, and Catri liked him, and already her parents and mine had held discussions about a marriage between them. Danrith, as the headman's firstborn son, who would be headman himself in time, was already being eyed by the parents of girls both older and younger than Catri. And Catri — the middle daughter of the village metalsmith — was not just my best friend, but pretty in a way I could never hope to be, and with a much sweeter disposition. From her father's successes and her mother's skills and talents in the home, she would bring a good dowry with her and many prized wifely skills. Plus, now, magic. If we survived the Spire as we had survived the dragon, anyway.

Whether those talks ever came to anything or not, both of us would have been glad of Dan's presence.

"I don't hear anything," I told Catri after moments that seemed like hours.

"I don't, either. Do you suppose the lights are magic, the way the lights in Arrienda were?"

"The dragon made it sound like we would be the only people here," I said. "So we can hope."

"We have to do more than hope, for if we don't find a privy soon, I'm going to burst."

I wished she had not mentioned that. I had managed to push that particular need out of my mind. But she was right. And if the sun wizards whose place this was used the same designs in their homes in the Spire as they had in the sun wizard's lair that Dan, Yarri, and I had slept in, then they would have privies inside.

When the two of us had convinced ourselves and each

other that the lights had come on of their own accord, we told each other the dragon's rhyme, and I volunteered to open the blue door beside us.

I grasped its door handle and tried to open it. A man's voice snarled, *"Hak geen korok!"*

Catri and I both screamed.

The man's voice mimicked our screams, then shouted back at us, *"Hak tomartyk korok!"*

We grabbed for each other's hands and dragged each other at a dead run back the way we had come, back to the relative safety of the slightly known — the city's grand entry hall.

And once there, we shoved ourselves into a niche from which we could see if anyone burst out of that passageway in pursuit. We wrapped our arms around ourselves and stood shivering and staring at the doorway, waiting for the angry man to emerge.

"The dragon did say he was the only one here, did he not?" I asked.

"I thought he meant that," Catri agreed. "But I was awfully scared. I might not have understood, and considering how many dragons he seemed to think he was, would he even have noticed real creatures?"

"I don't know." I leaned against the marble wall of our

niche, and I'm sure that it was as beautifully shaped and lovingly placed as everything else in the city. At that moment, though, all I noticed was that it was cold, and it was hard, and it was knobby, which made it an unpleasant place to lean. If I'd felt any steadier, I would have stood on my own power. "He didn't say anything about the blue doors at all but that we were to go through them when we wanted a place to stay."

Catri said, "Can you remember the words the man shouted at us?"

I closed my eyes. *"Hak geen korok."* Master Navan's drills came back unbidden. *"State your name,* Tagasuko command case."

"Imperative case," Catri corrected. She was better than me at languages. She had managed to pick up a fair amount of nightling, too, in the three months she had lived in Arrienda, while my grasp of nightling was shoddy. She frowned. "But why would anyone *here* speak Tagasuko? The language has been dead for a thousand years, along with the people who spoke it."

"Maybe they're not all dead."

"Everyone knows they're all dead," she said.

It was my father's opinion that anything "everyone knows" was likely to be wrong. Standing in a sun wizard city we had thought empty but that proved to have at least someone still at home, I hoped this was an exception. I did not want to meet a real sun wizard while trying to break into his house.

I said instead, "I have met ghosts who spoke the lost languages. The warrior ghost that haunts Dan both speaks and reads Tagasuko — we found this out when he helped us read the covers of books in a sun wizard's library." I shivered a bit, remembering that adventure. "And the ghosts the bard summoned from the war harp spoke a language from those times. You saw them in Letrin's arena. And heard them."

"I remember," Catri said. "But they're all dead. Do you think there are any alive who still speak it?"

"Doyati," I said.

"He couldn't come here. He's half nightling."

"But he's still alive," I said. However, she was right. He was half nightling, so he could not enter the Spire. According to the dragon — who might, I thought, not be the most reliable source — the Spire would kill any who were not human who entered it.

Then I had an idea.

"The sun wizards bound the ghosts to a harp so that the ghosts would be an army forever. Could they not have bound ghosts to the Spire, so the magic of the Spire could run forever?"

Catri shuddered. "Oh, wouldn't that be simply perfect? Imagine this place full of the ghosts of the people who lived here, all of them waiting behind their doors, and in this whole city, not a bed for us to lie down in."

"Or a privy which we might use."

She looked at me and started laughing. It was nervous laughter. "This place is so huge. Would ghosts be bound to all the doors, do you think?"

"I don't know," I said. I peeked around the corner. "We might be the unluckiest girls alive to have chosen to try to open the door we did. Maybe it was special somehow. But there were countless others down that corridor." I stopped leaning on the wall and stood on my own two feet again. "Why don't we try another?"

"And if it's haunted, too?"

"Countless other doors, Catri. Countless. So long as no one — or no *thing* — comes charging out at us, I say we try them."

She nodded.

"All right, then," I said.

We lifted our chins and straightened our shoulders. And I thought we were willing to brave a lot in hopes of finding a privy.

We went back the way we'd come, down the close

corridor, and we did not stop at the first blue door. Or, by silent agreement and for no logical reason I could find, the second, or the third. Catri pointed to the fourth door, though, and I nodded. Reached out. Touched it.

A man's voice snarled, *"Hak geen korok."*

This time we did not scream, though we did jump.

"Hak geen korok." The voice was imperious. Demanding. But not angry, really.

We crept away from it and worked our way down the corridor and around the corner of the very first intersection we came to.

We stood next to a blue door. Right across the hall from it was a green door. Green was food, and at that moment I wanted food almost as much as I wanted a privy. But the blue door would most likely offer a privy — so blue first. And straight across the hall to green second. "This place would be perfect," I said, pointing to the blue door beside us.

Catri nodded. And gave it a tentative shove.

The man's voice snarled, *"Hak geen korok."* The *same* voice. The *same* man. Same.

"Catri," I whispered, "that is the very same voice. I think . . . I think it's magic. Not a man. And not a ghost. A sort of magic door guard."

She nodded. "I think so, too."

"*Hak geen korok,*" the man repeated, still sounding bossy, but sounding much less angry now that I was expecting to hear him.

Tusu geen? meant "What is your name?" It was the politer way of asking. It was what people who thought they might be friends said to each other. *Hak geen korok* was a command.

"*Geen sha Genna,*" I said. "My name is Genna."

"*Geen sha Catri,*" Catri told the door.

"*Genna so Catri, hak tomartyk korok!*"

Which meant "Genna and Catri, state your purpose."

I frowned. Our purpose was to move in and live there, but I had no idea how to say that. I fell back on what I hoped would work. "*Hak jaskatyk benino!*" It was not a polite form. It was a command form that said, more or less, "Let us enter."

"*Sokpatora jaska, Genna so Catri,*" the door said. A lock behind the door thudded, and the handle did not move, but the door opened.

I almost cried right there. *Sokpatora jaska* meant "Welcome and enter," and the voice did not even sound the littlest bit bossy when it said it.

We crept in, ready to flee at the slightest hint that something was wrong. But the door didn't say anything else.

We stood in the first room, which held two long, padded, high-backed couches, both pale green, and both facing a long wall covered by empty shelves. The rest of the walls in the room were of a green darker than the couches, but plain. Nothing painted on them, no carved wood beams, no borders or decorations. The floor was marble, smooth and snowy white, and also very plain. Across the room from us, an open arch led into an area for cooking and dining.

From there, directly in front of us lay three closed doors, while to our right lay two closed doors, and then around a corner to the right from there, a big room with a single round couch sunk into the floor in the very center. And all around, walls painted the same white as the marble floor.

My mother would have looked at the place as a challenge. Something in need of painted flowers and carved magical tokens and carpets and wall hangings and silver plates. I could see it the way she would have made it.

Me, I could only think that behind one of those doors might await a privy.

I led us forward, to the first door on the left. When it opened, a light came on, and we both shrieked a bit, but this time we calmed quickly.

We faced shelves — lots of them — and a handful of boxes with pictures of food on the outsides. "Larder," Catri said.

I nodded, and we backed out.

The next door proved to be the privy I had hoped for, along with other things I did not recognize. I greeted it with a glad cry, and Catri eyed me and said, "Oh, do hurry." I saw my own desperation reflected in her eyes.

I hurried, and then so did she. We each managed to figure out the taps on the washbasin — wiggling our fingers beneath them made water come on, and moving our hands to the right made it warmer, while moving them to the left made it colder.

When we were both done, we explored the privy-room further. A tall box made up of countless glass tiles in white and yellow and shades of light green stood in the far corner of the room, and poured water on anyone who stepped into it. It was very like a waterfall, save that the water was warmer.

I found this out by accident, but stood there getting my skin and my clothes clean at the same time, until Catri pulled me out and stepped in herself.

I decided afterward that it was probably meant to be used without clothes, but right then neither Catri nor I cared. The water, faintly perfumed and lightly soaped when we first stepped in, washed and then rinsed us, and rid us and our clothes of the stink of dragon breath and human sick. We walked out of the privy much happier than we had walked in.

The next room proved to be a bedroom, its wide bed complete with a mattress as good as anything the nightlings in Arrienda had. It was in the bedroom that we discovered the first real ornamentation in the rooms. One wall was made of glass and metal — the glass was wavy, thick, and brilliantly colored, and the metal took on the textures of tree bark and branches, and defined the sky above and the ground beneath. The left side of the glass wall was the moon, a quarter full, in a dark blue night sky dotted with stars. The right side was the sun, in the sun wizards' curly-rayed style, in a bright blue sky with the hills below green and meadowy and covered with flowers. And in the center was a tree, its leaves silvered and moonlit on the night side, and the green and gold and red and burgundy of autumn on the day side.

Daylight poured through this incredible creation, scattering colored beams of light everywhere in the room. I had never seen anything like it. I moved forward, my fingers reaching out to touch the colored glass — and the tree split in half down the center and opened on invisible seams worked into the picture to let us out into a courtyard.

A perfumed, warm breeze blew in.

"Oh," I whispered, "how wonderful."

Catri and I stepped into one corner of a broad common that led to a tall rail. And the tall rail lay at the edge of the Spire. The sun was setting on the horizon, the long light casting huge shadows behind us into the room we'd just left. If we walked out onto the railed promontory that jutted from the very edge of the commons and we looked southeast, we could see a world bathed in purple. And beneath us, the fluffy tops of clouds slid by, brushing through trees or making them disappear entirely.

"Fog," Catri whispered. "That's fog, only from the top."

Any people below us were actually inside of those clouds. The sight made me shiver. The world was a very different place when viewed from above.

We crept back to the bedroom we'd found, feeling small and inconsequential.

But that feeling passed quickly, for as we explored further, we discovered, at right angles to the bedroom we'd been in, another exactly like it, with the same glass and metal wall and the same wondrous hidden doors.

"We could each have our own whole room," Catri whispered.

"And a huge, fancy bed of our own," I said, awed by the thought. She and I had shared a room and a bed in the

Arriendan suite, and she kicked and stole the covers . . . though she accused me of doing the same. I'd had my own bed in my parents' house, but it had been a narrow cot with leather straps woven through to hold up the thin cob-filled mattress. I'd been grateful for my own space up in the eaves, but it had not been a room of my own. Or a grand bed.

Beside the second bedroom we found a second privy. And that took us back to the white room.

Neither Catri nor I could figure out what it might be for. I was tempted to wander through, to look at that odd white couch set deep into the floor. But Catri was the more practical of the two of us right then. She said, "Food," and at the word, my stomach rumbled.

To be clean, to have food, to sleep comfortably; all those things were within our reach.

"The green door?" I said.

She nodded. "And if it talks to us, too?"

"We say '*Hak meggo korok*,'" I told her. "We require food."

"And *skop*," she added. "Drink."

It worked. It worked only as well as it should have — which is to say, the green door let us in. We stood in a surprisingly small room filled with closed cabinets, all of them the same stark white as the white room in the little home we had chosen.

I opened one cabinet, and it was empty. I opened another, and it was empty.

"This does not look promising," I told Catri. "Perhaps food was here once, but why would it be here now?"

She sighed. "Will we have to walk all the way to the ground to find food?"

"I hope not. I would give anything for a huge bowl of hot stew and hot bread and jam and black grapes and an apple, and hot sweet biscuits, and some of Mama's tea."

Catri eyed me sidelong. "Right now, I'd be happy with some bread crusts, if they were not moldy."

I opened another cabinet. It was empty.

"Genna," Catri said, "do you smell that?"

I thought I had been imagining it because I was so hungry. It smelled exactly like the stew Mama made, rich with mutton and potatoes and carrots and leeks and long beans, spiced the way she did it.

"You can smell it, too?"

"I can."

We opened all the cabinets, then, one after another, until we had looked in all of them, save the two I had opened first.

We exchanged glances, and I opened the first cabinet again.

It was filled with a huge bowl of steaming stew, with hot bread, with still-warm sweet biscuits, with grapes and apples and black currant jam in a big glass tub, and a full pot of Mama's herb tea. And stoppered flasks, like those Mama made vinegar and honeyed water in.

"Noooo," Catri said, sounding awed.

Something made me open the second cabinet again.

It was full of dried bread crusts.

"Noooo," Catri repeated, but this time she sounded dismayed.

The bread crusts vanished.

"Help me carry all of this over," I told her. "There's enough here for both of us and all my family as well."

The food we carried back covered the whole table. The water we drew from the taps smelled safe, but neither of us could be sure of that. Water in the village, drawn from the community well in buckets and carried home in water skins, had to be boiled before we drank it. Otherwise, sometimes terrible sickness would follow. Sometimes not, but it was impossible to tell. Perhaps water in this city, like water in Arrienda, would be safe straight from its silver taps. But we didn't know that, and I had no wish to die clutching my belly, as some did when they drank bad water. If we could not figure out how to boil water in our dwelling, we would carefully test the contents of those stoppered flasks.

We would not starve, though, in this city of plenty, and we would not die of thirst.

While we sat and filled our stomachs, we talked through our day. Yarri's note, the dragon and his assertion that the sun wizard magic had been behind that note and the attempt on our lives, the Spire, our victory over the doors, our grand luck with the food, the wonderful rooms we would each have. Most of all, our laughter and our delight came at finding ourselves alive and so well-off after such a day.

For a while we managed to forget that, to our parents, to Dan, to Yarri and Doyati and the cat and all our friends, to everyone who had ever known and loved us — or hated us — we were both already dead.

CHAPTER 6
THE CALL

"Genna . . ."

"Genna, we're waiting for you. . . ."

"We've missed you. . . ."

"We're waiting for you. . . ."

Soft and sweet, the voices calling me, leading me toward them. I could smell the voices, faint as spring violets, promising as apple blossoms. I could taste them like rain on the tip of my tongue. They were not friends, but waiting to be friends. We did not know one another, but we knew we wanted to.

I moved toward them, toward radiant silver light from my sad and lonely place in darkness. They were waiting, and I was going to them as quickly as I could.

The curving rain sill on the inside of the glass-and-metal

doors snagged my bare toe and pitched me face-forward out those doors and onto rough-cut granite.

I woke falling — and there are not many worse ways to wake — with the ground coming up fast, not knowing what's happening, not remembering where you are, with no idea how you got there, and to a bewildering sense of loss. I'd been . . . somewhere wonderful, my still-half-dreaming self insisted. Doing something amazing.

I hit the ground hard, but not as hard as I would have had my eyes still been closed, had I still been sound asleep. I managed to catch myself just enough to keep my face from slamming into the stone pavers. Barely. The shock of the crash slammed through my hands and arms and shoulders, through my back, up and down my spine, and the pain in my knees and right toe lit me up like a torch set to flames. I shrieked with the pain and the surprise.

Once. Only once. And then the hunger caught me.

A sliver of moonlight lay like an arrow shot across my outstretched arms. Moonlight. Unaware of what I was doing, I pulled myself forward and let it bathe my face, and the hunger inside of me jumped and stirred and grew. The moon, nearly full, hung overhead, and when I looked right at it, I caught my breath and my heart raced.

The moon. The moon — my beacon, my friend — shone full and fat, high in the sky, and it surrounded me with the scents of flowers that had been in my dream, and sang to me a song my heart knew. The moonroads called to me. They were in my blood, and my blood was on them; when I listened, I could hear them coming to me; I could smell them even if I could not yet see them.

The moon wanted me. It sent not-yet-friends racing in my direction. I'd missed the moon. I'd missed the roads. I simply hadn't known it.

Beneath the ground in Arrienda, there had been no moon, no moonroads, and no temptation; I had, perhaps, felt an edge of restlessness. But I had forgotten the sharp yearning, the ache to step into the wildness borne by the flickering lights and let it carry me someplace new. I had forgotten the hunger in my heart that cried out as I stood there in the darkness, bathed in silvery light.

I did not have to call the roads. In my sleep, they had found me, and needing me as much as I needed them, they were coming. Some of them — I could feel them reaching for me — some of them were as hungry as I was.

I stood, dressed only in the thin linen underdress and the underthings I slept in, barefoot, my braid heavy between my shoulder blades, and I spread my arms to embrace the moonlight. I lifted my face and closed my eyes to better feel it against my skin.

I was lost in the hunger of the roads, lost in the nameless desire that knotted my gut and made my heart race. Lost — and glad to be lost.

And have you not yet learned that the roads which hunger for you are not the roads you want?

I jumped and shrieked at the mocking voice inside my head, and turned around in circles. And there he was.

The cat.

Gray and reddish-brown with swirling black stripes and neat white fur on chin and belly and all four paws. He sat out of the moonlight, along the top of a decorative wall, watching me with eyes that reflected bright green.

I would have thought you'd learned that lesson, he said inside my head.

The cat. At that moment, I was torn between being grateful for his presence and frustrated that he had caught me.

The moonroads called. They *called,* and I needed to feel them again, to step onto them, to drink in their magic. The moonroads felt like a part of me that had been ripped from me and that I had just miraculously won back — and he was trying take them away again.

I tasted them on my skin and the tip of my tongue, I smelled them, I felt them, I drank them.

"Everyone thinks you're dead," the cat said.

I knew this. But talking made it harder to focus on the moonroads.

"You have to step inside, Genna. The roads that want you could be the roads that long to take you to those who wish to kill you. Who *tried* to kill you."

"You said the moonroads aren't sun wizard magic," I said. "That the sun wizards didn't use them."

"That's right."

"A sun wizard tried to kill us," I said.

The cat laughed. He should never laugh, haughty know-it-all that he is. It makes me want to pull his whiskers out. "The sun wizards are long dead and gone."

"But the dragon smelled sun wizard magic on the note that led us to Fallowhalls and to him."

The cat tipped his head. "Come here. Show me the note."

If I went to him, I'd have to step out of the moonlight and into the shadows. I didn't want to.

I said, "The note is in the pocket of my skirt. Which is hanging beside my bed, still damp."

"You really want to step onto the moonroads wearing nothing but your underthings? Without even shoes on your feet? You *do* remember some of the places the roads took you, don't you?"

1 did. Lands of ice and snow. Lands of steaming, red-glowing rock. Lands with sharp grass and sharp rocks and deep mud.

Not places to wander without shoes or clothes. Not places to step into unprepared. Or alone.

I took a step toward him.

Good girl, he said softly, straight into my thoughts. *One step at a time.*

The moonroads called to him, too. And he had been walking them for a very long time. He said the call got stronger the more you walked them. I believed him.

I took another step, and he said, "The word is that the cave dragon devoured you. That it was an unfortunate accident."

"The dragon says not. That the note I received wasn't from Yarri, but from a sun wizard who wanted me dead."

"And the dragon let you go."

"Not exactly. He, ah, grabbed Catri and me and carried us in his mouth from the cave to a ledge below here. He flew. It was awful. When we got to the ledge, he told us a few things he said we needed to know. He called me Sunrider before we left him."

The cat backed up a step, urging me forward. The moonlight on my skin tingled, and I could hear the soft ringing of bells behind me. I could smell rain and sunlight and a meadow full of wildflowers. I could taste winter with its snow coming, and, deep within me, I felt the bubbling of laughter. The moonroads were there. They had come for me, and the cat was right. They were the roads that wanted me, and that were hungry for me. So I needed to walk away.

I took a half-step toward him. He nodded feline encouragement.

The dragon devours all who fall within his reach, the cat said. *So how do you still live? Think your answer — don't say it aloud. The moonroads have ears.*

I nodded. *He said he owed a favor to her. But he did not say who she was.*

Cats cannot frown. They can hiss and flatten their ears against their heads, though, and the cat did. *Don't trust favors, or those who carry them out. Favors always come with strings attached.* He backed up, so that his haunches were up against the little step-up into my bedroom.

I took another step toward him. It hurt. I wanted to turn, to slide into the little ring of sparkling lights waiting for me, to follow the lure of the waiting moonroads.

He brought us here — and gave us her message, though

I don't know who she is — and then threatened to have us for his lunch if we did not run to the Spire.

I've met the dragon. Does he still talk to himself?

Yes.

That's a shame. He's hard to reason with like that. He was much saner once.

I couldn't imagine how he could be much less sane. I did not say this. I was creeping into shadow, and the shadow felt so cold it burned. I needed the moonroads. The pain of moving away after such a long separation hurt so much I turned and saw them glittering there. Tiny firefly lights of green and red, silver and gold, yellow and blue, all dancing, sliding, swirling. Half a dozen roads had come for me, and I could take any one of them.

I took a step toward them.

In your bare feet, the cat warned. *In your nightdress. Going you know not where.*

I know, I told him, and I thought I'd stopped, but my feet stepped forward without me.

We need to know who — of the many who would love to feed you to a dragon — was the one who actually tried.

I'd like to know that, I agreed. I fought my feet. They inched forward. I dragged them back. They inched forward again. I was losing ground to the magic that called me.

A living sun wizard — one who should side with you because you are the Sunrider — tried to kill you, Genna. You have to find out who. You have to find out why.

I stood in moonlight, and more roads came to me. The tide of the moonroads pulled at me from a dozen different directions at once. All I had to do was move forward, move backward, move sideways, step on one. Any one, and the magic would spirit me away someplace new, someplace fantastical. . . .

Someplace dangerous. The cat's voice was a blade inside my head, cutting at the wonder of the moment, hacking at it.

The roads want to eat you, he said. *They're hungry, you fool. Wake up!*

My feet, my body, my skin and bones and muscles all ached to move, to touch, to fall into one passage or another. I wanted. I wanted.

Gold to my right, ruby before, emerald and sapphire to my left — and I turned, circling, caught in a spell of yearning not even the blade-sharp irritation of the cat could cut.

In Arrienda, surrounded by friends and guards, I was supposed to have been safe. Safe from Banris, who had sworn to kill me. Safe from the kai-lords of other nightling cities, who had reason to kill me, for I had been part of freeing the slaves in Arrienda.

Safe from some rogue sun wizard — when everyone believed there were no more sun wizards — who would have fed me to a dragon.

I was not safe. Even in this magnificent sun wizard city, even high above the rest of the world — thought dead, locked away — I was not safe. The cat had found me and found a way to reach me, so others would be able to as well. And as long as Catri was with me, she would not be safe.

Enemies wanted me — the Sunrider who knew nothing about being a Sunrider. The only enemies I'd had before were girls my own age. Now the most powerful creatures in the world wanted my head on a pike.

Thanks to the dragon and the woman to whom he had owed a favor, I still lived. Those who hated me thought I was dead, and that was a good thing. But half a day after the rumors of our deaths had begun to spread, the cat, who had believed us dead, had found us anyway. And had come to us.

Secrets do not last.

Boldest, richest summer green, the road I wanted most sidled toward me.

I breathed in the scent of it — the richness of a hot middle-of-the-afternoon meadow full of black-eyed daisies and Maiden Lace, tall grass going to seed, earth baking beneath the sun. I saw firefly flickers and the embers of some memory of fire. I heard wind rustle through drying leaves.

The yearning to step onto that road, to flee to wherever it might take me, enveloped me, and I started to move, to embrace it, to let it carry me away. I would be gone, and everyone I left behind would be safe. And I would find my own way.

The cat had other ideas.

Screeching, claws out, teeth bared, he launched himself at me like an insane, furry little demon. The needlelike fire of his claws raking across my bare arms, and the shock of his small, angry body slamming into me broke the spell. I screamed with the pain of his claws, and with the pain of falling again and battering already-wounded palms and knees.

The emerald road disappeared. All the roads disappeared.

"Idiot," he growled. "Self-pity is going to be the death of you — and with you, the death of hope."

I stared at him, saying nothing. The dragon had spoken of the death of hope, and of how perhaps it would be better dead. But he had let me live.

"I saved you from yourself," the cat said. "The hungry roads cluster around you like a pack of starving wolves around a spring lamb, and you go toward them like you'd . . . like you'd . . . seen your mother. . . ." He leapt to my shoulder and clung there, hissing and sputtering, his fur standing out all over, his eyes wild, his back arched, his tail straight out.

I knew he spoke the truth. I knew he was right.

But I stood in moonlight — the moon still full and fat overhead — and already I could feel the stirring inside of me, that yearning calling again. While I was in moonlight, the roads would feel me as I felt them, and they would come.

Catri's doors swung open and she stepped into the courtyard, rubbing her eyes. "I heard shouting," she said and looked from me to the cat. "*You're* here?" she said to him. The smile that spread across her face shone like the sun.

"Hmmmph. A decent welcome from one of you, in any case," he said. "Get inside," he spat at me.

"I do not want —" I stopped myself. I did not, at that moment, know what I wanted. The moonlight held me captive, pouring promises into my soul that I knew it would not keep.

With his claws sunk into my shoulder, I remembered the horrors that lay in wait on the moonroads. The dangers. The patient death. I had walked the roads, I had needed them, but the cat was right. I should never have been so overcome by my insatiable hunger that I was ready to step onto a road that had chosen me.

Moonroads fed strange worlds beyond, and sometimes those worlds got hungry, too.

Catri said, "Inside?" and the cat said, "Now, please," and she obeyed right away, turning and walking the few steps back to her room, disappearing through the glass-and-metal doors.

I hesitated.

I'll hurt you, the cat said in my head.

I believed him. I followed Catri in. She drew curtains over her doors so the moonlight did not come in after us, and we headed into the kitchen, closing her room. No moonlight made it in there. I began to breathe a little easier.

The cat was watching me. "You have to learn to control that," he said. "It gets worse, not better, over time — each walk you take on a moonroad binds you more tightly to all of them."

"But *you* walk them."

"I know what they've done to me. I know what I once was. I know what I am now. That's how I know about the hooks they've set in you. I feel them, too — worse than you ever will, if I can protect you from them. I do not want for you the pain they have brought me."

Catri said, "What's going on?"

She didn't feel the moonroads — she had not been with me when the cat and my brother and Yarri and I stepped into that first sparkling road and fell from our own world into another. Like me, she had survived the wrath of a kai-lord, had been a part of the magic that had overthrown him, had wandered the astounding realm of Arrienda, and had flown in the mouth of a dragon. But she had not moved into the mystery and the wonder of the twilight worlds that existed just a half-step from our own.

I had wanted to show her the moonroads. I had promised her.

Right, the cat said inside my head. *That's a fine idea. Drive her crazy with the hunger for them, just as you are, so that the next time the moon wakes you from a deep sleep to tempt you into stupidity, she'll trot willingly at your side. Keep her off the roads, Genna. She can keep you safe if you don't let them enchant her the way they've enchanted you.*

I told Catri, "I just about got myself killed. I told you a little about the moonroads, and how we used them to find Doyati."

She nodded.

"And I told you about how dangerous they are."

"Yes. The taandu monsters, and the creatures of the twilit worlds . . ." She shivered a little and wrapped her arms around herself.

I had, in fact, relished telling my stories to her. I hadn't needed to embellish the details a bit to make them horrifying, and she'd been a gratifying audience.

"Tonight, the moon called me out, and roads came for me," I said.

She frowned. "I did not see anything."

"Be grateful. As long as you cannot see them, you are still safe from them. When you *can* see them," I told her, "they can find you." I twisted the tip of my braid. "Sometimes, they find you in your sleep."

She shivered.

The cat murmured into my thoughts, *You have other work than moonroads to think about. You can't go back to the nightling city to study. You're going to have to learn here. And not even Master Navan can come here.*

That was worthy of a cheer, but I didn't cheer aloud. A thought occurred to me.

Could Master Navan be a sun wizard? I asked the cat.

The cat's laugh in my head was suddenly and startlingly human. *That old fraud? I'm unconvinced that he's even a scholar. I think he managed to convince important people that he knew what he was talking about, and I think he used those connections to find himself a comfortable place to stay in his dotage. He figured as a scholar teaching you something no one alive knew anything about, he would have a pleasant job doddering around with old books, and he would never have to produce results. Who alive could tell him he was teaching you wrong?*

If he were a sun wizard, though . . .

If he had anything to do with trying to get you killed, that would be a dangerous sign of how vulnerable you are. But he has no air or scent of magic about him. None. I have a good sense for these things.

"Master Navan knew where we would all be, because he gave us the assignments himself," I said aloud. "He knew how Yarri wrote, for he had gone over many of her reports. He didn't like me, and he didn't think I was worthy of being the Sunrider. I agree with him, but nobody seems interested in that."

Catri said, "You're right. He could have written the note in Yarri's hand — or a bad imitation of it."

In my mind, the cat added, *You've given me something ugly to think about. Not that he is a sun wizard, but that he had been bought. That someone used him to get to the two of you.*

His ears went back again, and his tail began to lash. *I need to hunt. And then I'll find out where Master Navan went.*

What should we do while we wait for you to return? I asked.

Stay here. Stay out of the moonlight. Learn what you can.

"While I slept, before the moonroads woke me, I dreamed of a silver door," I told Catri. "I saw it clearly. Silver from top to bottom, and it is not plain like the blue doors. Or the green ones. It has no handle, but is carved with wizards, men and women alike, with lightning and fire shooting from their fingertips. In the center of the door, there is a sun — the emblem the sun wizards used. And around the edges of the door are carved suns and roses."

Catri said, "The dragon's riddle held a silver door."

"'Sleep behind the blue door. Eat behind the green. Learn behind the silver door the truth that has been hidden,'" I quoted.

Catri chimed in. "There were beds behind the blue door. And food behind the green, once we figured out how to get it. And doesn't it make sense then that if we can find a silver door — like the one Genna has seen in her dreams — we will be able to learn magic behind it?"

The cat's ears flicked, and he hissed a cat laugh. In my head, he said, *The mad black dragon of the Spire gives you a riddle, and you turn it into how you're going to learn magic? Good luck with that.* He stood up and stared at me, unblinking. *Can you stay out of the moonlight, do you think?* He turned to Catri. *More important, can you keep her out of the moonlight?*

Catri nodded. I could not hear what she thought to him.

Lock and bar those doors to the outside. Shove furniture in front of them. If you pull blankets off one of your beds, you can cover the glass so moonlight will not shine in. You don't need to have any more of these incidents while you sleep.

Catri and I studied each other. I wanted the moonlight. Even there, out of the night, away from the moon. I still hungered for what I should not have. I cannot explain it.

Catri said, "We can share a room and bed again, I suppose. That way I'll most likely know if you get up."

I sighed, because my shins would have fresh bruises, and my ribs would end up with her elbow marks on them, and she'd wake up with all the covers. She was worse than my sisters in that regard.

But the stupid cat was right.

"We'll do that," I said, because the cat was staring at me, and I made myself think that I would obey him, because I was almost certain he could read every thought I had, no matter what he might have told me. In my belly, though, I hid a knot of defiance.

He studied me, and huffed, and said, *Of course.*

CHAPTER 7

SPIES

After he watched us block the beautiful doors with one of the green couches from the entryway and hang the blankets from Catri's bed across my beautiful glass wall so that no light came in, the cat said, *Show me the note.*

I pulled it out of my still-damp skirt pocket. It was wet, and the ink had run on the parchment so no words remained. The cat, though, sniffed the parchment, and his fur stood out from his body until he looked twice as big as his usual self. His back arched and his ears went flat to his skull. *Sun wizard indeed.* He hissed.

He poured himself to the floor in the boneless manner of cats and told me, *I'll return as quickly as I can. I have several questions I must pursue while I still have the moon-roads at my disposal.*

The door into the corridor opened for him, and he left.

Catri saw the wistful glance I gave my big bed. Like me, she'd spent a lot of years sharing room and bed with sibs, and the luxury of a whole soft, huge bed with a thick, wonderful mattress and thick, fluffy pillows to herself was not something given up lightly.

"When the moon isn't so strong, we'll sleep in our own rooms. But you and I both know you should not sleep alone tonight."

What I knew and what pulled at me were two different things.

"You had better stay," I agreed at last.

We slept well enough. And my dreams were . . . forgettable. Some nights, I think that is the best you can hope for.

If sleep went well, waking did not.

Light blazed suddenly all around us, and *"Hak bas gokmat!"* a woman shouted, which brought us awake and upright and sent us diving for the floor looking for a place to hide in almost the same motion.

No one was near us. But the woman was still shouting.

"Hak bas gokmat! Hak bas gokmat! Hak bas gokmat!" She sounded impatient. Annoyed. And then she, wherever and whatever she was, fell silent.

We lay on the cold, hard floor, on opposite sides of the bed, still as mice, waiting for whatever was about to appear wielding axe or sword or wizard staff. I held my breath, and I would guess Catri did, too. *"Hak bas gokmat"* meant "Wake up now," and not in the nice way your mother said it, either.

But no one appeared, wielding an axe or anything else. No other sounds came from any of the rooms.

After a while, pressed hard against the bed and jammed as tightly against the wall by the bed's head as I could get, I started to feel a little silly.

Catri, though, regained her courage before I did. "Why was she yelling at us?" she whispered. I could hear her moving on the other side of the bed, but I could not see her.

"I don't know," I whispered back. I still hugged the floor, but I'd stopped wishing there were a way to get underneath the solid block of a bed.

"'Wake up, wake up, wake up, wake up!' What a horrible woman."

I agreed.

"She sounded a little like a mother," Catri said after a moment's thought. "Not a very nice one, though."

"Could people have wanted a voice to wake them? The same way a voice guards the doors?" I suggested this, but it seemed unlikely to me.

"I can't imagine anyone wanting *that* voice to wake them," Catri said. "Mama would sing up the stairs at us."

Mine did the same thing. I nodded.

We got up, took turns showering because the water was deliciously warm and adjusted itself to the temperature we wanted if we only thought about it. We washed our faces and cleaned our teeth with little cloths we found on the shelves, and thought of the little boy in the primer and how he had used a sort of brush to clean his.

Our foray into the green-doored magical pantry yielded up a rasher of bacon, still sizzling, eggs, fresh asparagus, fresh-baked biscuits, and a huge rainmelon.

The cat did not show up for first meal. We did not expect him.

"What should we do today?" Catri asked.

"Look for the silver door," I answered. It was the only thing I could think to do. If it held the secrets to magic, or the secrets of being a Sunrider, or whatever truth it was that had been hidden and that we needed to know, then it made sense that we ought to find it as quickly as possible.

"Perhaps the cat could help us find it," Catri suggested, spooning jam onto a thick, hot biscuit.

I kicked her under the table and she yelped. *Not here*, I mouthed.

The cat did not come back. When we finished, we piled our dishes in the washbasin and went outside through the door in Catri's room. "We dare not talk inside," I said. "Not about the cat, or anything important."

"Why not?" Catri asked.

"Don't you feel the room listening?"

"I do," she said, "now that you mention it. But I only wanted to say the cat might lead us to a silver door. He seems to know his way around."

"*He* knows Tagasuko," I said. "He reads and speaks the sun wizard language." We walked to the city edge and leaned on the railing, looking down.

"What do you think he really is?" Catri asked. "Some ancient wizard who angered another wizard and was thrown into the body of a cat as punishment?"

"I see him more as the sort of wizard who did a spell wrong and accidentally turned *himself* into a cat," I said. "He seems the sort to make big mistakes. And he said he was not as old as Doyati, that he was not around when Doyati's father was killed and his mother was exiled, for example."

We both considered this.

"Perhaps he is a foreign prince," Catri said.

"Perhaps he is a thief who got what he deserved for meddling."

"He could be something other than human. . . ." Catri

said. "A nightling, or one of the little gods who fell afoul of another."

"He can't be a nightling, or he would not be able to come into the Spire. All I know is that he's not really a cat." I was trying not to think of him as having once been human. He was curiously careful for a cat. He was never around when I dressed. And though he had sometimes slept in the same room with me when we were in Arrienda, he always found a spot on a table or on the lintel over the door. Most cats I'd known, given the opportunity, would drape themselves on your head while you slept, or across your chest, or, on cold nights, burrow under your blanket.

On cold nights, truth be told, I hadn't minded that. A cat was better than a fire in the fireplace for keeping warm.

The cat might actually have been human once, I realized.

"Maybe he's handsome," Catri said wistfully.

"Maybe he's pocked and scarred and old. That he's not as old as Doyati doesn't mean he's young. He might be . . . seventy. Or forty."

She stuck out her tongue at me. "I'd rather think of him as a handsome, green-eyed prince who was transformed by an evil wizard. He could just be waiting for us to find the right spell to save him, and when we have, he'll fall in love with one of us and marry us and one of us could be a princess. Of a kingdom."

"If he's waiting for *us* to rescue him, he's in deep trouble," I said. "We were such idiots we got eaten by a dragon. It was through no brilliance of ours that he spit us out."

I saw a sudden resolve cross her face, and a gleam flicker in her eye, and my heart sank into my belly.

"We can learn," she said. "And we can save him."

I wondered how the cat would take the news that we were going to rescue him from himself. I did not think he'd be pleased.

But Catri, who has been my best friend forever, was in the grip of an idea, and nothing but exhaustion and complete failure would serve to shake her out of it. She had decided the cat was a poor, enchanted prince in need of her rescue. Clearly, she did not know him well.

We went back inside and scrubbed the dishes, and she led me out the door, dragging me by an arm. "We shall find a silver-door room, and we shall discover the way to free *him* from the enchantment."

I, being dragged, was already off balance. So the fact that I tripped over a rolled tube of paper did not suggest that I was merely clumsy. Really.

I picked up the paper, unrolled it, and a chill passed through me that took my breath away.

"Catri, look."

She looked exasperated, but when she saw what I pointed to, her expression changed to the same fear I felt.

"How . . . ?" she whispered.

Our portraits were on the paper, in full color, pushing open the doors to the city and staring inside, as we had stood in the grand entryway to the Spire.

We looked tiny.

I unrolled more of the scroll.

Where I found a portrait of the two of us hiding in the niche after we ran away from the door that spoke to us.

And a portrait of me standing beneath the moonlight, with the cat off to one side.

Another page.

A portrait of Catri hiding on one side of the bed and me on the other.

A portrait of the cat killing some hapless bug in some long city passageway.

I pointed to that one. "Prince Bug-Eater," I said.

"He cannot remember what he was," she said. "That's part of the enchantment."

I rolled my eyes, but my amusement did not last. Around each of the pictures, there were words printed in the sun wizard language. We had managed to learn some of the writing of the sun wizards, but it was complex — much harder than learning to read Osji, our own language. Nevertheless, the script over my picture — ⟡ — was the way Master Navan had taught me to write my name, while ⟡ was the way Catri had been taught to write hers.

"Someone is watching us," I said. "And knows our names."

"And was close enough to paint our portraits."

"How could anyone paint so perfectly and so quickly? You look in each of these exactly like you. Exactly."

She stared at the portraits of us done before we found the showers. "Oh, no! We are both covered by dragon spit and . . . and . . . sick." She turned to me, horrified. "What artist would paint our hair so tangled or our clothes so filthy? Or . . . oh! That is disgusting!"

Yes, this was Catri. Becoming distraught at the fact that the artist had painted us filthy and forgetting to worry that we had been painted *at all*.

"Catri," I said. "How do they know our names? How do they see into a bedroom when we first wake up? Why were they watching us come into this city, and why are they watching the cat? And who is writing these things about us? And where are they?"

She had been muttering under her breath about people raised so poorly that they would paint someone covered in vomit and with her hair sticking out at all angles and her clothes sticking to her skin, so that she looked not like a girl at all but more like a drowned rat.

She stopped muttering, though, and said, "Right. Watching us." Her face paled. "Were they watching us as we showered?"

I had not even considered that. I stared at the pictures in the scroll and imagined one of me in the shower, and I resolved from then on to only shower with some sort of clothing on. "There are no portraits of that," I said. "Perhaps they have *some* decency." But they did not. Not if they watched us as we slept, watched us as we woke, watched us without our knowing, and made portraits of us that we had not asked for, and wrote words about us.

I was beginning to dislike the sun wizards. They had made a wondrous city, but they had filled it with some ugly things. Had there been these watchers who had kept track of all of them? Who had the men been who had painted portraits of strangers who did not know they were being observed, who wrote words about those strangers without ever knowing them, or speaking to them, or asking their permission?

I looked at the portrait of Catri and me done as we cowered on both sides of the bed. We looked terrified. We looked like small children about to cry, in truth — both of us — and I was ashamed to see myself like that, and ashamed to know that somewhere, someone else had seen me look so foolish and helpless and cowardly.

Catri leaned over and whispered in my ear, "Leave that. When the cat comes back, perhaps he can read it to us and tell us who these people are who are spying on us. Now, though, we must find the room with the silver door."

"Must we?" I asked. I did not want to move, or go anywhere, or do anything, for fear of receiving another roll of paper like the one in my hands. I wanted nothing more, in fact, than to find a hiding place where the unseen watchers could not follow me. I wondered how the people who had once lived in this city had managed to accomplish anything if they had also lived knowing that eyes were always on them.

Catri was braver about it than I was. She said, "If these hidden people are going to watch us, I would rather they see us doing something good. Let's go find that silver door."

And of course she was right. I decided if I had no choice in whether they made portraits of me and wrote words about me, then I did have a choice in what they painted and what they wrote. I could have a portrait of myself bravely charging forward at whatever came at me, or I could have one of me hiding away from everything.

My voice sounded grim even to my own ears as I told Catri, "You're absolutely right. We shall go find that door."

CHAPTER 8
NOT SILVER, BUT GOLD

We went to the entryway through which we'd entered the Spire. It seemed the reasonable place to start. From it, we looked into the vast corridor-ringed space around us.

"Which corridor?" I asked.

Catri shrugged. "I think the one with the monster carved over the arch."

"I think one close, so we don't lose our own little corridor and have to find a new place to sleep at night," I said.

She frowned at me. "If you look in little places, you'll only find little things."

"If you look in big places, big things can find you!"

We argued outside our door about which way we should go to find a silver door, until finally we did cho-bo-do to decide it. The rhyme is:

Cho! Bo! Do!
Ta-ma sa-ta ni-la no!
Ni-ra ba-pa ca-ra ro!
Da-sa hi!
Da-sa jo!
Cho! Bo! Do!

And what you do, of course, is point with each word, or each syllable, to one of the people who wishes to be chosen, including yourself in turn. There are tricks to getting the count to come out the way you want, especially if there are only two of you, and by the time you're fourteen, I suppose everyone knows them. Including me. Including Catri. But perhaps she didn't want to win as much as I did, for she didn't protest when I did the chant and my hand chose me.

I won — I will not even pretend it was fairly — when I took us to the first small corridor left of the grand entryway. Not one big enough an army on horseback could march through — if ever an army on horseback could get up here.

I looked down our chosen corridor. It went so deep into the Spire that I could not see the other end of it, just the soft glow of white, and the bright colors of doors, and that magical light that came from nowhere. "We go in only in straight lines. And only three intersections deep. If we don't find a door, we come straight back out and go down the next corridor. That way we can be sure we won't get lost."

Catri fished through the pockets of her skirt and came out with a large spool of strong, shimmery, blue thread. "I found it behind the mirror in the privy-room," she told me. "I thought we might tie it to something, and let it unwind behind us, then roll it up as we come back."

That, to me, sounded even better.

So we tied the thread to one of the bits of decorative stonework at the entry to the first corridor, and Catri let it unravel out of her hand as we walked. We still went three intersections deep, and found regular blue doors, and green doors, and doors of red and brown, both of which were locked to us and would not open no matter what we said. But no silver door. So by agreement, we went a little deeper, and then began to backtrack and go down the side corridors — but just a ways.

We found ourselves at the end of our thread a few times, and still no silver door.

"Next corridor?" I asked.

Catri nodded. "But we should stop at the next storage room we pass and get something to eat as we walk. We might be at this a while."

She proved herself a true prophet. Long hours later, we were staring at our fifth corridor from the great foyer, and the sun, which had been bright and morningish when we began, was falling through the sky.

"I'm tired," Catri said.

I could only agree. Walking was not working — I'd worked harder as a child helping my parents than anything we had done in the Spire. But all that searching without finding made the mind weary, and dampened the spirits, until I could only wish that we had some other, easier thing we might do.

Much depended on our learning magic, though, and on me discovering how I was to carry out the duties of the Sunrider. There were so many duties, and they were so hard. Yet we dishonored our families if we did not give our best effort to finding the silver door and then finding our way through it.

"We have enough time before dark to explore this corridor," I said, though I secretly hoped to hear Catri answer that we ought to go back to our little rooms, have a sit-down meal, and rest.

"We do," she said instead.

So we went, with the spool of thread unreeling behind us yet again. And as before, we found nothing of interest.

Catri said, "It's going to be more of the same, isn't it? We are going to wander down each side corridor, and nothing is going to be what we need."

"But we still have to do it," I said. "We cannot leave some area unchecked out of laziness."

"Oh, I know. And I don't want to start back here tomorrow. I want a fresh corridor, and a chance that it will hold a room with a silver door."

I agreed. "So we finish this one as we did the others."

"Yes."

We backtracked to the first intersection and headed down it, working around the gentle curve, hoping with each step to see a silver door revealed just ahead.

We did not. But we found something else instead: a room with a door the color of goldenrod in autumn, the most beautiful of golds I could imagine. It glowed — the whole door — including the silver bar that ran across the center of it and met another silver bar that ran up and down. And at the very center, where the silver bars connected, was set a ruby out of which light radiated.

We stopped dead and stared at each other.

"What do you suppose *that* is?" Catri whispered.

"I wish I knew. At least it's something different."

"I'm out of string," she said. "It's beyond our limit. It could be trouble, and perhaps the fact that it's beyond our limit is a . . . a sign."

I pondered that possibility. I believed in signs. "The fact that we found it at all could be a sign, too," I said. "We could have run out of string just a little ways before, and we would have never found it."

We looked at the door, and looked at the string.

"If I drop the string, it will still be here when we get back," she said.

"I know."

We looked at the door a little longer.

"It isn't silver. I've dreamed nothing at all about bright gold doors," I said.

"Nothing," Catri agreed. "But we found it."

We looked at each other, both scared, and I said, "We have to take a look." I stared at the string, then looked back at the door. "It's the only interesting thing we have found all day."

She dropped the string on the floor, knowing it was tied to stone at the entry to the corridor, and we walked slowly forward, with the glowing ruby and the glowing door beckoning us forward.

We reached it, and Catri told the door to open.

The door stayed closed. The door voice, which we had learned to expect, said something long and complicated and neither of us understood a word of it.

"Dare we touch it, do you think?" I asked.

"I don't think we should."

I didn't, either. But there it was, right in front of us. A mystery. Something exciting, something different, with its beautiful ruby badge glowing from a sturdy silver bar that crossed the door from side to side and from top to bottom. It called to me. It made my fingers itch to reach out, to feel the warmth of the glowing gemstone, the cool smoothness of the metal. It said *Touch me* in so many wordless ways.

I reached out a hand and heard Catri catch her breath. My own heart galloped like a horse chased by wolves.

My fingers hovered over the ruby. My mouth went dry, the hair stood up on the back of my neck, and it seemed for a moment that all the air went out of the room. I knew in the back of my mind that the spell that guarded the door might hurt me, that whatever made it glow might kill me. Fire might shoot from the ruby, or the door might open and loose trapped monsters upon Catri and me, and instead of doing something that would save our people, we would die horribly and no one would ever know what happened to us.

Well, perhaps the cat would find our bodies, but that thought gave me no comfort.

And yet, I wanted to touch it — wanted it so badly that I finally would not, could not, stop myself. My hand shook like an aspen leaf, but I touched the ruby.

It *was* warm.

I heard Catri make a noise, a tiny whimper, and I gasped as I felt the light flow around my hand like a warm, furry animal rubbing up against it. The instant I touched the ruby, the compulsion to do so vanished, and I yanked my hand away. But if damage would be done by my touch, then I had already done it.

The light that flowed over the door and the light in the ruby flickered, then died.

"Oh . . ." Catri whispered.

I exhaled and realized I had been holding my breath.

"Oh, why did you do that?"

I looked at Catri, who was pale and shaking.

"I don't know," I told her. "I had to."

We watched, and for a moment nothing happened at all except that the lights were gone.

Then the bars clanked and pulled away from the ruby in the center and retracted into the four sides of the door like the claws of a cat that had decided to play nicely.

"Well," Catri said.

I couldn't think of anything to add to that.

We waited. The door did not open on its own. No monsters came bursting through it. Except for the huge ruby in its silver setting in the center of the door, and its bright gold color, it could have been any door. It sat there doing what doors do.

"What would happen if you touched the ruby again?" Catri asked.

"I don't know. I don't think I want to know."

But I stepped forward, curious. This time, though, the door voice demanded the usual information, and we told it our names and commanded it to open. It did.

The room inside was bright, dustless, as clean as all the other rooms in the Spire. Unlike the other rooms we had so far explored, though, this one had an inhabitant.

A boy who looked about our age, perhaps a little older, stood in one corner, not moving. But saying that does not begin to describe how much he was not moving. He did not blink. He did not breathe. He did not twitch or tremble. He was as still as any statue, as any piece of furniture in a room. He glowed with the same light that had flowed over the door. In the darkness of the room, though, it was easier to see the way the light moved. It swarmed around him, motes like a firefly cloud, making him seem more alive than either Catri or me, even for all his stillness.

He stared at us, frozen, his lips barely parted and an expression of such sorrow on his face that I wanted to weep. He wore clothing in the style of the sun wizard people: a fine white shirt embroidered with silver, a pale blue tabard over the shirt with the symbol of a great green tree in the center (the same tree, I realized, that graced the glass-and-metal wall in Catri's and my bedrooms), and, high on the right breast, the same sun that had been on the uniform Danrith had worn when he walked in to face Kai-Lord Letrin. His dark-blue long pants sheened like silk as the light flowed over them, and he wore the sort of light shoes that would only be appropriate for people who lived in the Spire and whose feet never trod through farmyard muck or over dirt roads.

His hair was long and silvery blond, pulled back in a ponytail at his neck the way some traders and outlanders wear theirs, and his eyes were the palest shade of blue, like shadows on snow, but with the irises dark-ringed.

Catri and I stepped toward him, enchanted.

She whispered, "He's . . ." But she said nothing else.

My thoughts finished the sentence for her. Beautiful. He was beautiful, as some boys can be. Not feminine. Simply . . .

perfect. Square-jawed and fine-featured, taller than either of us, lean and strong-looking. His hands were long-fingered and very clean and not calloused — they were nothing like the hands of all the boys I knew. They were, I thought, something like Doyati's hands.

Standing there, lost in staring at him, I thought for just a moment of Doyati made young again, and how I had thought him the handsomest boy I'd ever seen.

This boy made Doyati plain.

While I was standing there, stunned and captivated, Catri had walked all the way up to him. She was standing before him, at an angle to me, with her mouth a little open and her eyes as wide and as unblinking as his.

I thought of sad-eyed does staring at the salt lick in our pasture, kept away by our dog.

I thought of our dog, looking at the ham bone on our table after the meal was through, as my mother picked it up to carry to the pot to make soup stock for us.

In Catri's eyes were all the things we want but cannot have, and know we cannot ever have. All the dreams that are forever out of our reach because of some accident of birth, some moment when Fate passed a hand over us, then moved on, leaving us untouched. I could feel her hunger in my own heart.

The same hunger I'd felt when I touched the ruby on the door.

She leaned forward, eyes still wide and staring, lips parted, and I suddenly realized what she was going to do. She stood on her tiptoes, and her face dipped through that blanket of sparkling lights, and I fought the stillness that held me — a bit of magic, perhaps, or just my own yearning — and I managed to cry out, "Catri! NO!"

I lunged for her, trying desperately to stop her.

But I did not reach her in time.

She kissed him.

As soon as her lips brushed his, she threw herself backward and covered her mouth with her hands and screamed, but it was too late.

The damage had been done.

I stared at her. She stared at me.

"You do not even know him," I whispered.

"I could not stop myself."

"I'm your *guardian*. Your parents will have me beaten for this."

"I did not mean to," she told me.

I knew. I knew. She had been drawn to him as I had been drawn to the door.

But that did not change the fact that she had not been made an adult of our village, and that she had been in the presence of her guardian when she — still by law a child — had betrothed herself to a complete stranger frozen in a blanket of flowing light in a place far away from her family, who had not even met him to pass judgment on him.

"They are going to kill me," I said.

"They think you're dead already," she reminded me. "For that matter, they think I'm dead as well."

The boy stood there, still frozen.

"We could just not tell anyone," she said.

"We could leave him in here, and try to lock the door again, and pretend we never found him."

"A kiss, though," she said, and buried her face in her hands.

"Maybe he's dead," I said, and I fear my voice sounded hopeful when I said it.

She stared at me, horror written on her features, and shuddered. "I think I'm going to be sick."

Kissing the dead is only a little worse to my people than an unmarried girl child kissing a stranger. In truth, I am not entirely certain that it would be seen as worse.

Without warning, the light that flowed around him flickered once, then went out as abruptly and finally as the light on the door had. At the same instant, all the lights in the room we stood in came on.

The boy's eyes focused above us, behind us, and he sobbed, *"Kem beno mozaru!"* which I was almost certain meant "Don't leave me."

In Tagasuko. The sun wizard language that nobody spoke.

Then he actually saw *us*. Catri first, then me. He made a sound, a little cry of shock or fear or surprise.

And then he fell to the floor and lay there unmoving.

Catri shrieked.

"He wasn't dead," I whispered. But he looked like he might be as he lay there.

I ran to his side and touched him. He was warm, and his chest rose and fell. But it moved quickly — so very quickly. I rested my head on his chest and listened to his heart beating. His heart raced, going far too fast.

"Is he dead?" Catri said. I heard the tremor in her voice, and turned to see her standing where she had stood before, but with her hands over her eyes.

"He is not dead," I said. "He's not exactly well, either, but he still lives."

She opened her eyes and came over and knelt beside me. "Alive . . . What are we going to *do*, Genna?" She shook her head. "What do we do with him?"

"We'll worry about the . . . the . . ." I could barely make myself say the word. ". . . the kiss . . . later. We have stranger-duty to him. Get him fresh water to drink, I suppose," I said. "Some food to eat."

Spirit and little gods command that strangers who come offering no harm be treated well, welcomed, and cared for. The boy had done nothing to us and needed our help. So we were bound to help him.

Catri nodded and ran to the kitchen, and came back with a mug full of cold water. "There's no food in here, but I saw a green door nearby."

I nodded. "I will see if I can do anything to heal him. I can't find anything broken — that would be easy to fix. I'm not very good yet at mending the vague ills."

"I'll be right back," she said and ran off. I heard the door that led into the corridor swish open, and then close again.

Without the radiant light surrounding him, the boy seemed more regular and no longer enchanting. Something in that light had made us want him, I thought. It had, perhaps, been cast so that whoever found him would want to touch him — and touching him was the trick to waking him.

As I had wanted desperately to touch the door, Catri had wanted to touch the boy.

If he didn't know she had kissed him, was she still betrothed to him? She knew. I knew.

And there was the kiss itself — a thing shared only by two people who had sworn their lives to each other, a wordless promise between two souls who had vowed to walk through death and beyond together.

I had failed in my duty to Catri, and I had no idea how to fix the thing I had let happen. If she had acted from the compulsion of magical enchantment, still I had been the one who had allowed her to step into the room. I had been the one who had been careless with her virtue and, if the boy was not an adult among his people, with his.

I sprinkled some of the water Catri had brought on his face, and I watched him, and I worried. I could do nothing at the moment. I could tell my father what had happened when at last Catri and I were able to go home without endangering everyone and everything we held dear, but until then, I could only be guided by my own judgment.

Which did not seem to be working well for me.

I wondered how long he had been frozen in that room,

waiting for someone to come rescue him. I wondered who had left him there, and why.

His eyes fluttered, and I asked him, "Can you hear me?"

His eyes went very wide then, and he said something in Tagasuko that I did not even begin to catch.

That at least gave me another clue besides his clothes — which I'd thought he might have found in storage — as to how long he'd been frozen in that room. I shivered.

I was so startled, so confused, that I could barely recall the bits of Tagasuko I knew. I wanted words that would reassure him and comfort him, but we had studied nothing like those. I had commands. I had questions.

"*Hak skren skrezaru,*" I finally remembered, which was the bossy way of saying "Drink the water." I helped him to a sitting position and handed him the mug of water.

He stared at me like he thought the mug might be full of poison.

Of course he would think that. I was clearly not of his people, I barely spoke his language, and I probably looked threatening.

Well, being a girl and both smaller and most likely younger than him, I probably did *not* look threatening, but I imagined to his eyes I looked strange.

I took the mug back from him, took a long swallow of the water Catri had drawn, and handed the mug back to him again. *"Hak skren skrezaru,"* I said again.

He sniffed the contents of the cup and eyed me like a dog someone had beaten. *"Skren?"* he asked, which is just the word for "water." But when he said it, it didn't sound the way it did when I said it.

I repeated the word, pronouncing it as he had.

He nodded and carefully drank. And some of the fear left his eyes. "Water," he repeated.

And then a torrent of words.

I held up a hand, hoping he would recognize the gesture as "stop" and not think I was threatening him. I pointed to myself and, in laborious, slow Tagasuko, said, "I . . . do . . . not . . . speak . . . Tagasuko. Much. Speak . . . slowly."

Catri ran back into the room, her skirt pockets bulging and her arms full.

"I brought food," she said, and then she stared at the boy, whose color was better, who was sitting under his own power and drinking water from the mug, and her knees gave out. She sagged to the floor and buried her face in her hands. "Oh, Spirit and little gods, he's awake."

CHAPTER 9
THE SUN WIZARD BOY

We followed the string back to the grand foyer. And we watched the boy, who walked beside us silent as death, his face marked more by fear with every step he took.

Catri said, "What does he fear, do you think?"

I did not know. Except for the two of us, and perhaps whoever had been spying on us, we had seen no proof of life within the Spire. And during our long trudge through the empty corridors, I had found more than enough time to think, and I was convinced magic had been involved in both the portraits and the writing that had made the scroll. Magic, and perhaps the sun wizards' working ghosts.

The boy seemed to belong to the place, though. If he feared something, I thought Catri and I would probably be wise to be more afraid, no matter what the dragon had said about us being safe.

But as we walked along the edge of the foyer, heading back to our own corridor, with the boy looking wildly in all directions and growing more and more agitated, he suddenly grabbed me by the shoulders and screamed into my face, *"Hak gaenani dasna koro!"*

I turned to Catri, hoping her better skill with languages would help us this time. "Do you know the word *gaenani?*" I asked.

She held her hands wide. "Not even a little."

I turned to the boy and told him, *"Kem be worok . . . gaenani,"* which I hoped meant "I don't understand *gaenani.*" I might have been saying it wrong, though.

A look of purest frustration crossed his face, and he smacked his hand on his chest, and very slowly he said, *"Be. Gaena."* *Be* was a word I knew. It meant "I" or "me." He pointed to me. *"Su. Gaena."* *Su* meant "you." He pointed to Catri and said, *"Haen. Gaena."* *Haen* was "she." He waved his hands to indicate all of us. *"Beni. Gaenani."* *Beni* meant "we." So he and Catri and I were each *gaena,* and together the three of us were *gaenani.*

Catri and I looked at each other. "People?" I said.

She shrugged. "That seems right."

I tried that with the words I knew. *Hak* and *koro* meant

"tell me," and *dasna* was "where," from that list of question words Master Navan had made us memorize:

> Dasna, pasna, hasna,
> Jorna, norna, korna.
> Where, what, when,
> Why, who, how.

Tell me. Where. People.

It sunk in on both of us at the same time, and Catri whispered, "Oh, poor boy," and I suddenly understood his fear and his bewilderment. She and I turned to him at the same time.

He wanted to know where all the people were. He must have been in the Spire when it had been alive, when people crowded the corridors and inhabited all the dwellings, when it was as full of humans as the kai-lords' domains were of nightlings.

I did not know if he had felt time pass while the light had held him. I did not know if humans and nightlings had already gone to war when he had been left in that room to await the rescue of strangers. I knew only that he had stepped into that door in a world full of humans and had stepped out of it into a world where we were almost gone.

And I did not have the words to tell him what had happened. "We have to show him," I said.

"Show him what?" Catri asked.

"We have to take him through the great doors and let him look down at the world below. If he sees the taandu forests, if he sees the world as it is now, he'll understand that he's been . . . away . . ." I sought a better word but couldn't find one. ". . . for a long time."

"Seeing the forest and all the people gone from most of the world might kill him," Catri said. "Or drive him to kill himself."

He stood watching us, listening, frowning.

Catri looked sidelong at the boy, then looked away again and blushed. "I say we go to our dwelling and make a meal for the three of us. I'll share your room and we'll lock the door. He can have my room to himself. In the morning, we'll show him the world outside of the Spire, and we'll try to find a way to explain what happened to the people."

I considered that. I could imagine him looking out across the endless taandu forests, seeing nothing but trees where once there had been roads and cities filled with humans, and farmed fields, and I knew not what else.

"Well thought," I told her. "The cat will be back by then, maybe, and he can advise us. If not, we'll struggle as best we can."

"*Hak geen korok,*" Catri said to the boy. "Tell me your name."

He looked a little surprised. "*Geen Jagan,*" he said. "My name is Jagan."

Catri put her hand on her chest as the boy had done and said, "*Geen Catri.*"

The boy managed a small, tired smile. "*Astama, Catri.*" He turned to me. "*Hak geen korok.*"

"*Geen Genna.*"

"*Genna.*" He nodded. "*Astama, Genna.*"

"*Astama, Jagan,*" I said. I remembered *astama* as being the sun wizard greeting. Doyati had said it was something like "blessings" and something like "hello."

The three of us walked down the corridor together, not talking, and reached the door to our dwelling. At the door lay another tube of rolled paper, and with a glad cry, the boy Jagan leapt for it and unrolled it.

That scroll. No one had been near us. No one had followed us. In the corridors, we had heard our own footsteps and no others. "Sun wizard magic has to be what is making those scrolls," I told Catri.

She watched Jagan reading and said, "Working ghosts like the ones in the harp. And the one who haunts Dan."

"Maybe."

Jagan stood there, reading, frowning, looking from the sheaf of pages to us and back to the pages again. When he turned to an inside page, I saw what he'd seen on the front page, and my cheeks grew hot. I knew they were turning red. The top picture was of Catri and me standing at the point in the corridor where we could see the glowing door. We were holding the string, looking awestruck and a little sheep-stupid.

There was a picture of me opening the door, wearing an expression of unnerving hunger on my face as I did it.

Oh, and the third picture. Catri, rapt and lost and yearning, up on her toes, her face half buried in the flowing light that surrounded him, kissing Jagan, who, with his wide-frozen gaze and expression of great sorrow, looked like he knew what she was doing and wasn't sure he wanted her to do it. And there I was, in the background, with my mouth hanging open, looking surprised and shocked.

I was almost certain I'd been shouting, "No!" at that instant, but the picture didn't include what I said. Maybe the caption underneath it did, but considering the caption was written in Tagasuko, I did not think, if any of my people ever saw that picture, they would consider the words beneath important. The picture, after all, seemed to show the situation.

It was then that I realized pictures could lie.

The picture did not show who people were on the inside. It did not show what Catri and I had experienced, the magic, the strength of the hunger that had taken hold of us, or how that magic had released us the moment we had accomplished what that hunger had led us to do. No one would believe that the boy was senseless at that moment, that he no more knew she had been there than he knew a thousand years had passed since his last breath.

If Catri's parents saw the picture — if anyone from our village saw the picture — her family would be forced to have her marry the sun wizard boy, for the kiss is a sacred pledge, the uniting of two souls, a promise that must not be broken, and there she was, and there he was, and no one would be able to argue what it was they were doing.

I pulled that page from Jagan's hands, began ripping it to shreds, and let the shreds fall to the floor.

He made protest, a long and angry sentence that I did not understand and did not try to understand.

I said in my own language, "It is nothing to you, boy, but everything to her, and near as much to me. Silence yourself." He could not have known my words, but surely he caught the anger in my voice, for he fell silent.

Catri had seen the picture. Her eyes went huge when she saw me tearing it up. "It's your duty to tell them when we return. If you brought me forward for having shamed myself, you would not bear the blame at all."

I said, "Upon my head be the shame of this, Catri, but no one will know what you did. I will not tell anyone, and as your guardian I command that you will not tell anyone. I know the force of the magic that pulled you forward, and I know that you were innocent of what you did. If this lie that I will tell is mortal sin that will anger Spirit and turn little gods against me, then I will bear their anger. I was responsible. I failed you once by letting you go into that room. I will not fail you twice."

In that moment, I intentionally stepped off the path of the dutiful daughter, the dutiful citizen, and the good girl for the first time in my life. I committed a sin with full intent to commit it, as an adult whose sins were counted.

Catri had tears in her eyes. "I *wanted* to kiss him, though, Genna."

"And I wanted to open the door," I said. "But something

else wanted me to open it even more, just as something else wanted you to kiss him."

Jagan looked from one to the other of us, said something that sounded angry, and ran past us into the privy. A few moments later, he returned, but he did not speak. Instead, he went to the white room, went down the three steps into the couch pit, and sat down.

The instant he sat, the room went dark, and lights began to move through it. I could make little sense of what the lights were; they danced and shifted, layered in front of me. I caught something that looked like the glass wall in my bedroom, but the image was different. Not a tree, a moon, and a sun, but a great bird unlike anything I had ever seen before. And a moon and a sun. But mostly, the things I could understand disappeared behind blurs and smudges and streaks of other light.

Jagan kept saying "Show me —" followed by words I did not know, and each time he spoke, the colors and images changed.

Catri said, "Maybe it all looks different if you're sitting on that couch."

I felt a fool for not having thought of that.

We crept in, tiptoed down the three stairs, and sat.

Suddenly, all the blurring and smudginess resolved, and we were *in* place after place within the Spire, moving through different doors, seeing the insides of different dwellings very much like ours, except all empty.

Jagan spoke faster and more urgently, pleading, "Show me —," "Show me —," "Show me —," over and over again, and we began moving through public spaces, gliding beneath great statues, and over fountains, through rooms with grand tables and great arched ceilings, along balconies that looked down into courtyards. I began to understand how immense the Spire was, how much lay within it, and how very simple the little dwelling we inhabited was compared to all that was out there. But while every place was perfect, new-looking, and always magnificent, every place was empty.

I realized tears were running from the boy's cheeks, down into his mouth. That he was breathing hard. That his hands were balling into fists as he spoke.

He said "Show me" one last time. *"Hak be haw jat."* "Show me . . . *haw*." I did not know what a *haw* was, either, but I caught a flash of a room with the silver door I had dreamed of, with wizards and roses and lightning and the sun in the center — and suddenly, there was someone. A man, in the room. With us. Catri yelped and I grabbed my dagger, but he did not move forward. He did nothing to threaten us. He was tall and stern-looking. Silver-haired, dressed as Jagan was dressed, except his tabard was a brilliant scarlet, and the rest of his clothing was the gray of a dove's breast.

Jagan's face didn't brighten at seeing someone alive in this place. He spoke desperately, asking what had happened to the people, where everyone had gone.

The man began to speak, far too quickly for me to understand, and as he did, he faded away until only his voice was with us.

I, frustrated by too much Tagasuko, and not enough *understanding* Tagasuko, shouted, "Wait, wait, wait, *wait*! *Kem be Tagasuko korok! Kem be Tagasuko korok!*" Which meant "I do not speak Tagasuko."

The man studied Catri and me for a moment, then turned to Jagan and said something about *gaenani*. People.

It was too much for one day. Being wakened so badly by the shouting woman, finding the spying scrolls, and then trudging endlessly about looking for the silver door and discovering Jagan instead, and then carrying the burden of Catri kissing him and what we would face if her actions were discovered, and finally coming home to have a stranger magically appear in the room with us, and not knowing what he said, was more than I could bear.

My cheeks burned, and hot, angry tears ran down them.

The pictures vanished, and the man was standing in the white room again, in the open space in the center of the couch. *"Siroeth suno journa?"* he asked.

I did not behave well in the face of that question or in the presence of that voice. In fact, I lost my temper. "I do not know what you ask me! I do not *speak* your stupid language! I want to go home and be with my parents and be a child again and let someone else be the Sunrider. I want to leave this stupid place and find Papa and have him tell me what to do, because I *do not know!*"

Inside my head, something . . . popped. It was the littlest thing, a nothing. It was almost unnoticeable, just a slight shift, as when you yawn and your ears pop. Only it was not that exactly. It was something else.

It made me stop my screaming and ranting and making myself a fool. It made me hold my breath, because however small it might have felt, it came from outside me, and it happened inside me, and it was . . . different.

I did not know if it might be a good sort of different, or if in the next instant some monster would erupt from the whiteness of the room — as the man had erupted from nothingness — to devour me. I said something about monsters.

The man said, "There will be no monsters today."

No. That was not what he said at all. What he said was, *Kem skrabaruni ashanzi stah.*

And that is what my ears heard, too.

But what I understood was, "There will be no monsters today."

And then he said something else, and I understood him to say, "I am Neth Kosae Haw, teacher and trainer of wizards, Sun Wizard of the First Order, and by my will and the power of the Ag, monsters cannot come here."

I said, carefully, "You are not speaking Osji, are you?"

"No. I speak Tagasuko. The True Tongue, the language of art and magic."

"And I am not speaking Tagasuko."

"No. You speak Osji. The Defiled Tongue. The slave language of your owners, the nightling kai-lords."

I wanted to snap that I spoke no such thing. I wanted to be angry, insulted, enraged.

But if I had understood anything Doyati and Master Navan had taught me of the history of humans following the nightling triumph in the Long War, the man was correct. Rude, but correct.

Catri elbowed me. "I can understand him," she whispered.

"I have done a small magic," the man said, "that will permit you to understand speakers of the True Tongue, and, as long as you are within the Spire or the ground it controls, will allow them to understand you."

"That's better," Catri said.

I had to agree.

The man told all three of us, "Watch, and I will show you where the people went."

Without warning, we stood on the deck of a great bird-winged ship sailing through the skies, and the ground below us was farmed in places, and covered with networks of roads dense as the threads in a spider's web in others, and marked all over with cities above the ground, built of glass in every color, built of shining white stone, built of gleaming black metal, built of brick and painted wood. The ship-of-the-air in which we stood turned and dipped until I started to feel dizzy, and then I saw the Spire, looking as it still did, but with a vast and colorful city built at its base, where now nothing but grass and trees remained, and roads ran out from that city in all directions, like spokes of a great wheel. There were pockets of forests, a handful of taandu trees in the distance, and I pointed the place out to Catri. "That's where Arrienda is, I think."

She nodded.

The ship turned toward the Spire again, though, and moved toward it. I could feel myself sitting, but I could see myself standing; the sense of movement and the simultaneous feelings of falling and floating were making me sick.

And suddenly the picture changed.

I was looking through someone else's eyes as he walked through the Spire — but a Spire busy with life, wild with noise and color and movement. I had been in Arrienda, so I knew how enormous a city could be. But the Spire was huge in a different way. It was loud. It was . . . cheerful. It was human in a thousand tiny details I could not even name. Arrienda, built and occupied by nightlings, was magnificent. It inspired awe. It stunned all the senses, a feast for the nose and the ears and the tongue and the fingertips as much as it was for the eyes. But it was something from another world, too, a cool, twilit, shivery world as alien to me as the worlds of the moonroads.

The world that surrounded the Spire — and even places in the Spire itself — was warm and bright, a little messy, a bit jumbled at the corners. That world had room for mistakes, for chances and risks, for foolishness and laughter, even though I could see all the places where it was serious, fierce, strong. I could have lived in that vibrant, busy time and found my way to calling it home.

And then the pictures changed again.

"This was the war, which Jagan remembers in small part. This was the battle between Sunkind and Moonkind," the man's voice said, though he had vanished when the images returned.

Before my eyes, the long-dead war lived again. We stood on pinnacles beside wizards who cast down spells, cringed as nightling armies moved past us through the twilight, watched as fires burned forests beneath a smoke-filtered sun, and in the dead dark of moonless night beheld forests of taandu trees growing forward at an impossible rate, maturing and taking ground, devouring first roads and farms, and then towns and cities, and everything and everyone in them. Ghosts marched. Explosions and screams echoed; the dead burned where they had fallen.

"The world of humans died, and the bent and twisted shapes of monsters slipped from the moonroads into the dark corners of the ruins, and took up residence beneath the perpetual shade of the taandu forests," the man said. I could see their shadows slipping between the massive trees, and my skin crawled.

The room appeared around us again. White, bright white, and in it, before us, the stern, calm man who knew what had happened.

The man said, "So it ended."

And Jagan said, "No. I saw all that. I knew all that. The Spire still lived then, and so did everyone in it. But when my parents dragged me down here to the Warrens, and hid me in a safety room, and promised to come get me when everything was over, something had changed. They were afraid, right then, of something terrible that was coming right then. They went, but they didn't come back. What happened to them?"

"The Fall," the man said.

And Jagan said, *"Hak jat."* "Show me."

CHAPTER 10
ALL WE LOST

The cat rubbed up against my legs, and in my head, said, *Careful, now. Watch everything, say nothing.*

I looked down to find his round, furry face tilted up to me, his eyes huge and unblinking.

Never speak to me in front of the wizard. Or the boy. Or if you speak to me, never say anything you would not say to the cats in your barn.

I looked up and found myself not in a plain white room but out on the broad, wide landing of the Spire, where Catri and I had come when first we climbed the path away from the dragon and the ledge.

The sky was full of dragons and ships-of-the-air, and the landing was covered with people who were dressed in the fashion of the sun wizards. I was close to a rail and could see below, and what I saw bewildered me. It was the world of humankind, with the thin ribbons of roads flowing in all directions, with towns and cities scattered as far as the eye could see . . . but with flames and smoke below, and explosions, and trees. Spreading. Spreading so quickly I could watch them growing.

This is the day of the Fall, the cat said in my head.

I stared at the trees. From the great height of the Spire, I could watch a forest spreading in long, curving lines. First a single tree would burst through the surface of the earth some distance away from a main mass of trees. Then another one would erupt some distance from it, and while it was growing broad and wide, a third would appear some distance from it. And on and on, in a line that curved gently to follow the ridgeline of a particular hill. Where roads or houses stood in the way, the tree came up beneath them, destroying whatever resided on top.

And when this line of trees stopped moving forward, branches started shooting out on either side of the main line. Those lines were shorter, and when they had filled out, side branches began spreading from *them.* I was watching the forest spread the way a puddle grows in a hard rain, filling in everything in one area, finding a place where it could break free of its boundaries, spreading again.

And erasing everything that had been there before.

I found myself leaning forward, trying to grip a railing that was not there. Willing the spread of the forest to stop, because those beautiful towns and cities were falling before it.

There was a sound to the forest growing. I would not have thought such a thing was possible, but there was a sound. It was a low rumble, so low I could barely hear it, so vast I could not help but feel it.

At the edges, I could see men with fire weapons setting the spreading forest ablaze. I could see the great ships-of-the-air soaring over the advancing line and the men aboard them pouring liquids on the trees that withered some of them and stopped them from growing.

But the forest went around the areas where men fought, and there were not enough men to fight everywhere.

As the terrible battle advanced toward me, I saw places where the trees spread behind the men who were fighting them, and lines of trees filled in, and suddenly dark things were moving beneath the trees, reaching out, grabbing the humans who were unlucky enough to get too close, and dragging them into the spreading shade.

The nightlings and worse things, safe beneath the canopy of spreading forest, were destroying everything the trees did not.

I jammed my hands into the pockets of my skirt and fought back the tears that threatened to spill from my eyes. I swallowed against the lump in my throat. I blinked and blinked, and still a few tears leaked out.

Mindful of the cat, I said nothing out loud. People on the balconies passed through me, going about whatever they had done that last day. Dragons landed, spoke to men, landed again. They were overseeing the evacuation of survivors, I realized. Getting everyone they could into the Spire.

Below me, the line of trees stopped advancing. It began filling in, and as it did, it made the same perfect circle around the base of the Spire that still existed.

The magic is holding it, I thought. If the Spire has this magic, why do the cities of men not have it? Why are they falling, crashing to the ground before my eyes, disappearing into the spreading blanket of unbroken green?

Before the trees finished filling in, people were still getting through, running wildly, dragging children and nothing else, reaching the safe ground and still running, because from the advance points of the forest, the dark shadows beneath shot at them, and many fell.

The clear ground was littered with bodies but also with survivors racing closer, pouring into the passageways that led upward.

And dragons were flying into the open spaces, scooping up the injured in their mouths, and bringing them to the landing, where they spit them out and went back for more.

The nightlings did not shoot at the dragons.

But the tighter the forest filled in, the more I could see a seething mass of shadows forming a wall between the forest and the clearing.

The humans who successfully broke free and ran to safety stopped being a flood and became a trickle. And then no more came through.

I could not stop myself anymore. I cried, wrapping my arms tight around myself, trying to tell myself that I had not seen the terrible things I had, wishing for all the world that I could believe they were all pretend.

Those people down there were dead a thousand years before I was born, I thought.

I know how this story ends. Some of them survived.

But not in the Spire, unless, like Jagan, they were still frozen by magic and hidden away.

Catri took my hand, and I saw she was crying, too.

The man said something, and without warning, day was night. Dark night, with a full moon riding high overhead. I stood in the same place. Below me, the world lay dark and silent, save for a few places where lights still glowed or where forests burned. The rumble of the spreading forest had stopped.

I was not quite alone. A line of silent men dressed in the uniforms I had come to recognize as the dress of the sun wizards stood, more or less evenly spaced, along the rail, facing outward.

No panicked people ran to shelter within the Spire. No dragons delivered survivors. The men, holding objects that I knew had to be weapons — though they looked like nothing I had ever seen before — stood grim-faced and alert, watching the ground beneath. The clearing below had been lit with the same sourceless light that still filled the Spire's corridors. Someone or something had cleared away the bodies of the fallen.

Nothing moved.

And then something did.

The wings of dragons thundered overhead, and I thought, More survivors, and dared to hope that the worst was over.

But the dragons landed all together, at the same time, and opened their mouths, and out crawled . . . horrors. Some I had seen the likes of before, shambling through the twilight worlds. Some had clearly once been human, but were no more.

Whatever magic had protected the Spire from the night-lings, it did not protect them from the nightmares that spewed out of the dragons' mouths and lunged forward, all together, and quickly killed the wizards who had been guarding the landing.

My knees gave out.

The dragons had been helping the humans. They had fought against the nightlings. Well, they had not fought, but they had rescued the injured.

They brought distractions to keep the uninjured busy, the cat said in my head. *Most of the greatest talents in wizardry were deep in the Spire as what you are watching happened, fighting to save the lives of those who had been injured by nightling magic. They didn't know that magic was turning each human they were fighting to save into another of the very monsters you see here.*

And as those humans changed, they turned on the people who were trying to save them. And they destroyed them.

I could not look at the bodies of the wizards, being thrown over the rails by the creatures who had once been human.

I could not look at the dragons, who had betrayed the people who trusted them.

I could not look at anything.

I sat, eyes squeezed shut, arms wrapped tight around myself, while a silent slaughter came and then went. The dragons flew away. The killers they had brought with them crept into the heart of the Spire.

Now I knew why the Spire had been empty when Catri and I arrived.

I opened my eyes, and the room was white. Featureless. Brightly lit.

Some of the humans here lived, the cat told me. *They were lucky, and they managed to destroy the monsters before they were completely overrun. They hid for a while. And then they tried to go to the villages where the last humans survived — the villages held and owned by the nightlings. And the Spire, nearly abandoned, waited.*

I turned to stare at him. *The dragons . . .*

They had their own goals. They were not allies of the nightlings. They were not allies of the humans. They played their own game, and in the end, they were wiped out. All save the last dragon.

That stopped me. I almost spoke out loud, but the cat hissed. So I thought, *The last dragon? MY dragon? The one who saved me and saved Catri when the nightlings were trying to kill us? He was not part of what I just saw, was he?*

He was, the cat said. *He has suffered much for the*

treachery of his kind. He suffers still. But he was as much a
part of it as any of the rest of them.

I thought of his mutterings and whisperings. Of how he
argued with himself in dozens of voices about devouring
both of us, of ending all hope. He had fought with his kind
to destroy my kind, but in the end, he had saved Catri, and
he had saved me. Why? Whose will did he serve? His own?
Some other's?

He spoke of another, but I had thought that was most
likely another of his mad voices.

Now I was not so sure.

Don't worry yourself about it, the cat's voice purred in
my head. *For whatever reason, you lived. He has gone his
way, and you have gone yours. It's done.*

"What happened then?" Jagan asked. I dared to open
my eyes. He looked sick. The room was bright again; the
pictures of the Fall were gone.

The man said, "Nightlings rounded up the surviving
humans and marched them to camps and put them to work.
They slaughtered any who complained or resisted, any who
tried to escape. They slaughtered adults wholesale and those
older children who showed a streak of independence.

"They raised a generation of human children to be
slaves, bred them to one another, made them speak a

language that was neither that of the sun wizards nor that of the nightlings, and when the second generation — docile and obedient — grew to adulthood, they set these humans to work on farms in little villages, making cloth and growing animals. And every year, drawing daylight sap from the taandu trees. For a thousand years, it has been so."

These, I thought, were my people. Slaves bred for captivity, slaves who had known nothing but slavery, and like sheep and cattle, had not known they were beasts penned and tended for the benefit of others.

The boy whispered, "A thousand years. I've been locked in sleep for a thousand years?"

"Yes," the man said. "You have." But he — the cat had called him a wizard — was not finished. "There was a second story. In the Spire, a handful of wizards had survived. They had children; they trained their children to be different. Rebels. And they carefully sent their children into the villages, using the tiniest of magics to make sure it seemed to the villagers that they had always been there. These rebels married, raised children, taught, wrote, gave law and justice, passed on their books to their own children."

I realized I was a descendant of this second lineage, too, that I was born of both the slaves and the free wizards. My family had been lawgivers for generations. My family had been full of women who knew little magics, careful magics.

Each had chosen to risk everything to pass on the knowledge to the next generation, even though much of what they passed on was the knowledge that humankind had once been free and strong, and the idea that humankind might one day be again.

This had to be my destiny, I thought.

But Papa told all of us, "Your destiny is what you make it. Every moment, you choose who you will be, if you will be someone better and stronger and braver — or someone worse and weaker and more cowardly — than who you are right now. Your choice is all the destiny there is or ever will be."

So I was born of slaves and of wizards, and my destiny was choice. The choice to save my people, or the choice to hide. *Choice* is a big destiny.

The pictures of the war and its aftermath had ended, and for an instant, I saw the boy talking to Neth Kosae Haw. The man answered, bowed slightly, and faded slowly into nothingness. It was then that I realized he was a ghost. Another sun wizard ghost.

The sun wizards had left little behind them. Books, ruins, a handful of tools they'd created, and one standing city that the taandu trees had not been able to devour and the nightlings had not been able to invade.

Plus a boy who had lived when humans ruled, and who lived again.

That boy who might know something that would let us find the way to free humanity from nightling power for good.

CHAPTER 11
JAGAN, THE CAT, AND ME

The cat lurked around our dwelling after Genna and I carried a meal over from the green door cabinets.

When we sat down to eat, Jagan, who had said nothing and done nothing but sit and stare at his hands since the wizard had vanished back to where he came from, looked at the cat and smiled a little. He took a bit of food from his plate, dangled it near the floor, and said, *"Hak tok, tewi, tewi,"* in the sort of soothing, crooning voice people use when trying to get a cat to do something. Anything. "Come here, kitty, kitty."

Because cats do only what they want and need to be wheedled.

Well, this is embarrassing, the cat told me.

He was staring at the dangling food, and he started sidling toward it. He took it from Jagan's fingers with delicate care, and purred blissfully, eyes closed, while Jagan scratched him between the ears.

How dignified you look right now, begging scraps.

If you laugh at me, I'll scratch you, the cat threatened.

You could just tell him you're not really a cat, and then he wouldn't treat you like that.

If I had turned into a barking dog, the effect on the cat could not have been more severe or more astonishing. He turned and hissed at me, his back arched, his fur stood on end, his ears went flat against his head, and he launched himself from the floor to one of the low kitchen cabinets, and from there to the top of a high one.

From his perch, he glowered down at me.

Catri said, "What in the world has gotten into him that he acts like that?" She started to say something else, but her face went blank, and I realized the cat was talking to her in her head, the way he talked to me in mine. She glanced once at Jagan, and her lips thinned.

"Genna," she said, "could you get him and toss him outside? Maybe he'll be in a better mood when he comes back."

In my head, the cat said, *I told her to say that.*

I sighed and stood up from our very fine last meal, which was hot and savory fish soup, greens and herbs, and mutton pie just the way Catri's mother made them. I did not want to bother with the cat. I wanted to eat. But first meal had been extravagant, and we'd eaten middle meal as well — something usually reserved for men working in the fields. The food was tantalizing, but I could push myself away.

I stood up and turned to face him. "Cat, whatever is the matter with you? Come here."

The cat said nothing out loud. In my head, though, he said, *He cannot know about me, Genna. I can only be a cat to him. Because the wizard knows him, and he trusts the wizard.*

The cat glowered down at Jagan and said nothing else to me.

"What happened?" Jagan asked.

"I don't know," I said. "He's an idiot cat. Who knows why cats do anything?"

But I asked the cat, *And if the wizard found out you were not truly a cat? So what?*

Then I am in danger again from the sun wizards, and after a thousand years of being free of their animosity, I would rather stay that way.

I was so busy wondering why the sun wizards could possibly be interested in the cat that I almost missed the *really* important part in what he said. Almost.

But when I had been running the moonroads in a crazed panic to save my family and my village from the Kai-Lord of Arrienda, the cat had told me that he wasn't old enough to have known Doyati's mother, or to have seen the assassination of Doyati's father. Doyati's father had died roughly a hundred years before.

Yet the cat had just stated that the sun wizards had been dangerous to him a thousand years earlier.

My blood grew cold, and something twisted my stomach, so that for a moment I felt as I had when I'd been in the dragon's mouth — sick, and dizzy, and scared.

I stared at him and said, "Here, kitty, kitty. You and I need to go outside. *Now*."

I wiggled my fingers as you do with cats, but I wasn't thinking calming thoughts. I was thinking, *You and I need to talk away from these two, and we need to do it right now.*

He was an impossible animal, that cat, but to his credit, he did a good enough job of smoothing his fur and lifting his ears, and he jumped down to where I could reach him and pick him up.

I took him out into the corridor, and from there into the dwelling directly across from ours. I commanded the door to open, and when we were inside, I locked it behind us. I put him down, and thought to him, *You haven't been in danger from the sun wizards for a thousand years?*

No. But nobody else has, either. I just don't want things to change. That's the tiny little question that has your fur rubbed wrong? You're not concerned that you don't know this boy, that you don't know why he was locked away in a hazard containment room, that he's still alive after a thousand years or perhaps more? You're not concerned about telling him what I am, but you wouldn't think of telling the same thing to some boy you know from Hillrush.

They would not believe me.

Better for me if this one wouldn't, either. That's wizard apprentice garb the boy is wearing, my girl. And blazoned with the Tree of Magic, which marks him as from a family of high importance.

I chewed on my bottom lip and watched him, waiting to see if he would suddenly realize what it was that was bothering me. But he was focused on the boy.

He paced in tight little circles, his ears halfway back and his fur once again fluffed out so that he looked bigger and angry. *Some of those people were dangerous — and not just the adults. Some of the children were veritable nightmares, too. Oh, most of them were fine, as far as that all went, children and adults alike. Only a few were ever* entrusted with magic. *Most learned cooking and building design and how to purify water supplies and how to plant crops and how to write books and on, and on, and on. Harmless, most of them. And most of those who did have access to magic learned it in a responsible manner. They were taught how to use power wisely before they were ever entrusted with any; they didn't go off chasing moonroad monsters for what they could learn from them.* He hissed. *Some of them, though —*

And then he looked up at me and stopped. One of the few expressions a cat does well is surprise. That cat looked surprised.

Whaaaaat?

A thousand years, cat?

He sat carefully before me, putting paws neatly together, wrapping his tail around his feet. And then he looked up at me, clearly puzzled, head cocked to one side, ears pricked forward, green eyes wide. His little round face with its dark stripes and its neat white muzzle, the swirly black stripes of his body, his perfectly clean white bib and paws, and the neat brown and rust-red of the rest of his fur made a picture that was . . . well . . . cute. Almost unbearably cute.

I was not thrown from my track; I was not misled by his cuteness.

He might look the part of the most adorable of house cats, but he was nothing of the sort.

I sat cross-legged on the floor and stared at him — a game one should never play with cats. But I said, *You told me you weren't old enough to know Doyati's parents, or to see the assassination of Doyati's parents. And yet, moments ago, you admitted having been around long enough to get yourself in trouble with sun wizards.*

The cat broke our little staring contest, raised a paw, and began to wash it vigorously.

Caaat . . .

He stopped licking briefly to correct me. *I did not,* he said, *get* myself *in trouble.* He resumed licking the paw as if the world itself would end if he did not get that fur clean in that very instant.

I glowered. *I find that hard to believe. But right now, I don't care whether you were guilty or innocent. I want to know why you lied to me. And I want to know what you are.*

Lick, lick, lick.

I could pull your whiskers out one at a time, I told him.

He looked up at me, unblinking, challenging me with his gaze. *You could try.*

I thought of the magic he wielded, of the power I had seen him command before, and I realized that I would not be able to pull out even one of his whiskers if he did not let me.

I took a deep breath. *Maybe I could not. But I can take Catri and the boy Jagan and go hunting through the moonroads, away from you, and let you find us if you can.*

I cannot say what change I saw in him — it was too small for my mind to define — but he no longer looked so sure.

I built on that. *You know I want to. You travel the roads yourself. You know how they call to you, how that hunger to be on them builds. You know I can feel them pulling me toward them. How some part of me is calling them to me even now, even without my conscious will. They are in my blood, cat, and my blood is on them. It is only because of my respect for your wishes that I do not take to them right now.*

The cat blinked once. *Only? The safety of your family does not call to you? Banris's desire to destroy you and use your death to claim immortality does not keep you here?*

Thanks to the dragon, Banris thinks I am dead. I could take to the roads, hunt him down, and find a way to kill him before he even knew his danger.

The cat sighed. It was a long sigh, weary and dispirited. *I do not doubt for a moment that's what you think would happen. So I must consider your threat real. But I can tell you with certainty that Banris would destroy you utterly, even if he now thinks you dead. You'd have no chance against him.*

I could still try.

And die in the trying.

And you could carry that guilt on your tiny shoulders for however much longer you live.

His eyes narrowed, and the tip of his tail began to flip back and forth with agitation.

I don't much like you, he told me.

Nor I you, right at this moment. What are you, cat?

I cannot tell you. I am not saying I will not tell you, but I cannot. Words do not exist for what I am, and what you see is only the smallest part of me.

Are you Spirit?

That's a word. The cat sounded irritated. *If I were Spirit, then I could say, "I am Spirit," and you would understand me.*

One of the little gods, then?

His ears went back. *Also words. Let us save ourselves some time, shall we? If you can ask a question about whether*

I am this thing, or that thing, then the answer is already no, because anything you can name is a thing that I am not. That's what "There are no words" means, you idiot.

I curled my middle finger against my thumb and flicked him on top of his head.

He hissed. *Why did you do that?*

Don't call me an idiot, I said. *If you cannot tell me what you are, then show me.*

That I cannot do because it would be the instant death of all of us.

Oh, really?

Yes, really. Do you think I have gone around in this form for . . . well, a very long time . . . because it amuses me? I am in hiding, far more than you are, and from a much greater enemy.

An enemy greater than Banris?

The cat stood up and paced again. *Your enemy dreams of controlling the world. Mine already does. It is bigger, more terrible, more monstrous than any creature living today can imagine, and it is everywhere. And it is waiting.* The cat's ears went back. *For me. To destroy me, and everything I represent, and everything I fight for — everything that lives right now only through me. It knows I am not dead. It simply does not know where I am or how to reach me. Were*

I to make my presence felt as what I truly am, here and now, it would move the world and everything in it to put an end to me. You cannot imagine the fury it could unleash.

Has it something to do with the Green Sorceress?

Never ask that question again, never speak that name aloud. Never. Do you understand?

I did. Something about the cat's demeanor, something about the fear that radiated off him, something I could not put a finger on convinced me that everything he had said was nothing less than the truth.

I might be gullible. I might. And trusting the cat did not seem the safest of bets. But then, nothing in my life had been safe since well before my brother Danrith and I walked into the woods one night to gather taandu sap to save my mother's life.

I had come to discover that "safe" was an illusion, a pretense that adults wrapped around their children — and sometimes themselves — to make the world seem comfortable. I had discovered that under that thin cover of let's-pretend, monsters and nightmares lay, and that not all of them came from places like the moonroads or the nightling cities. Some of the monsters were people we knew. People we thought we could trust.

Who is your enemy, cat?

He chirped, that little cat sound of entreaty, and crouched and wiggled his hindquarters. And he leapt gracefully onto my shoulder and rubbed his head against my cheek. *Some things I cannot tell you, girl. That thing I will not, because if you know the monster, you will pay attention to it when you pass it — as you passed bits and pieces of it most days of your life. You will know it for what it is, and when you know it, then it will know you. And in the instant that it knows you, it will destroy you.*

How do you pass it, then? I asked.

He leaned around my shoulder, digging his claws into my skin to hang on, and stared into my face. *You hurt my head, do you know that?*

It is an honest question.

It is an annoying question. You couldn't do what I do. When I am near the enemy, there is a part of me that is in my skin that no more knows the enemy than you do, and so passes safely. There. Do you find that helpful? Can you use that to go where the enemy is and not die? Or will you now concede that some things are beyond what you have learned in your twelve miserable years of existence —

Fourteen, I interrupted.

He yowled. Right in my ear, the cat yowled. And launched off my shoulder with his claws digging deep, and shrieked to the door as if I'd trampled his tail while wearing boots. *You dare quibble with me over how long ago an eye blinked? You dare argue the value of a year, of two years, you who are a babe in arms to me? Out! Let me out!* he demanded.

Annoying creature.

I opened the door for him, and he shot down the corridor as if someone had tied rocks to his tail and was gone before I could be certain which corridor he'd taken.

So I went across the hall, thoughtful. He was not a cat, he was not immortal, he was not Spirit made flesh, he was not a little god, and he had an enemy that I knew but did not know. And one that if I knew it, would kill me instantly.

That was going to bother me.

"Where did you go?" Catri asked.

"To calm the annoying beast, and then to see if I could find the little idiot when he wandered off." Yes, I lied to her. I am not proud of that, but I could not explain to her what the cat and I had discussed. She knew a little about him, that he was old, that he was not what he appeared to be. She did not need to know what I had discovered. Yes, she was the same age I was, the age the cat dismissed with such scorn.

She'd had her own share of responsibility and duty. But she had not been through what I had been through. She had never walked the moonroads, and she did not know how they bit. She had never had the burden of the lives of her entire village in her hands.

She did not truly comprehend the awful danger that waited outside of our still-protected lives. The dragon was the worst thing she had ever seen. It was not the worst thing that had ever come after me.

And I was her guardian. I had been made an adult by my village, and she was still a child. It was my duty to keep the truth from her.

So why did I feel so vile for doing that very thing?

The boy Jagan was once again in the white room, surrounded by things that were not real. "What has he been looking at?" I asked.

"I cannot even tell you the half of it. Animals the like of which I've never seen, and men pale as milk and strong as trees sailing ships through the air. Cities above the ground — oh, Genna, such beautiful cities, and with streets white as snow, smooth as glass, and filled with people like us. You cannot imagine so many people so beautifully dressed. He asks questions about his family, his friends, and sometimes the old man answers, and sometimes shows him pictures, and then he cries a little, and then he talks some more."

"It must be awful to be him, and to be so alone."

Catri nodded. "Once he called me over and bade the old man talk to me. And he did, Genna. He looked right at me and asked me what I knew about magic trans . . . magical trans . . . transpo-something. Transmo —? I don't know. I did not know the word, and said so, and he frowned, and asked me something else about magic. And I kept saying I did not understand, I did not understand, until finally he returned his attention to Jagan and told him to bring us both to *aglak*, whatever that might be, in the morning."

I watched Jagan. He no longer talked to the old man. He was, instead, staring at two adults — a plump woman with hair the color of his, and a tall, handsome man whose pale blue eyes looked worried. They wore the same tabards he wore, with the big tree in the center. They did not speak to him or seem to be aware of him. They were working on a ship-of-the-air such as the one we had seemed to fly in when the wizard had shown us the past, only this ship was small. It had a long, arched neck, a peregrine head with a brass beak and obsidian eyes, green metal feathers almost as fine as a bird's feathers, and a long, sleek boat body covered by what looked to me like polished emeralds cut in feather shapes and banded with silver. The little ship held its wings tight to its sides and crouched on four sturdy legs that ended in big silver bird feet. It was all emeralds and silver, and rich dark red wood the likes of which I had never seen. The ship should have looked strange, but to me it was simply beautiful.

Jagan said nothing. He simply watched the people, his eyes sad, his lips pressed tight together. I could tell he'd been crying again because his eyes were once more red, and his cheeks had fresh tear streaks on them, but he had his shoulders hunched like someone who had been beaten and his head thrust forward. He was not crying then.

I wondered who the people were and guessed they might have been his family. And I stared at the lovely unfinished ship they were building with a hunger that I would not have suspected in myself.

Since coming to the Spire, I had been high above the ground, looking down from the balconies, seeing the world so much larger than I had ever imagined it, so full of space and possibility. I could imagine, suddenly, what it might be like to fly. And I discovered that suddenly, I wanted to.

CHAPTER 12
THE AGLAK

I stood before the silver door and said, "Let me in."

All around me darkness pooled, but the door and I stood in light — cold white light, like the light of the moon.

"Are you sure?" a voice I had heard before whispered.

"I'm sure," I said.

The door swung open without any sound, revealing nothing but darkness within. I had to go in, though. Once the door opened, I could not stop myself. I floated out of the light, into the darkness. Floated. The fact that I was floating frightened me, and I tried to turn back, to step back into the light, but I could not.

And then a full moon raced up over a horizon and silhouetted the vaguely manlike shape of a huge creature with horns growing out of its head, with wickedly curved claws.

The moon illuminated him, and he grinned at me with a mouth full of jagged teeth.

Banris.

Banris the taandu monster, the would-be immortal, who had once been human and my father's best friend, who was my father's attempted murderer, who sought to kill me because my death would somehow fulfill the requirements of the spell he needed to cast in order to live forever.

"Little Genna, come to die," he said.

And I awoke, screaming.

Catri, next to me in the bed, flailed her arms and legs, shrieked, and dove for the floor.

I sat up, clutching the covers around me, shaking.

"What?" she wailed. "What was it?"

Jagan burst through our door, and the lights came on, and we saw him standing there, blinking, holding a chair by its back, looking around the room with fear and fury on his face.

I could not shake the fear that clung to me. I could feel Banris, just on the other side of wakefulness, waiting to grab me, waiting to kill me.

But this time, it had not been real. No smallest beam of moonlight crept through the thick blanket that covered our glass wall. So the moonroads had not touched me. I had just been dreaming.

I let out my breath in a gasp, and in doing so, realized that I had been holding it. "Nightmare," I said. "Just a nightmare. About Banris."

Catri shivered. "I have nightmares about him, too, sometimes. About being chained to the wall again, with Kai-Lord Letrin on his throne, and the huntress and her hounds, and the harper and his ghosts, and Banris, chained close to us but not really captive. He was close enough to reach out and grab me."

"I know," I said. "I remember."

Jagan was puzzled. "The kai-lords are . . . nightlings."

I nodded. "The kai-lord of Arrienda took all the people of my village prisoner. He was going to execute them —"

Jagan interrupted me. "Both of you, too?"

Catri said, "I was his prisoner. Genna was the one who killed him. She and her brother Danrith." Her expression softened a little when she said Dan's name. "They brought Doyati back, too."

Jagan turned to me. "So . . . you killed a kai-lord?"

I nodded. "I had help."

"Even so." He looked impressed. "And" — he turned to Catri — "you were the kai-lord's prisoner."

"One of them," Catri said.

"And you both live." He looked wistful. "What adventures. And you mention this . . . Banris. Who is he?"

"He was a man," I said. "Now he's a taandu monster, and he has a spell to become immortal, but he needs to kill me in order for it to work."

Jagan's eyes went wide. "Really?"

I do not think he believed me. In truth, if I had not lived through the past months, I would not have believed me, either. "It is a very long story."

He nodded with all seriousness and said, "When we have time, you must tell me all of it. I have had no adventures, experienced no danger, done nothing of worth or merit in my entire life. I have studied, I have learned, and I have been kept safe."

"Be grateful," I said. "Adventures are only interesting once you've lived to see the end of them. Before that, they are nothing but fear, and being too cold or too hot or too wet or too hungry, and getting hurt."

Jagan said, "Sleep while you can. The Morning Call will wake us early, because you'll need time to prepare yourselves before we go to Aglak. While you shower and fix your hair, I will get appropriate clothes for you. Neth Kosae Haw, the wizard you met last night, said you both come from families of high status and both have already trained in some magic, though he was in part unfamiliar with the forms you know. So you will present yourself to Aglak as foreign students of magic and will wear the badges of rank. It will make Aglak less . . . daunting."

Daunting. I did not really wish to hear that Aglak, whatever that might prove to be, would be daunting.

I did fall back to sleep, but Catri and I awoke what felt like only moments later to the angry-mother voice demanding that we wake up. Catri jumped, flinging covers everywhere, then groaned. "I forgot she was going to happen." She sat up and studied me. "You look terrible, you know that?"

"I was awake for a long time after my nightmare. I am as weary as if I had been working in the fields with Papa."

Catri stretched like a cat and made all sorts of noise doing it. When at last she stood, she grinned at me. "You should think less, you know that?"

She had a point. I should also not keep company with talking cats, I should hide from all future dragons, and I should have no enemies. Then my sleep would be calm and my waking hours serene. I have never yet figured out what to do about good advice that you get, and that you know right away would help you, but that you cannot follow.

I did what I do. I said, "I'll try that tonight."

"Should we bathe or go have first meal?" she asked. "I'm so hungry."

I still lay beneath the covers, wishing that I could close my eyes and sleep the day away.

I could not, of course. Outside the tall, safe fortress that was the Spire, Banris plotted the conquest of the world, and the kai-lords still owned most of humanity and most of their fellow nightlings. And I was no closer to how to do what I needed to do to be Sunrider.

Catri bounced out of our privy dripping wet, toweling herself off, grinning at me. "Still abed. What would your mother say, Gennadara?"

"That I'm a lazy girl certain to come to no good end," I said, and yawned and stretched.

"Perhaps Jagan is already up," Catri said as she dressed. "We have the Aglak today, whatever that proves to be." She skipped out the door, and I looked after her, resenting morning and all people who woke not tired.

I lay abed until she poked her head in and grinned at me and said, "Hurry, lazy girl!" as cheerfully as if someone had given her Longnight sweets. Then I mumbled under my breath and crawled grudgingly from beneath the covers and went to stand beneath the water, turning it to cold so that it might do a better job of waking me up.

It did.

When I got out, my skin had turned pale blue and my teeth rattled. But I was awake. I put on the same clothes I had worn since the day we had fallen into the claws of the dragon and stepped into the kitchen.

Jagan had brought pots and plates of foreign food to the table and was covering the dishes so they would stay hot. The food smelled . . . strange. Spices and herbs I did not recognize, and much more sweetness in the smells than my people liked.

He smiled at me. "You can change into the clothes I brought for you either before or after you eat," he said. I could still clearly hear the Tagasuko that he was actually speaking, but it did not get in the way much. Being able to understand him was, at least, well worth the odd two-voices-at-the-same-time problem it caused.

Catri was sorting and folding clothes. "He brought these with the food," she said. "He got them out of the same cabinets, actually. We can get clothes there the same way we get food — will what you want, and there it will be."

"We *can*?" I looked at what she was holding. The fabrics of the clothes were beautiful. Colorful. Silks and velvets, brocades and broadcloth, wool and cotton and fine linen and I knew not what else.

Catri held up a dress in front of her and said, "Do you not think this would be lovely on me?"

The dress was as fine as the nightling gown I had worn during my first stay in Arrienda. Of brightest blue silk, it was cut as strangely as the rest of the clothing the sun wizards had worn. The skirt of the dress looked impractically long and full to me — a definite waste of very expensive material. The bodice, on the other hand, was tightly fitted to the waist, with a low, square neckline and sleeves full at the top, slitted and lined with red, white, and gold fabrics that were designed to peek out between the slits, and embroidered in gold thread with roses and suns. Below the elbows, the sleeves were designed to be quite tight.

Jagan said he had been told we were from important families, but looking at that dress, I was inclined to tell him that they were not *that* important. I tried to imagine whether Catri's parents would even recognize her if she wore that dress.

But truth is truth, so I told her, "You'll be beautiful in it." Of course, unlike me, she was beautiful all the time anyway.

"He brought one just like it for you," she told me. "Only green." She handed me the enormous pile of clothing, neatly folded. "He got us underthings, too, and shoes, and the most wondrous socks. . . ."

I tried not to think about what my parents would say about a boy picking out dresses, socks, and underthings for me. I was fairly certain they would not approve.

But the dress that hung in my arms was clean, and soft, and elegant. No dragon had held it in his mouth. No one had ever puked on it. It looked as if it would fit me; and like Catri, when I held it up to myself, I could imagine myself being beautiful in it. And to me, being beautiful was something special, something that I did not take for granted. The shoes that matched the dress were little green silk slippers, embroidered in gold thread with roses and suns. I thought they might be too small for my feet, but they stretched.

Catri and I decided, with food before us, to wait until we had eaten to change. I did not want to get anything on the beautiful green dress.

Jagan's food was very odd. There was little of it, and it was all very pretty, but I could not actually recognize anything. If you have mutton stew, you can see cubed mutton, and cubed potatoes, and sliced carrots, and other vegetables, a bone for flavor, and lots of gravy. You could learn to make stew just by eating stew.

This food was . . . mysterious. It was shaped into cubes, but when I cut into one, I saw that it was made of tiny layers of different colors held together by some sweet sauces, some sour sauces, and the firm icing that folded over and around the whole.

I did not need to eat much of it to be full, though. I was not used to all the odd spices or the unexpected combinations of flavors.

Jagan said, "So? How do you like it?"

I thought wistfully of my mother's cooking, and of nightling dishes that were savory and enchanting, and I said, "It's very good. I've never had anything like it before."

I kept myself from saying, "What is it?" because Mama had taught me that was rude, that some people are simply not very good cooks. I did not think that was the problem with this food. Nevertheless.

Catri finished almost as quickly as I did, and we scurried into the room we shared to help each other get dressed.

It proved not nearly as complicated as getting into Mama's bride dress. No buttons, no hooks, no fasteners of any kind. The silk of the dresses, like the silk in the shoes, stretched when we pulled the dresses over our heads. Much quicker than I would ever have thought possible, we were arrayed as princesses.

And Catri had been absolutely right about the socks. I could hold them up and see my hand through them, and they were thin and comfortable and wonderful.

And then Jagan said, "You both look just right. Now we go to Aglak."

We walked back to the grand entryway where we had come first, and crossed the sun emblem on the floor, and went to the very largest corridor on the opposite side from the corridor down which we lived.

"It's the first door," Jagan said. It was a bright red door. "Red doors," he told us, "are always government. Aglak is where you'll find your place within the Spire, and how you may get to move out of the Warrens. Anyone," he said, "can live in the Warrens."

He said that as if it were a bad thing.

He pushed the door open, and we followed him in. There was an enormous waiting room with a long maze of gold-colored fences. "This was always completely full," Jagan said. "We'll go in that end, walk all the way to the front, and then do each of the *aglakari* in turn."

So we walked, back and forth, back and forth, along a path that would have held hundreds of people.

"What is the purpose of this?" I asked.

"When barbarians and strangers and new wizards and craftsmen from the Belows and immigrants and everyone else came to the Spire, it was the duty of the Spire to find out who they were, what they could do, and where they might be of service to the Ag —"

"Stop," Catri told him. "You say Ag, and Aglak, and *aglakari* as if we knew what these things are, but we don't."

"Neth Kosae Haw said he had given you the understanding of Tagasuko."

"He did. But if the Ag, or an Aglak, or an *aglakari* are things we don't have at all in our language, how can we know what these are?"

Jagan considered that. "Well, yes. It's the problem of the thousand words for wings," he muttered, looking down at the ground. When he looked at us again, he said, "The Ag is the gathering of master wizards, master craftsmen, and governors of the empire of humankind. It is the government that takes precedence over all lesser governments. Members of the Ag are chosen by the Spire itself on their merits, for their genius in their particular skills. The Aglak is a series of tests done by magic to determine the skills and merits and much more of the people it tests. And the *aglakari* are the . . ." He paused, trying to come up with the right words. "Booths of testing," he said finally. "You step up to one, rest a hand on it, and it determines certain things about you. It then passes this information on to the next *aglaka*, which will base the questions it asks of you on what it learned from the previous *aglaka*. And so on, and so on. No sense, after all, testing those of barbarian bloodlines for places within the government, or those without magical talent for all the professions within the Spire that require magic."

We reached the end of the corral — that was what it had come to feel like to me. We used something similar, I realized, for branding livestock.

We walked through a door, one after the other, into a corridor that contained booths as far as the eye could see, but only a very narrow space in which to walk along them.

"I'll go first," Jagan said, "to show you what to do."

He stepped in front of the first booth, placed his hand atop the gold dome in front of it, and waited.

"Jagan Akajirri, Level Three Wizard's Apprentice, registered bloodline of Ambath Prime, accepted for Ag training by petition. You are already registered. You may pass."

He pulled his hand off of the golden dome and said, "That's it for me. I can wait with you if you'd like, while you go through the tests."

"Yes, please," Catri said.

Jagan smiled at her, and she smiled back — and I thought Dan would be a little hurt if he could see them.

I nodded, though. "You are very kind. But why must *we* do this? There's no one left in the Spire."

"Oh." He nodded. "Of course. The most important areas of the Spire, including all those where you can obtain magic training, are only accessible to those who have registered. The more valuable you are, the more things you'll be able to do, and the more places you'll be able to go. This is very important. You cannot even go to learn with Neth Kosae Haw until you can travel to the Magics Department."

"Does the Magics Department have a silver door? Wizards and lightning, a big sun in the center?"

"Yes," Jagan said. "You can't have been there."

"No," I agreed. "I can't have. But I dreamed about it."

Catri followed Jagan and put her hand upon the dome.

"State your first name," the voice of the *aglaka* said. It sounded womanish, but not as if it came from a real woman.

"Catriana."

"State your second name."

"Weaversdattar."

"State your third name."

Catri looked puzzled, then shrugged, and said, "Ot Hillrush."

"Have you any other names?"

"No."

"Hold your hand very still."

Catri did, then suddenly jerked it away, saying, "Ow!" She looked at her hand, which had a red, angry-looking line right across the base of her palm.

"Put it back," Jagan said. "The next part takes the sting out."

Catri gave him the same look she once gave her older brother after he'd pinched her and teased her in front of her friends.

But she put her hand back on the dome and said, "Oh. Now it doesn't hurt anymore."

"You have to hold it still when the *aglakari* say to," he told her.

The first *aglaka* said, "Catriana Weaversdattar ot Hillrush, registered bloodlines of Nelhath Prime and Spaj Segundus, acceptable for all positions within the Spire. Initial test for Magics and Ag suitability. Recommend Prime access."

"Nelhath Prime!" Jagan said. "One of my best friends ever was Nelhath Prime. I thought you might have been a barbarian, but . . . that's amazing. He was tracked to become a *haw*! And Prime access is very good. It means you can go almost anywhere — and you're eligible for Magics and Ag, which means we could end up studying together."

"That's good, then," Catri said.

"That's *wonderful.*"

Catri turned to me. "Your turn. It stings for an instant or two."

"I saw," I told her.

I put my hand on the golden dome nervously and answered the questions about my name. I wished I did not have to be there. I realized that the *aglaka* could say anything about me, about my bloodline, about my rights to travel through the Spire, and I would be hard-pressed to argue with it. I dreaded it saying that I had terrible bloodlines and ought to be kicked out of the Spire.

And then the dome bit the palm of my hand. Hard. It was nothing like a sting. No wonder Catri had jerked her hand away. Even knowing what was coming, I needed every ounce of my will not to pull back my own. But then, as quick as the pain was there, it was gone again.

The Aglak paused, then said, "Gennadara Yihannisdattar ot Hillrush, direct descendant of Sator Kizen Haw, registered bloodline of Ambath Prime, acceptable for all positions within the Spire. Initial test for Magics and Ag suitability. Immediate Ag access granted."

I said, "Well, there, then. What's next?" and turned to see Jagan with his mouth hanging open.

"Sator Kizen Haw." He bent on one knee and bowed to me. "Satimaja."

I frowned. "Don't do that."

He looked up at me. "You are a direct descendant of the only haw ever made Ag for life in the Spire."

"And he has likely been dead for at least a thousand years by this time, and no one is going to make *me* Ag for life."

But Jagan was worrying. "I did not get you the Tree of Life cloth. We shall have to do that when we return to gather your things. You'll have a great suite in the High Reaches — it's Ag only, but you can, of course, invite companions and retainers. I'd be pleased to be one of your retainers."

I narrowed my eyes. "Let us get through this line of tests, and then we three need to talk."

CHAPTER 13
THE SILVER DOOR

The Aglak took surprisingly little time. Catri and I each had to stand in front of only four other *aglakari*, one which told us about our health and spelled us against diseases to which we were not naturally immune, a second which tested our vision, strength, speed, and ability to respond to threats signaled by each of our senses — smell was the truly interesting test there. The third said it was testing our decision-making ability, but I did not see how asking me about some boy I'd never known doing things he should never have been doing had any connection to that. Fourth was magic, and while Catri's test took a few moments before she received notice that she was accepted, I put my hand on the gold dome of that *aglaka* and was told immediately that I was accepted.

I was given Ag access, which I learned would allow me to go anywhere in the Spire. Catri received the same Prime access Jagan had.

"Satimaja," Jagan said, bowing at me again, "we can have the finest food in the whole of the Spire if you wish. And we need to travel up to Neth Kosae Haw, who will be *very* glad to see us."

I looked at him and said, "My name is Genna. I don't want to be called Satimaja, please. I don't want to be bowed to. Bowing makes me sick to my stomach. Nightling slaves bow to their owners. Humans are — or will soon be — free. We bow to no one, and no one bows to us."

Jagan looked both startled and worried. "It is a sign of respect."

I nodded. "When I have done something with regard to you that is worthy of so much respect that you believe you need to act like a nightling slave, we can discuss bowing again."

I realized as the words fell out of my mouth that, first, I had sounded just like Papa handing down the law to someone who should have known better, and second, that I had been harsh with Jagan. Bowing might have been his people's way. It was not ours — it would never be ours. But I know ours is not the only way.

Forgive me, however, if I think our way the best.

Jagan took us deeper into the wide corridor, to a black door. "This," he said, resting his palm on it, "is a room of transport. An *okunaeso*."

My ear heard the word as *okunaeso*, though, and *room of transport* was not the image the word made in my mind. Magic was involved.

"The *okunaeso*," Jagan continued, "are only for use by sun wizards and the Ag. They lead to places within the Spire where only *we* are permitted to travel. And to guarantee that the *okunaeso* will be used correctly, only those with Prime and Ag access can use them." He smiled at this.

He liked being above everyone else, I realized. He liked being able to go places others could not go and do things they could not do. He was very happy to be important.

For just a moment, he reminded me of Banris desperately wanting Papa to become a judge in Greathaven, because then Banris would be able to return to Greathaven, too, and would be a man with an important friend.

For just a moment, I did not much like Jagan. But I realized he was just a boy. Boys are easily enchanted by things that most grown men shrug off as not important.

I smiled at him. "You spoke of food," I said. "I would dearly love to sit down and eat a meal."

Catri added, "I am so hungry, I could eat half a cow." She laughed, and I laughed, and Jagan smiled politely.

"We'll have something much better than that."

He told Catri and me, "You will both have to learn to use the *okunaeso*. You'll need my help to begin with, because you don't know any of the places you can go. But once you have been to them, you'll be able to go anywhere and in an instant. The *okunaeso* uses your magic and your focus and intent to take you where you desire to go."

"Does it move up and down through the, ah, tower? Er, pinnacle?" I asked.

"Oh, no! It doesn't actually move at all. You can go to any other *okunaeso* in any other pinnacle in the Spire. Once, you could go to any city that had *okunaesoni*, but toward the end of the Long War, all the Spires stopped allowing that, because the Ag feared enemy combatants would come in through them."

I looked around the small, pale-blue, featureless room in which we stood. "That seems to me a sensible worry. Considering how . . . warriors arrived by dragon."

The boy nodded.

And Catri asked, "Can you use them any time of the day or night?"

Jagan looked puzzled. "Of course."

"They're better than your moonroads, then," Catri said.

Jagan looked from Catri to me and back to Catri. "Moonroads? What are those?"

I said nothing. Silence is the best friend of surprise, Mama says. Of course, according to Mama, silence is the best friend of a lot of things. Anger. Exuberance.

Children.

Well, my sibs and I were a loud bunch. And we had always fought among ourselves. And played loudly together.

Silence, then, might only be the best friend of mothers, I decided, but I kept my mouth shut anyway.

I wish I had been able to talk straight into Catri's head the way the cat could talk into mine. I would have shouted at her for saying so much.

But I could not, and so she kept right on talking.

"Genna can stand in the moonlight and call magical doors to her that take her anywhere she wants to go. Even to the nightworlds."

"Nightworlds. How strange. Perhaps that is the interesting magic Neth Kosae Haw said you had. The sort of magic he could not explain."

"I do not think so," I said, hoping to change the subject. "I have never used that magic here."

"Hm. Something else, then," he said. "You must show me these moonroads someday."

"If I can."

"Back to the *okunaeso*, though. You press the palm of your right hand to the sun in the center of the door. All doors within the Spire now know you, Gennadara Yihannisdattar. You are living Ag, the first among the new sun wizards. Any door, including the *okunaeso*, will open for you. To use the *okunaeso*, you step into the chamber. And you *will* yourself to the place where you would go. See the image clearly in your mind and in as much detail as possible. When the door opens, you will usually be where you willed yourself."

"Usually?"

He winced a little. "Your attention, if it wanders while you are in the chamber, can end you up in unexpected places. But no harm done. Mostly. You simply wait for the door to close again, then pay better attention while you will yourself to your destination."

I waited, hoping he would explain that "mostly" of his without me having to ask. But he did not, and so I asked.

"What do you mean, 'mostly'?"

He looked from Catri to me, his expression solemn. "Do not think violent thoughts while in the chamber," he said.

And then he said nothing more about the *okunaeso*. The door opened, and we stepped out. But Jagan had given me a little more than I had anticipated. I knew how to work an *okunaeso* — at least I hoped I did. And I knew that the sun wizards did not recognize moonroads.

I also knew that the black doors were not to be trusted. That they might deliver me where I wanted to go, or that they might dump me into trouble. I knew this last thing as a guess more than as a fact. But my gut called it true.

In the corridor, Jagan stopped and frowned. "This is not where we were supposed to go," he said.

I looked around. The corridor in which we stood had a balcony on one side that overlooked the grand entryway, far below us. The rest of it was done in tiny stones of blue and green, set in silver and laid out in wave patterns. All of the doors in the corridor were exquisitely carved, elaborate, and red. Government doors, I thought.

All of them save one, I realized.

Catri spotted it at the same instant I did.

"The silver door!" we shouted at the same time, forgetting that we were hungry and that we were not where Jagan had planned to take us.

Jagan was no longer the one dragging us forward. We dragged him, right up to it.

"We were going to come here after we ate," he protested, but neither Catri nor I cared about that. Here was the silver door, beautifully carved, each tiny wizard on it with an individual face and an individual tabard with his or her own insignia in the center, each blasting away at unseen enemies. Not all used lightning, I realized. Looking at it closer, I could see that the jagged lines were done in dozens of styles, each of which no doubt symbolized the user's preferred magic. The sun in the center was carved in loving detail, each ray curling away and splitting off in many directions.

I pressed my palm against the door, and it swung open.

The three of us stepped into the room together. The door closed behind us with a finality I did not like. And Catri and Jagan vanished.

I screamed. Not the scream of a brave warrior charging an enemy, either. Not even the scream of a girl beating a giant worm to death with a long-handled fry pan.

No. I screamed like a little girl who had just lost sight of her mama. I turned, screaming, and turned some more, until I could no more have guessed in which direction I had been heading or in which I needed to go than I could have guessed the road to the moon.

A voice that, like the light, came from everywhere and nowhere, surrounded me. "*Siroeth suno journa?* Why are you crying?"

I took one slow breath to calm myself and asked, as politely as I could, "What have you done with my friend Catri, and the boy Jagan?"

Which of course was not as polite as it could have been, for as I heard the words come out of my mouth, I heard myself blaming the room.

"I have done nothing with them. They are exactly where they were. You simply fail to see them."

I looked around the room, but they were still gone.

"I do not understand."

"No, you don't. That's why you can't see them."

Riddlers, teasers, people who say one thing and mean another, and those who say nothing and try to make it sound like something all aggravate me. I suspected Jagan's former teacher, Neth Kosae Haw, as the ghost behind the voice, and he seemed to me to be one of those kinds of people. Standing in that room, alone in the whiteness, alone in the world, knowing my parents, my family, my village, and my people were in trouble and that they were depending on me to help them, and that I was depending on what I might learn from this . . . voice, this ghost, this *thing*, I snapped.

"Then tell me what I do not know!" I snarled. "Tell me what I must do to get them back!"

"You must *will* them to you."

In my head, memories of my mother's voice. *That which you want is nothing. That which you will, will be.*

I had willed the hurt out of Yarri's damaged leg; I had willed the sinews and muscles and bones right. I had willed the making of spells. I had willed the protection of my family.

I knew how to will things.

It required calm. Focus. Attention. Control.

And I was angry and upset, flighty, desperate, afraid, distracted, and at the very edge of panic.

So I sat. *That which I will, will be.*

I closed my eyes and stared at the middle of the inside of my forehead until I became dizzy. I counted my breaths slowly, in to a count of eight, hold to a count of sixteen, out to a count of sixteen, and hold out to a count of eight. Then in again.

Simple, steadying things. I had to have faith that nothing horrible would attack me while I sat there, blind and helpless. I had to believe that I was safe, that Catri was safe, that Jagan was safe.

I had to let my anger seep down my spine and into the floor. I had to pull blue, still calm from the air around me.

I sat. I breathed. I embraced the darkness and did not think about anything but the slow counts.

Inhale . . . two . . . three . . . four . . . five . . .

And on and on, while my lungs filled and emptied.

I was no longer angry. I was in that place inside myself that is like the first day beneath a new snowfall. All the world is silent and crisp and peaceful there. Untouched. New-made. I stood in the center of my mind, and I held my will, my determination, my focus, and shaped it to my cause.

I will have Catri back before me now. I will have Jagan back before me now. I will see them, and they will see me.

All around me, the room murmured, "Nicely done. You are not new to this, I see."

I opened my eyes, and Catri was there, her arms wrapped tight around her, her face pale and still a little frightened. Catri was not the daughter of a yihanni. She had been taught sewing and cooking, tending flocks and rearing children, making cheese and butter, weaving and knitting and the rest of the arts of the household. She had not been taught magic from an early age.

I *was* the daughter of a yihanni, and if I was no longer to grow up to wed a headman and be the yihanni of a village, I was on the path to something even more difficult. I was the Sunrider, whatever that might prove itself to be, and I had set myself on the path to stand between Banris and humanity, to stand between the slaving kai-lords and their countless nightling slaves. And for me to do what I imagined I might have to do, I would need magic the likes of which the world had not seen since sun wizards by the thousands flew through the air in their great winged ships.

I understood the fear in Catri's eyes.

"You were both gone all of a sudden," she said. "Where did you go?"

And Jagan said, "It's a test. Every apprentice test is different. Since we're all together again, I suppose you both passed."

The voice said, "Catri will have to be retested. Genna went far beyond the test I had prepared for her and broke it, bringing you both to her."

Catri and I both stared at each other.

Jagan raised an eyebrow. "I've never heard of anyone breaking a test."

Neth Kosae Haw appeared right in front of me and off to the side of Catri and Jagan, and I thought, Ha! I was right about the source of the voice!

He said, "It has happened before, though only rarely. Genna, your ancestor, Sator Kizen Haw, was notorious for breaking tests. And other things." He chuckled a little. "That blood has run true for a long, long time, I see. You have a grand future with the Ag, my girl." And then he shook his head. "So. Students have come seeking me at last, in this lonely place. I cannot tell you how long I have waited to teach again, or how tiresome the company of the ghosts in the walls has become."

I reached out to touch his arm, and my hand went right through it.

"Young bringer of trouble," Neth Kosae Haw said, "have you no manners? One does not touch those of us in the spirit world. It disturbs our focus and is most unsettling."

"I have never spoken to a ghost in a situation where manners were required. I fear I do not know the custom. But I know manners well enough. My full name is Gennadara Yihannisdattar of High House, firstborn of Jhontar, Caer of Hillrush, and Seldihara, Yihanni of Hillrush, and I am honored to make your acquaintance."

The man — no, ghost — before me looked amused. "Charming girl. And you have neatly put me in my place, too, for I must realize that — raised as a barbarian as you have been — you would have no knowledge of the forms and niceties of the Prime and Ag classes, or any way to know my rank and status and how . . . well, never mind that. The past and who I was matter little. This is a new day and a new world. And you make clear my own error, that I have not formally introduced myself to you. I am Neth Kosae Haw, Prime citizen, Sun Wizard of the First Rank, Master of Investigations. You may call me by my common title, which is Haw."

Haw, I somehow understood, meant "master." Royal. Wizard-Who-Teaches-Wizards. It was a complex word, and no matter how fine the magic that had slipped inside my head to make the words of the sun wizards work, I could not grasp all the depth and color of it. Whatever else it meant, *Haw* meant "important."

Jagan bowed. "Thank you for your help last night. I apologize for my . . . distress."

"Under such terrible circumstances," the haw said, "you bear no shame. The spell I cast on you will ease your grief for as long as you need it. When you don't, let me know, and I'll remove it for you." He shook his head sadly. "I remember your parents, and their decision, against every bit of advice and every piece of wisdom placed before them, to hide you away to wait for them. They thought they'd be back. They thought everyone would be back."

Jagan stared at the teacher, the haw. "What happened to them?"

"The darkness below devoured them. The forced ignorance, the filth, the evils of the nightling kai. I do not know their specific fate, for they, like all the rest, were lost to me once they stepped beyond the circle of the Spire's influence. They might have hidden all they knew and been accepted into one of the human villages that were set up by the nightlings after the Fall of man. They might have survived for a while or even lived out long lives. But they never made it back here. None who left did. The nightlings set up watches in the middle of the great taandu forests all around this Spire and the rest of them, and killed any who tried to cross into the lands protected for humans."

"So I am the last."

"No," the haw said. "You do not even approach being last. There are, throughout the Spire, the unbreathing children of other parents just like yours, who thought they were leaving to save humanity and instead left to be destroyed along with it."

Catri took my hand, and I held my breath. Other children just like Jagan, frozen in the light, waiting, waiting, waiting for parents who would never return. Parents who had died almost a thousand years earlier.

They could go to human villages, I thought. In Hillrush there were parents who had lost children to the nightlings, to the forest, to sickness, to an endless number of small tragedies, and who would welcome them. Families in Hillrush always had room to foster orphans. They would gladly take in these abandoned ones who had been forgotten by time.

I said nothing, though, for how could I suggest that the children of this place of magic should leave it to go live in the wood houses on the ground, where magic and the comforts the Spire offered were all but lost?

Catri spoke. "We could hunt for the others who have been . . . frozen," she said. "We could wake them."

The haw said, "You could. But you should not. You three have much to learn, and I have much to teach. And the children who are frozen in time will wait a bit longer. They have waited this long without harm. The three of you must learn all the secrets of the High Spire, and the magics of the great libraries and the vast hidden rooms that still hold their secrets. And you must find your way to the Deep Spire, where the engines of the sun wizards sit silent, waiting to be wakened. Those engines will do far more to save humanity from the depredations of nightlings and Moonkind than a noisy clutter of children. The children can wait until those arrive who can care for them."

I considered that, and knew it to be true. My heart cried out to free those who, like Jagan, had been locked away for centuries. But my mind yearned for the magic of the sun wizards, and the great tools and weapons they had borne against the nightlings a thousand years earlier.

Their weapons did not win the war a thousand years ago, a doubting voice whispered in my head. *Why would they now?*

I knew not. I knew only that I had to learn everything I could as quickly as I could — that somewhere in the midst of something that seemed like nothing, the secret that could save my people from Banris and the slaving kai-lords might await.

CHAPTER 14
LEARNING OLD MAGIC

Neth Kosae Haw looked at the three of us with interest. "You, Jagan, were destined from the beginning for sun wizardry, and you were making fine progress. Before the Long War wound to its terrible conclusion, your parents had hoped you would join them in crafting ships-of-the-air, but your talents and interests lay . . . elsewhere. What I must know is, do they still? All avenues are now open to you, lad. And some of them may be more interesting than what you chose when the Spire was full and the world belonged to humanity."

Jagan said, "There will be people here again, Haw. I will stay my course."

The haw smiled. "Very good."

The smallest of smiles crept across Jagan's face.

The haw turned his attention next to Catri. "You're a bit of a mystery. I sense talent and intelligence in you, but you haven't been tested, you haven't been trained in anything, and you truly have no idea where your aptitudes or interests lie."

Catri frowned at him. "Yes, I do. I want to marry and have a family. I want to raise children, tend a flock, and weave and knit and cook and do all the other things wives do."

The ghost shook his head. "There are no flocks in the Spire, so there is no need to tend them. You will not need to weave or knit here, for the systems of the Spire still function perfectly, and they can make fabrics finer and more beautiful than the best work by the most talented human. There is no need for men and women to raise children; that task has been given over to the norites when the children are infants, and to the sabites when they are able to walk, and finally to the haws when the children are able to think rationally."

Catri gave me a pleading look, and I shrugged. I did not know what to say or what to do. She had always known the life she wanted — it was like the life her parents had, and not even living in the unending luxury of Arrienda had changed that. Hiding out in the Spire did not seem to have changed her dreams, either.

I knew some of what she felt. My path had always been planned to take me away from my family and my village — the firstborn daughters of yihanni are trained to be yihanni, too, and they almost always go off to marry the sons of the headmen of villages that had lost their own yihannis, whether by death or by disaster.

But I had known my future from an early age. I had known that I would learn healing, and how to cast spells to protect the village and the villagers, that I would be responsible in many ways for the lives of all those who would one day depend upon me. I had been taught to accept duty, to carry my own burden while still watching to see that the burdens of others did not become too great.

And then, when I took on the responsibility of saving my mother's life, everything I thought I knew about my future came to a crashing end.

Since then, all I had known about my future was that every day would be different from the one before it, that I could count on nothing but my own wits to keep my skin attached to my flesh — and often enough my wits were barely sufficient — and that trouble was coming. And would keep coming.

But Catri suddenly smiled. "That is well enough, Haw, but since I do not plan to stay here any longer than I must, the faults of this place will not bother me."

"You're not staying?" Neth Kosae Haw looked thunderstruck. "You would leave the crowning jewel of civilization to crawl back to the dirt and the muck, to beasts roaming everywhere . . . and to your firelit world?"

Catri said, "Yes. I would. I love my family and my village and the life we have there."

I did not like the measuring look he gave her then. But his reply was innocuous enough. "I'll see if Jagan and I cannot win you to the virtues of civilization."

Neth Kosae Haw turned to me. "You are an unusual girl. You have a strong grounding in magic of a form that descends directly from the teachings of the People, yet you have within you currents that are . . . otherworldly."

"I have walked the moonroads," I said.

He pursed his lips. "Yes. That dangerous wild magic is part of what I sense. But there is something else about you. Something . . . placed on you. Or in you somehow . . ."

He stared into my eyes, and for the briefest moment I had the same feeling I got when I was falling into a moonroad, when the compulsion was upon me to flow with it, when I was enchanted by all the magnificence and magic that moonroads held. I took a half-step forward and . . .

Yelped!

I felt a sharp pinch on my arm, and any desire I had to look deeper into the haw's eyes vanished. I stepped back, rubbing my arm.

And I suddenly remembered the audiomaerist who had sent the cat with Dan and Yarri and me, and how, when I had saved her life, she had given me two gifts. One of them had been a hard pinch on the arm, right in the exact place where my arm still stung. I looked at it, and was startled to discover red skin there, and along with it, the start of a bruise.

The pinch had not been in my imagination.

"Well," the haw said, sounding suddenly irritated, "there's some odd force around you, but it does not seem to respond to the magic I have available."

I said, "I'm sorry about that."

"Not to worry," he told me. "You and I will have plenty of time to get to the bottom of your mystery. The new sun wizards will need every magical trick and strategy they can acquire if they are to reclaim the world for humanity."

"And the good nightlings," I added.

His eyebrow rose. "There are no good nightlings. There are conniving masters, and there are conniving slaves, but they are all, in the end, dedicated to the utter annihilation of humankind."

That thing my mother said about silence? It's good advice. I kept my mouth closed.

"You don't agree with me," he said, looking at me with that unnerving intensity I did not like.

"I do not know enough to agree or disagree, Haw. I have not your years of experience or your history. And certainly, my dealings with Kai-Lord Letrin were . . . most disagreeable."

"Which of them is he?"

"Was," I said. "He was the kai-lord of Arrienda, after he murdered his brother. My brother, a friend of mine named Yarri, Doyati — the son of the murdered kai-lord — and I killed him."

"I should have known all of that from your tests," the haw said. "Why did I not? Why did I not see that you had dealings with the nightlings before you came here? How were you granted Ag access, when you have had contact with those villains?"

"I thought the Spire chose whomsoever it wanted," I said.

"It does. I find myself wondering if, during the Fall, something happened that twisted the spells that guide it, so that now it works toward its own self-destruction."

He paced, and fretted, at times becoming so agitated that he grew transparent. The more distressed he became, the more he faded. Twice he disappeared completely.

The second time, though, he didn't fade back and keep pacing. He appeared suddenly and solidly, right in the middle of us. "I will send work for you to your hovel in the Warrens, and you will do it. I will be watching you, and punishment will be forthcoming if you do not attend to the tasks I set you. Now, however, you're to leave. All three of you. You're to return to the Warrens, and stay there, until I have tested the integrity of the spells. You may be the direct descendant of the greatest of sun wizards," he said, turning his attention directly on me, "but until I have seen to the spells and reassured myself that neither time nor malice has altered them, I will no longer believe it. Or that you deserve Ag access to the Spire."

"You have Prime access," Jagan told him. "You have no way of verifying anything about someone with Ag access."

"Some of the spirits who served the Ag in their lifetime remained here. They will work with me, I have no doubt."

Jagan started to say something else, but Neth Kosae

Haw raised a hand in warning. "While you are still in my good graces, boy, keep silent and leave."

That sounded like a fine plan to me.

My head hurt. Catri groaned and rubbed her neck. Jagan sat at the table staring at his hands. We had a dinner before us of fresh fruit and my mother's sort of cooking — baked trout and bitter greens and hard black bread — hot, still smelling of wood smoke — and fresh-churned butter, salted just a little, and red cheese. And sweet biscuits, which my mother only made a few times a year, but which I had discovered I could have with every meal if I wanted them and have them hot and soft and crumbly and dipped in sugar, too.

And the sad thing was, with that magnificent meal before us, all three of us sat around the table and picked at our food, too exhausted and dispirited to eat.

"I hate this," Catri said. "Word lists and word lists and more word lists. Read the word, write the word, say the word. Even if they are all words about magic, this is not moving you toward being a Sunrider, and it's not moving me toward being . . . well, whatever I'm supposed to become, besides your friend."

Jagan leaned on a hand. "Your future is in the Spire, Catri. The three of us are the first here in this new time. We are the only living people, so we become the first new wizards and the first new masters. The Spire and all its wonders are *ours*. The present and the future are *ours*. We can learn *anything*. Be *anything*. Do *anything*."

"Perhaps not," Catri said. "If Neth Kosae Haw stands in our way, we may sit here for the rest of our lives looking at words."

Jagan waved away the possibility of that grim future with a flick of his hand. "Neth Kosae Haw was a respected teacher. He was an acceptable wizard. He was not Ag, and he will never be Ag. He had not the skills to win the Spire to his cause, and he had not the power to win the members of the Ag to his cause. So he lived and died — and lingers — a respected teacher and acceptable wizard. The jealousy he must carry in him that you are a descendant of Sator Kizen Haw, and that you were chosen Ag before you were even a full wizard, must burn in his gut like fire."

He smiled a little and shook his head. "I'm a little jealous myself. The whole of the Spire is yours, and though I think we are wise to do his little busy tasks, I have no doubt the spirits of the Ag will look at all you have accomplished and uphold the Spire's decision to make you one of its own."

That all painted a tempting picture. I imagined myself wielding the vast power of the Spire against Banris. Against the evil kai-lords. Against the taandu monsters and the nightmares from the nightworlds. I could see myself dressed in a lovely sun wizard dress and matching shoes, with fire blasting from my fingertips down on the arrayed armies of the twilight people. And Banris.

Yes. Tempting.

"We shall learn," I said to Jagan and Catri. "And we shall wait." And I shrugged. "We cannot go home yet anyway. Cannot and *must* not. It is only by our being hidden away here that Banris and the kai-lords think us dead. We buy our families' safety with our absence."

Catri tapped her knife on her plate. "I know this is a place full of fine things." Her gaze slid to Jagan, and then away. "But I miss my family. I miss the sheep and the goats and the dog and the cats."

"I do, too," I told her. "I miss them so much." Just admitting that out loud brought the full weight of it home to me, and I had to swallow tears.

Catri rose from the table. "I have to go into the privy," she told me. "Come with me."

"Come *with* you?"

"I'm . . . not quite well."

I stood up and followed.

As soon as I was through the door, she closed it and locked it.

I frowned at her. "What are you doing?"

"There are no watchers or listeners in privies," she told me. "Nothing that hears our words, nothing that paints our portraits."

"There . . . wait. None? You're sure?"

"I asked Jagan."

I felt a deep admiration for her right then. Perhaps she had not been planning to talk to me in secret, or perhaps she had, but she had managed to find the one piece of information we desperately needed and the one I had been sure simply did not exist. "How in the world did you ask him?"

"I told him that I was shy," she said. "That I did not want to see images of myself bathing or sitting on the pot when the next scroll came to our dwelling, and I was becoming afraid to use the privy."

I grinned. "And Jagan said . . ."

Catri grinned back at me. "He said, 'Don't worry. The Spire is designed to keep the personal rooms private.' "

I considered that for a moment. "You're sure?"

Catri's vehement nod made her braid bounce. "They

cannot see us or hear us in here, and with the door locked, we need not worry about the cat showing up."

"Good," I said. "I'm glad you thought to ask him."

"Seeing all those pictures of us from everywhere else, I knew they could see and hear everything we did and said. And I really *was* worried about . . . you know . . . the other thing."

Seeing ourselves naked in the morning scroll. Yes. I knew.

"So . . . when the haw started being impossible, you stopped talking," she said. "And you've barely said three words all evening."

"And . . ."

"Any time you stop talking, you start thinking. I know you."

She was right. I had been thinking. I'd been thinking I could take the two of us home by moonroad, just until morning, and who would be the wiser?

"You and I will go home tonight when the moon rises," I said. "Just until dawn, just to let our parents know we're alive."

She hugged me. She rushed me right there, and threw her arms around me, and shrieked.

And that was when Jagan began banging on the door, shouting at us. I could barely hear his shouting. I could hear his fist pounding on the door quite well, though.

Catri and I looked at each other.

"He is going to want to know what we're doing," she said.

"He will get in the way and be a nuisance and a bother," I said.

"He is a decent sort of person, for a boy," she argued.

"We *cannot* tell him what we're doing. He no more understands moonroads than we understood the Aglak, when he was talking to us about that. We could only show him, and if he panicked when he stepped onto a moonroad, and something went wrong, would we chase after him? We want to see our families."

She bit her lip and twisted the skirt of her magnificent dress in her hands. "And if we took him and something went wrong, we would have to go after him."

"Of course we would," I told her. "We do not want ill to come to him."

"No. We do not."

He was still pounding on the door and had started shouting "Neth Kosae Haw! Neth Kosae Haw!"

I thought right then a little ill could come to him. "Pretend you were throwing up," I said.

Catri leaned over the privy seat and pushed the handle that made the water empty. And she made little retching noises.

I, meanwhile, opened the door with rage on my face. Part of it was real, and the boy Jagan stepped back.

He glanced around my shoulder, and the petulant expression on his face changed to one of concern.

Catri stood, wobbling a little as she did, and walked to the basin, then turned the tap and rinsed out her mouth. Then she leaned against the wall and held her head.

Behind the boy, I saw the shadowy outline of the haw, not so solid-looking at the moment. I hoped he was distressed. He stood watching us, and I did not like the wariness in his position or his knowing look.

"She was overtired," I said, sounding as curt and formal as I had heard my mother sound when talking to some demanding families who refused to believe too much work might make their children sick. "Your work today overburdened her, and when she ate her meal, it would not stay down."

Jagan turned to the haw, and the haw looked at me as if he wanted to kick me.

I refused to be intimidated. "She needs to sleep through the night without disturbance," I said. "And she needs more reasonable work on the morrow."

"We're in a hurry," the haw said. "And when did you end up in charge, child?"

"I am an adult in my village, made so for achievement and not by age. And I am Catri's guardian, made so by her own parents. So, where she is concerned, what I say is law."

"That children have become the guardians of other children suggests a depravity among your people, child, that I do not wish to fathom."

"You do not need to. Until she is well and has her strength back, Catri is my concern and mine alone."

The haw leaned close to Jagan and whispered something, and Jagan's eyes grew wide. Then the haw told me, "I will expect you to report to the Magics Department tomorrow, after you have had time to rise and prepare yourself, where you will receive my final judgment on your . . . situation."

I nodded, in acknowledgment of his statement. Not agreement.

If we were back from visiting our families, Catri and I would both be too tired to go traipsing around the Spire. And if we were not back . . . well, what could he do about that?

CHAPTER 15
BANRIS REAPPEARS

We said our good nights to Jagan, went to our room, and locked our door.

We agreed that we would sleep as much as we could, knowing the moon would summon me when it rose. Catri bound her wrist to mine so that, if the moon summoned me without waking me, as it had before, my movement would alert her, and she would be able to wake me.

And then we pulled down the blanket that covered the glass wall and both gasped at the same time.

The whole top of the Spire — from every window of every pinnacle — blazed with lights. The lights had not been on after dark before, but at that moment they shone almost as bright as the sun.

"It's beautiful," Catri whispered.

It was. And it was human, too. Not nightling. It was a symbol of all humankind could do.

I smiled. In fact, I think I probably smiled even as I slept.

I did not wake half so well.

The cat stood on me, digging his claws into my arm. *Up,* he said. *Hurry.*

I just got to sleep, I told him.

He shoved his face so close to mine, his wet, cold, pink nose brushed mine. He had cat breath, too, which is not as bad as dog breath but still not much like roses. *And the moonroads just opened. But Banris has been busy,* he said.

That woke me up. I shook Catri.

Mostly asleep, she regarded me through half-closed eyes. "Time? Already?"

"Trouble," I told her. "I don't know what kind."

We rolled out of bed and dressed in *our* clothes — sweaters and skirts and sturdy boots. The cat waited until we were finished, then trotted out of the room into the kitchen.

The cat told both of us, *Don't mention me at all.*

Jagan was already out there, leaning against a wall, blinking at us and looking bewildered and sleep-rumpled.

Neth Kosae Haw was there, too. Again. He stood at the far end of the kitchen from our rooms, and he glared at

Catri and me. And pointed into the white room. "In there. Be scated."

We were good children, Catri and I, and raised to be obedient. Up to a point, anyway. So we and Jagan went into the white room and settled on the round, sunken couch. The haw stood in the center space again.

"Your presence in the Spire has been found out," he said, "and your enemy Banris and the creatures he commands have moved against the human villages that surround the Spire."

"Which would those be?" I asked, willing them to be anything but Hillrush.

"Your village is among them," the haw said. He seemed smugly pleased to be able to deliver the horrible news.

"Our families . . ." I whispered. Catri made a mewling noise in the back of her throat, and slid her hand into mine, and we hung on to each other with all our strength.

The haw closed his eyes and sighed. "Monsters from the moonroads have been pouring through the forest since moonrise, led by Banris and his allies, aided by the strength of the full moon, and the monsters have wreaked devastation on the human villages."

My heart blocked my throat, so that I could barely breathe. "What about our families — ?"

He stared at us then, unblinking and unsympathetic. "Your village had some warning, and its inhabitants fled. They are as safe as can be hoped for, at least for the moment. But they are surrounded by enemies and will need a rescue." The haw stared at me alone and added, "To survive, they will have to come here. This is the last of the living siege cities, the last sun wizard fortress that survives with spells intact. Humans who arrive here will be safe from the kai-lords, the nightling armies, and the creatures of the moonroads."

"We can rescue them," I said. Catri and Jagan both nodded.

The haw closed his eyes for a moment and stood in silence. Then he returned his attention to me. "We have assets that we will have to gather. There are a few surviving living artifacts from the age of the sun wizards. Some tools, hidden here, and some even better hidden in the dead sun wizard fortresses."

"We can go get them *right now*," I said again. "We do not need to wait for anything."

The haw ignored me. "There is a harp that will be quite useful against these creatures of the twilight. And a very fine pair of boots. Several swords. A copper horse. Several other things. I will need to recruit other haws to locate these creations, and then we will need to find humans who can go and retrieve them. It should not take more than a month or two, at most."

"*We* can rescue them," I said. "We will do it this instant."

Finally, he heard me. He looked at me and shook his head. "There is no way," he told me. "The spirits of the Ag verified that you are exactly who and what the *aglakari* claimed you were. You are safe here, and precious. The city is awake because you are here. Your future is here, child. You will remain here, protected, to rebuild the Spire."

"Who will save our families then, if we do not?" I asked. "You?"

"I cannot," he said. "As a spirit, I am bound to the Spire. I can never leave it."

"*We. Can.*" I glared at him. "We can find them. We can save them."

"You think so? Let me show you what you face in trying."

Without warning, we stood in the middle of a taandu forest but with cropped grass growing between the trees. I stepped forward and discovered pieces of Hillrush's Treaty Stone, shattered by an enormous tree that had pushed up beneath it. I could see threads of the road that had led into our village, but trees as wide around as houses had grown in the middle of it.

And I only knew it was our village because I could see the outline of my house and, sitting next to it, Catri's.

But all that remained of the places we had lived most of our lives were empty, broken shells. I stepped forward, my heart in my throat, and looked in all directions. The village had been in a clearing, and in the center of the clearing, there had been one tree. Our Justice Tree, beneath which my father had sat to hear the problems of the villagers and to deliver judgment.

That tree, older than the village, had been ripped out by its roots. It lay toppled on its side. And behind it, our house had been overrun by taandu trees. One had grown straight up through the heart of it, becoming massive. Its branches burst from the walls and through the windows, and they were lifting off sections of the roof.

No one would ever live there again or call the place I had loved home.

Months before, when Catri and I still lived there, there had been no taandu trees in Hillrush. It was, I thought, nightling magic that had pushed them to grow so quickly. What I could not understand was why they had done so in the taandu forest that surrounded Arrienda. The kai-lord there was a half-human boy whose mother was fully human.

She would never have done anything to destroy a human village.

Catri, with her hands over her mouth, stood up, clearly intending to run to her own house. "Catri, wait," I shouted.

Neth Kosae Haw said, "You cannot move within this picture. But I can move it around you. You're seeing images of the place, not the place itself, and if you stand up or move, the magic that makes them look real shatters."

Catri turned on him, her face a red fury, her shoulders hunched, her fists clenched.

"What happened to my family?"

The haw shook his head. "Anger helps nothing here, girl. This is an image of what is. It is nothing I have done; it is nothing I could control. I and the other haws can only protect that which resides within the magical shields of the Spire. Such allies as humanity still has must be entreated to bring them here."

"Can you show us our families?" I asked. "Catri and me? Can you show us where they are hiding?"

The haw frowned. "I can show you them. I cannot show you how to find them, for I will find them through their echoes in your flesh and blood. But I will not know where they are and neither will you."

"Show us," I said.

"Close your eyes and see your parents in your mind," he said.

I focused. I pictured myself standing with my mother and father, looking from one of them to the other. I had seen them in Arrienda, but they surely would have returned to the village when they got the news that Catri and I had died. They would have had to tell Catri's parents, and our families would have mourned together. They would have been in the village when everything went bad. I missed them so much, and I thought I did a good job of seeing my mother's smile, my father's square jaw, the light furring of hair on the back of his hands, the way sunlight caught her braid and her eyelashes and turned both gold.

"Oh," Catri whispered.

My parents crouched in the center of a room, and my mother placed her hands on Old Rifkin Deerskinner, pushing huge slashes in his chest together with her fingers, making the ripped skin mend.

Behind her stood a huge copper horse, lit by what looked to me like wizard light.

"The horse," the haw murmured. "*There* it is!"

On the floor around Mama lay the dead and the dying. She moved steadily from one to the next, healing where she could, passing by when nothing remained for her to do. Hadgard the priest should have been following after her, doing such things for the dead as he always did. But neither he nor any of his assistants were anywhere to be seen. Surely, they had not all died.

I had no idea where that enormous horse might be. I had never seen anything like it. So I did not know where to find my mother, or my father, or my sibs. I could not see, either, who else from my village might live and who might have died; the dim light in that room prevented easy identification, and the faces of the dead were covered by the scarves of women from the village. I felt helpless.

Catri's hand holding mine came near to crushing bones. "Show me mine," she said.

She closed her eyes and thought, and the haw rested his hand on the top of her head. I wondered if he had done the same thing to me while my eyes were closed.

The instant her eyes opened, he was back in the center of the circle, and suddenly we were with Catri's father, standing by a barred door with other armed men from our village.

"Where's my mama?" she shouted.

And just like that, we were back in the room with the copper horse, where Catri's mother and my brother Danrith tended my sibs, and Catri's younger sibs, and other small children from the village.

"They live," Catri said and released her grip on my aching hand.

"They live," the haw agreed. "Now you can get on with learning magic, knowing that you will be doing them more good that way than you will by worrying pointlessly."

"We shall not worry, pointlessly or otherwise," I said. "We're going to go get them."

The haw stared at me. "And how will you find them, child?"

"I already know where they are."

I had recognized the barred door where Catri's father stood as the one that Yarri and Dan and I had barred, before spending a miserable night worrying that the wizard who owned the place would come home and discover we'd tampered with his magic room.

"We'll go by moonroad and bring back as many with us as we can each trip. It will be safe enough."

"You'll go nowhere," the haw said. "It isn't safe."

"There is no such thing as safe," I told him.

"I forbid you to go."

"Then stop me." I stood up and looked at Catri and Jagan. "Are you coming with me, or are you staying here?"

Both of them rose.

The haw tried to stop me. He waved his hand, and a warm, furry light surrounded me. I felt sleepy and still, and my mind started to fog. I was drifting. Drifting. And then . . .

A pinch to the arm. It hurt, and I yelped, and all that light that had been pouring from the haw's fingertips flashed back on him and surrounded him. He blinked out of existence.

Jagan shouted, and Catri jumped. And I wondered whether I had killed him — can you kill a ghost? — or banished him, or simply chased him away for a while.

The three of us looked at one another. "We should hurry," I said. "We don't know how much time we have."

I went into Catri's and my room. Jagan followed us. The three of us moved the couch away from the doors.

I thought, We will bring them here — my people, and then other people, gathering up humans until this place lives again. But when we are all here . . . then whatever had happened to the sun wizards who had populated this place might happen to us. We would die. Be gone. Be lost forever.

Humanity would vanish from the world, and with us would go all our human hopes and dreams, our songs and art, our history and our science.

Sunlight would hide away, and twilight and darkness would rule.

The world would become the home of nightmares from the moonroad, and nightlings, both masters and slaves.

Freedom and the dream of freedom, like my people, would die.

With that dreary thought, I led us out into the moonlight.

CHAPTER 16
ON THE MOONROADS

The chill air out in the commons nipped at the bare skin it found. I was grateful I had dressed warmly.

On the birthday that I received chapel shoes — thin-soled, beaded, and embroidered — I wanted to wear them everywhere. My mother had said, "Never go anywhere questionable wearing impractical shoes. You might have to run, you might have to fight, you might have to walk through mud."

Jagan had no such practical clothing, and beside Catri and me, he shivered.

"Are you ready?" I asked them both.

They assured me that they were. I took their hands.

The moon already sat high in the sky, waning but not yet by much. The missing sliver was thin. But I could feel the press of time, and out in the night air, I could imagine refugees in the forests below and everywhere else — those from villages that did not sit close to a for-gotten wizard's lair — hiding from hunters who wanted them dead.

Catri hugged herself and stared down into the silver-lighted trees. I saw her shiver. On my other side, Jagan swallowed hard.

Yes. I felt it, too. Something down there had changed.

I pointed to the cliff that hid the tiny cleft that led to the wizard's lair. We said nothing out loud, because those crea-tures that watched and listened within the Spire knew what we intended to do . . . but did not know where we would go. They did not need to know where I planned to go.

We wanted to say nothing that other, perhaps more pow-erful, haws could use to stop us, for instance.

I had traveled the moonroads without the experienced cat or Doyati along before. Well, I had been on the moon-roads once without a guide, and that time, my choice had been to freeze to death in the fourteen nights during which I could not catch a moonroad, or jump, right then and there, hoping for the best.

I had jumped, and it had turned out about as well as I could have expected. Which is to say, horribly, initially. Blind hounds, vicious huntress, mad kai-lord, and madder destroyer of my family and village . . .

I swallowed and wished that the cat were coming with me, and that he could guide me to the right moonroad.

But I could see the place I wanted to reach in the moon-shadowed darkness, and I could imagine the same place as it was when the cat had taken us there.

I held it in my mind: shape of crevasse, color and texture of rock, feel of ground beneath my feet, way the light fell through the clearing. I could feel the moon touching me, could feel the pull of the roads, their hunger, my hunger, the yearning and the wildness that was a sharp taste in my mouth and a tingling on my skin, the smell of a field of flowers, the lightest sound of laughter. Lights sparkled at the corner of one eye, pale yellow, very faint.

My feet moved of their own accord, and I was only vaguely aware of Catri's and Jagan's hands clenching mine, of something behind us moving fast, of a solid thwack that knocked me to my knees, though I never quite fell. And I never lost the road.

And we were falling. Flying. Swirling and tumbling, weightless, in pale yellow. Not three of us. Four.

It takes, I discovered, exactly as much time to travel by moonroad from our world to the twilight worlds as it does to travel from one point in our world to another point that you are looking at and can see. This makes no sense to me.

None. But that is how the moonroads are. They twist the world inside out, backward and forward, stretch it, squish it, and shake you out at the other end to land on your behind, much harder than you expected to, with two people sitting on top of you.

And an angry cat beneath you. *Again,* he snarled in my thoughts. *Will you never learn to land on your feet?*

I yelped. *I had no warning you were coming.*

I had almost none that you were going. The cat's retort was sharp and angry in my mind.

Catri, who had never traveled the moonroads, clambered off me, ran a few steps away, and dropped to her knees, shaking. And the boy, that uninvited, unwanted, going-to-be-a-problem-if-we-brought-him-along boy, rolled to one side of me and promptly was sick all over everything.

Except me.

I knew just before he tossed his stomach what he was going to do, and for once I was fast and agile. Well, I was motivated, too — determined not to be soaked in someone else's sick. I had dealt with enough of my own.

I got to Catri first.

"That was nothing like magic," she said. "That was there, and then here, with nothing changed but with my stomach turned inside out. That was . . . terrible!"

I took her hand and pulled her along, grabbed still-retching Jagan, and dragged them to our destination: the crack in the cliff the cat had brought Yarri, Dan, and me to only three months before. I crawled in, then tapped the crystal I wore around my neck, the one Yarri had given me. Blue light filled the narrow, twisting passageway.

"Get in here. Fast. Before someone sees you," I snarled, dragging at their hands.

Catri followed, and with a moment's hesitation, so did Jagan.

We crawled on our hands and knees, across rough stone, through places too narrow for an adult to fit.

That gave me a moment's pause. Our families were in the wizard's lair. Everyone in our village, as far as I could tell, was there. But they had definitely not come in through the small crack we were using. Some of our villagers are stout. My father has wide shoulders. My mother might have fit, but not carrying my youngest sibs, who would have balked at the ground over which we were moving, and the darkness, and the bugs, and the worms.

Catri behind me was moaning about those. "Worms on my hands, Genna," she complained. "They're so sticky."

Jagan, too, talked. He muttered steadily, and I could not understand one word in a hundred of what he said. The few

I could catch were Neth Kosae Haw's name, and the word for "home" and the word for "people." I realized, much to my dismay, that my ability to understand Jagan had vanished when we left the Spire. It made sense, and the haw had even said something to that end. But it was horribly inconvenient.

Jagan was truly unhappy. I think he might have been wishing he had not come with us. But I could not be sure.

It was a long crawl. I had made it before with Yarri and Danrith, and I thought this time it would be easier because I had done it before, and I knew that it came out all right. No monsters. No bats — I hate bats. No suddenly falling off unseen cliffs and tumbling to my death.

I thought about such things. In such a place, with so much fear, anyone would.

But the crawl was as long as I had remembered it, partly because I had to keep stopping to urge Catri on. In fairness to her, there *were* a lot of worms. And nothing is quite as sticky as squished worms all over your hands.

But we came at last to the opening. To the vaulted part of the cave where stairs rose before us, and where the tunnel smoothed out tall and broad, and where, at the top of the stairs, a single door waited, and in front of that door, a long, straight passageway into darkness.

It almost felt like coming home.

I ran up the stairs and grabbed the door handle, forgetting in the excitement of knowing my family was on the other side that I had seen it barred.

It was still barred, of course.

I bit my lip to keep myself from saying things I knew were not permitted of children. And then I remembered that I was an adult and could say anything I wished. But I did not.

Instead, I borrowed Jagan's clever plan. I pounded on the door with both fists and yelled at the top of my lungs. The door opened almost instantly, and I found myself facing swords. But they were my neighbors' swords, wielded by my neighbors. Hormyn the butcher, Rosnith the miller. They recognized me, and behind me Catri busy wiping worms off her hands and onto her skirt. And they let us in. Jagan, too.

They closed the door behind us. And locked it. Barred it. They did not give us the warm welcome I had expected, though.

Instead, Hormyn and Rosnith grabbed my upper arms, two other neighbors grabbed Catri's, and two more grabbed Jagan's, and they dragged us across the deceptive front room of the wizard's lair — which looked like a very fancy dwelling for one person — then behind a tapestry of three women dancing in a circle holding hands, through another door, and down a long, poorly lit corridor.

Behind me, I could hear Catri shouting, "Ogmar, you know me. *You know me.* Let me *go!*" And, "You're hurting my arms."

Truth be told, they were hurting my arms, too.

We arrived in the room with the giant copper horse. They were, then, taking me to my father, I decided. Hormyn, who had the loudest voice I've ever heard, yelled for Papa, which removed all doubt. I saw him sit up. He had been asleep with my mother and brothers and sisters on a pile of mats spread out in a corner of that huge room.

Hormyn's deafening voice woke them. He woke most of the other families taking refuge there, as well. The injured stirred. Only the dead were not bothered.

I watched my father stand up, rubbing his eyes, looking tired and thin and miserable. And then he caught sight of me, and the first look on his face was one of shock.

That was when I remembered that he thought Catri and I were dead.

Yes. It took me that long. I had been concentrating so hard on simply getting to him, I had forgotten that he would not be prepared to see me when I arrived.

He stopped in midstep and looked at me, his eyes first wide, then narrow, then wide again. He frowned. And he said to me, "Tell me the name of your next-to-youngest sib."

I had to think for a moment to remember which of the twins had been born first.

"Yorni," I said after just an instant.

He considered that, staring down at his knotted hands. "Perhaps that was too simple. What did you keep under your pillow?"

I had a little bag on a string I'd knitted for myself, in which I kept my treasures.

A cardinal's bright red feather.

A shell given to me by a trader, who told me he had picked it up walking along the shore of a faraway sea.

A thin braid of hair from the tail of our riding horse — which I rarely ever got to ride, that I thought was beautiful. I'd pulled the hairs from the currycomb one day and braided them.

A scrap of paper on which a boy I knew had written, *I like you, and I think you're pretty.* He had said that. About me.

I told my father what I kept in the bag, and he did not smile. Or nod. Instead, without saying one word, he pulled the bag from beneath his shirt, lifted the string over his head, and put it around my neck. Then he burst into tears and grabbed me away from our neighbors, and hugged me tight.

"You live," he whispered. "You live."

"I live," I agreed. "I've come to rescue you and take you back to the Spire."

He pulled back and stared down at me. "The . . . Spire?"

"That tale is long enough to be told over dinner," I told him. "And far too long to tell now. Get Mama and the littles, and I will take you there."

"How?"

"By moonroad. But we have to hurry. The clearing feels dangerous. I do not think we were seen coming in here, but someone is sure to notice that little crack in the cliff we came through sooner or later."

"You came in through a crack in the cliff?" He frowned. "We're going to need to seal that off. I thought we controlled all the passageways."

"Papa," I said. "You need not worry. Let the others do it. Help will come for them, but I want to get you to the Spire, and we need to go now."

He looked down at me, suddenly the headman of Hillrush and no longer simply my father. He said,

"Gennadara, who are you that you would suggest saving just your own family —"

"And Catri's," I interrupted.

He was not mollified. " — when everyone here is in equal danger? You got into the Spire? You even got *to* the Spire? There were tales that it was still alive, and just this night, shortly before we got warning that Banris was invading, we saw the lights go on, but no one has been able to get there in time untold."

"It is . . ." I paused, a bit puzzled. "Alive? The Spire itself? Not just the ghosts and everything in it?"

My father nodded. "The history of the Spires is . . . not what you were told. There was no mountain worn away to the northwest. The Spires were the final and greatest achievements of the sun wizards — vast living fortresses summoned from the bones of the earth themselves to lift humanity above the reach of the nightlings, and spare them from destruction when it became inevitable that humans were losing the Long War. They were enormous; they would have held all the survivors, and those survivors' families, for generations to come. And they were, the sun wizards thought, impregnable."

But dragons and traitors and hostages had disproven that.

"I can get you there," I told my father. "But we have to hurry. The moonroads will only be open for a little longer."

"Genna." He looked at me so sternly, I wished I could simply disappear. "Can you take everyone?"

And there it was. I knew I could take two people. But could I take more? I'd never tried more than two. The cat had taken himself, and he had pulled either Danrith or Yarri through on occasion. And I had taken both of them as well. (At that moment, I realized I did not know where the cat had gotten to. But he was a capable creature and would have to take care of himself.)

Meanwhile, I knew that I could take at least two people with me over the moonroads.

But.

How many people were hidden away in the sun wizard's lair? A hundred? Two hundred? Our village had held five hundred and some, and I knew many had died. But how many had lived?

How could I take so many?

"I do not know, Papa," I said. "I know I can take two at a time. But I have never taken more, and I cannot say what would happen if I tried. I might kill everyone. Or nothing might happen at all. Or perhaps I would simply get us all lost in the twilight lands, where the monsters would find us easy prey."

Behind me, Jagan said something loudly and angrily, and I turned to see him struggling to pull his arms free from the two neighbor men who still held him. Catri was gone, and I guessed the neighbors had escorted her to her own parents.

But Jagan. He was an outsider, and no one had welcomed him. I cringed.

In the same moment, though, my father's face transformed. He turned his attention to Jagan and asked him, slowly and carefully, in the sun wizard language, who he was and where he had come from.

I should not have been surprised that my father knew the language. He knows so much.

Jagan looked at him, startled, and answered in a flurry far too quick for me to follow.

Evidently, the same held true for my father. Papa held up a hand and explained that Tagasuko was difficult for him. He spoke slowly.

I could understand my father.

And Jagan grinned. This time he spoke more slowly, too, gave his name, and said that he came from the Spire. This time, he was as happy, in fact, as I had ever seen him.

My father turned to me. "Where did you find this boy?"

"He was . . . frozen, or held by light . . . in one of the rooms of the Spire. We came upon him while we were searching the lowest open floor. What the boy, Jagan, calls the Warrens. We . . . Catri and I . . . we woke him. We thought he was dead, but he was not."

"Then he is from the time of the sun wizards? What he says is true?"

"So says the haw," I said, and that got another look from my father, one positively jubilant. "There's a haw still within the Spire?"

I nodded. "Neth Kosae Haw."

"I would not know names," my father said. "But the haws were the great teachers. The master teachers, who taught wizards."

"The haw is teaching Jagan, Catri, and me," I said. "Or he was, until we sneaked out to come here to rescue you."

"We shall make whatever we must right with him when we get there," Papa said. "But for now, we must get there."

"Everyone?"

Papa turned to Jagan and asked him if he knew anything about *natykni* and *natykaru*. I did not know those words, though they felt a little familiar. And Jagan nodded eagerly.

Papa told me, "Perhaps we have a way to take everyone who can go to the Spire. Some will wish to stay here. Some *must* stay here, for if the Spire lives, they cannot enter it, or they will die."

"All humans can enter safely," I said. "The haw said so."

So had the cat and the dragon, but I did not recall if my father understood about the cat, and it seemed a very bad time to be discussing my adventure with the dragon.

"Nightlings cannot," Papa said, "and some of them hide here, too. Our known allies. Our closest friends. They were caught away from Arrienda when Banris attacked, and we could not leave them in the forests to die."

"Is Yarri here?"

He shook his head. "She and Doyati disappeared shortly after we got news of your death. Her family does not know how she fares, or if she lives."

I closed my eyes against the lurching of my stomach and stood very still. She had to be safe. Somewhere. She was as dear to me as a sister. She was a friend. We owed each other our lives. She had to be safe. She and Doyati both.

Papa, however, had been talking to the boy, and he turned to me again. "Come, now, you and your young sun wizard friend. He says he knows the workings of the great ships of the sun wizards."

Ah. The magic that made ships fly was *natykaru*. The ships *natykni*.

"His parents built them," I said.

"Then they must have been powerful indeed. The *natykni* are considered among the greatest of the lost arts of the sun wizards. We have one here. Hidden away, waiting for the day when it might be used again. None of us has been able to figure out its workings, and we know not whether it still works, or if it died long ago, as some of the other sun wizard creations seem to have done."

"The war harp still worked," I said. I did not have happy memories of some of the sun wizards' creations.

But we were by that time hurrying up the passageway down which we had just traveled, Papa, me, Jagan, and the neighbors who had guarded the two of us. And when we reached the main room again, Papa said a word to one of those charged with guarding the door, and he ducked beneath a tapestry and hurried into the room where I knew the sun wizard had kept his library and his tables full of magical tools. And a giant statue that Yarri, Danrith, and I had accidentally awakened — one that guarded the chamber, and perhaps more.

Men came out in a hurry. Some were neighbors; some were strangers. I counted a dozen of them.

Papa led us beneath a tapestry of wolves and stags at the edge of a forest, with a magnificent city just visible over the treetops, woven in every imaginable color and beautiful beyond words.

Behind the tapestry, another door awaited, and another passageway. This passage had dozens of doors to either side, but we ignored them all. We wended our way down, down, and farther down, until I started smelling fresh water. And then I began to hear it falling. Pouring, gushing, turning into a deafening roar by the time we reached level ground.

The vast cavern we stepped into was unlit by any torches or lamps or the sun wizards' hidden lights.

But natural light from the moon overhead filtered in through the pouring of a waterfall. And outlined an enormous flying ship — wings tucked, head bowed, eyes closed — still and waiting.

CHAPTER 17
SHIPS & OTHER FLYING THINGS

One of the sun wizard ships sat before us all, and the sight of it took my breath away. Its metal wings rested close to its sides like a bird's, its metal legs pulled tightly beneath it, as cats settle on their paws when they are dozing. And its lean, long ship body rose high over my head. It faced the waterfall, so I could not see the prow.

It seemed made of precious gemstones cut and faceted; it glittered in the moonlight. And the metal bands that held the gemstones together gleamed, though I could not guess whether they were gold or silver or some lesser metal.

I heard myself gasp.

Jagan, however, shouted and raced toward the ship. Papa and the men ran after him, and I, with a moment's hesitation, followed.

He walked to the front of it, to the place where a graceful

metal neck arched swanlike up to a metal face carved to look like a bird. It had a head like an eagle's. He asked my father for permission to address the ship, and my father nodded.

Jagan pressed his hands together, and bowed, and said something to the ship. Words I had never heard, did not know, and could not guess at. I wished then that I knew the sun wizards' infernal language better, or that the Spire's language spell worked at a distance, for I felt as left out and bewildered as any human being could feel.

After he spoke, there was silence. The men who were with Papa all seemed to be holding their breath. Papa could have been a statue, he stood so still.

Nothing happened. Jagan waited, I waited, and the men waited — none of us daring to breathe — and nothing happened.

My father asked Jagan a question, and that at least I understood. He had asked him, "What did you say?"

Jagan repeated the words slowly, and my father nodded, mouthing them as the boy said them, then mouthing them over and over again.

He stood where Jagan had stood. He took the same pose Jagan had taken.

And then he said the same words.

"*Emerok agabaji, bagajan wanar ae ya.*"

This time, something happened indeed.

The ship opened its closed eyes, stared down at my father, its neck twisting and its head moving, and it spoke.

And what it said, I understood only too well. *Hak geen korok.*

"State your name."

"Jhontar Aldarsson ot Hillrush," my father said.

Jagan frowned a little and whispered a question to my father, and as he did, the ship moved its head down level with them and cocked its head as if listening.

They talked — almost all in words I had not yet learned. I could guess they were talking about the workings of the ship, and I caught a comment from the ship that Jagan was too young. But the rest was a mystery to me.

And then the men standing off to the side — all of them men who had come from the wizard's workroom — cheered.

My father turned to me and said, "The ship will take us to the Spire. It has agreed."

I thought, Wonderful, wonderful, but what was everything else you and Jagan and the ship have been saying? "Good," I said, though. I know Papa. He will answer questions when there is time, but I would have wagered a horse against used wool he would not think that now was a good moment for them.

The other men were already running up the passageway, opening doors, and shouting, "A rescue! A rescue! To the sun wizard ship!" so that Papa, Jagan, and I, following a little behind, had to fight an ever-increasing flood of refugees headed in the other direction as we climbed the stairs. We ended up hugging the wall and shouting at people to make way, and even so, we had to back down a step for every three or four we climbed.

And in the end, we need not have bothered. Mama and my sibs, including Danrith, were already coming toward us when we reached the throng in the main room. With so many people in it, all of them hurrying and pushing to get to the one door that led down to the ship, I feared we would be separated.

But we fought our way to them, hanging on to Jagan and pulling him with us. And then the horde thinned out, and we had breathing space.

And Mama and my brother Danrith saw me. "Genna!" Mama shrieked.

Mama is not a shrieker. She is a yihanni, and yihannis are dignified. So I knew she must have mourned me deeply, and it hurt that I had not been able to send her word that I still lived.

Danrith said nothing, but he grabbed me and hugged me, and from my younger brother, such a thing bordered on the miraculous. The younger sibs were happy to see me, too, but they were far enough younger that they were unlikely to have understood what "dead" meant. I was back, and that was good enough for them.

Papa stopped to speak to a nightling who had come out of one of the hidden doors.

"Some of the men will stay behind to continue guarding your people," he said. "But there is a haw within the Spire, and we will make better progress learning to use the sun wizard magic, and learning to fight the kai-lords and their armies, if we can learn from the haw and use the Spire's tools. Tell those who wait to keep faith. We will triumph."

The nightling, tall and green-skinned, with hair of darker green, nodded and said, "As you will." His voice was bells and chimes, and I shivered. I had forgotten the beauty of nightling voices in the time I had been gone from Arrienda.

The mind cannot hold on to their sound. Perhaps it is that they are simply too beautiful, or perhaps there is some magic that makes them impossible to recall.

I did not know, but when I heard his voice, I thought of Yarri and ached to know that she was safe. I could see her, tiny and so slender she was almost frail, with skin of palest yellow and hair the color of buttercups, that stood out in all directions as if she were a dandelion gone to seed.

I prayed then, to Spirit and little gods, that she would be safe until I could find her.

We headed for the ship room, and again the sudden freshening of the air and the growing roar of the water sang to me as we descended.

In that vast cavern, the people waiting no longer seemed a crowd at all. They did not fill up the room or even come close. They huddled together in family groups, parents counting children and keeping them near, young husbands and young wives clutching each other's hands, all of them holding the few belongings they had managed to carry with them. Little things.

I felt my throat tighten. They had been so quickly overrun, so desperate, that in many cases all they had was one another. These were my people. Friends and cousins and neighbors, folks I loved as well as people I had never much liked, but all of them mine. Even the ones I did not know, I realized. They were mine, too, by virtue of being human, by virtue of being hunted, under attack.

. We were all of us a sort of family right then.

And as we watched, the ship turned its head and told my father, "Bid them welcome for me."

And Papa said, "The ship, whose name is Kratak, bids you welcome."

My people stamped their feet and cheered approval.

Down from the sides of the ramp, steps unfolded. The cheer got louder, but even at their most jubilant, the people of my village could not compete with the roar of the waterfall. I could hear them, but the sound they made was so small.

When all whom we could rescue had been saved, I wondered how much of the Spire we would fill.

The first-level Warrens?

Just a few sections of the Warrens?

A single corridor?

I tried to imagine humans as numerous as nightlings, filling the whole of the Spire as they once had, and an unknown number of other Spires, too. And the cities beneath, and the villages all around.

It must have been wonderful, I thought, to rule the world.

Jagan and my family were last aboard the ship. Papa kept checking to make sure no one who needed to go had been left behind. A few stragglers came from hidden places: a courting couple who had slipped away from their chaperones; a mother whose husband had died fleeing the hunters, and who had lost track of one of her half-dozen children; and a handful of single men who had spent time chasing down everyone else and making sure they knew the humans were leaving.

Perhaps the sun wizards' great ship would return to the cave one day. But perhaps not.

Banris had brought monsters to our village and the other nearby villages. He was, at that very moment, hunting the people from my village and the others who had *not* found a hiding place in the sun wizard's lair, using his monsters and no doubt every other weapon he could bring to bear. We might never be able to leave the Spire again.

On board, we found a few grand cabins above the deck, but many down the wide stairs that led below it. Each of those cabins had room enough for four or five adults. Papa put Mama and Danrith and my younger sibs in one, kissed Mama firmly, and said to me, "Come. I will need your help."

He did not ask Danrith. He asked me. It was the first time in as long as I could remember that he had needed my help rather than Danrith's. I followed him to the front of the ship-of-the-air, where the great bird head had turned to watch us, and I felt almost giddy. He needed *me*.

Eldest *child* is a different thing than eldest *son* to fathers — something daughters learn early on. You can be a firstborn, but if you are a girl, you always sense your father waiting for the next child to be the son who will follow in his path. Danrith would one day be headman, of course. I knew this, and I did not envy him — I would have been a yihanni like my mother, had the world not changed so much around me. As firstborn daughter, I had once had a clear path and a clear place of my own.

But there was always the little pang when Danrith got to travel with Papa, or inspect with Papa, or hunt with Papa, or learn the laws with Papa.

That moment, *I* was special to Papa.

I cherished it.

We stood behind the great ship's head. The men who knew some portion of the sun wizards' language stood in the front with Jagan, speaking with him. One turned to Papa as we arrived, and said, "We had to convince the ship that the boy had our permission to fly it. He knows how, but because of his age and the fact that he has not passed some sort of test for piloting ships of this size, the ship would not accept him."

"So long as you convinced it," my father said. "I do not care to think about any of us at the helm."

Papa turned to me. "Your young friend will take the ship to the Spire. Meanwhile, you will tell us what we must be prepared to do once we arrive — what our families must do, how we can find food and shelter, how we will survive."

The men of my village began to gather around me, but just then, the ship made a soft noise. I would have called it a whicker if a horse had done it. The sound, though, had more metal in it and was followed by the ship asking my father another question, to which my father replied, *"Hak va,"* which even I knew meant, "Go."

I was expecting a jolt. But the ship rose gracefully on all four legs, ran forward with the din of metal feet on stone floor — but without anything like the up-and-down motions of a running dragon — and took us through the waterfall, with water spraying on all sides of us but not touching us, into the late night. The moon was near its zenith, hard and cold and bright. Morning would be a ways off yet.

The ship-of-the-air spread its wings wide, cupping the air with them, and we glided forward, then rose, glided forward, and rose again, no wind in our hair, no sound of flapping from the great ship's metal-feathered wings . . . and with no sick sense of nothingness beneath our feet or of being tossed around like a cat in a sack.

It was, in other words, as different to me from the flying I had experienced before as day is different from night. As humans are different from nightlings. As the sun is different from the moon.

I thought I might like this sort of flying. Staying warm and dry and on my feet, able to see where I was going. Quite a step up from dragon's breath and dragon's spit.

For a while, the men on deck clung to the railings as I did, staring down at the world below us. But, a few at a time, they recalled their duty and gathered around me again.

I told them of the Spire. Of the rooms in the Warrens, of the green-doored supply closets that spewed out whatever might be desired, of the Aglak, and the white room with its magic pictures, of the higher levels of the Spire, none of which I had yet explored. I described the haw, and told them what I knew of the Ag, and Prime and Ag access, and the *okunaeso*, and anything else I could recall. The men decided that everyone would spend a day resting in the Warrens before they would brave the Aglak — and when they went through, families would go in groups, a few families at a time.

The ship-of-the-air followed the course Papa had laid out, its wings spread wide beneath the disappearing moonlight, the feathers of them making their own music as we turned and began to rise.

Papa had talked of going a long way south beneath the line of the cliffs before we rose above them and turned north and a little west. We did not, after all, wish to give away the location of the sun wizard's lair. But as we banked and turned, I realized that I could no longer see any sign of the Spire. We had traveled a very long way indeed for it to disappear.

We rose quickly and smoothly. The people sitting in cabins might not even realize that we were already traveling, I thought. We would arrive where we were going and they would not even know they had left where they had been.

We finished our turn to the north and seemed to stop climbing in the air. I found my way to a rail and looked down, and nearly lost my breath. I'd thought Catri and I had been high above the world when we had looked down from the Spire, but from this new height, the river we had left was nothing but a glittering line drawn by a mapmaker's pen, and the world itself was a lumpy, silvered blanket.

We had seen the human lights of the villages before, Catri and I, when we looked out and down from the Spire. Now they were gone.

Humans had been shuttered. Hidden. Silenced.

I bit back my rage at Banris and his evil and his greed and focused on the men who would lead the people I loved into their new home. I told them about the parts of the Spire I loved — showers, privies, the comfort of the rooms, the wonderfulness of the food — and then I told them about the parts that I hated. The little spying scrolls that showed up on front doorsteps. The way the Spire and its ghosts listened everywhere. The Aglak line, with its enormous corral, and my feeling of helplessness facing it as it decided my future for me. Neth Kosae Haw's condescension, hostility, and suspicion when he thought I might not be related to his revered dead man.

That vague sense of being captive.

They had more questions than I had answers — I had not been in the Spire long, and I already sensed that if I had been there for the last thousand years, there would still be parts I had not yet discovered.

But I told them everything I could, offered my best guesses when those were all I had, and when I knew nothing at all, I said so.

They listened. I had earned their trust when I bargained with the kai-lord, and their respect when I beat him, even if it was with a lot of help. I had earned their consent to be called adult — even if in my own mind I was nothing like an adult yet — and I had been where they had not.

I do not know if they believed all I said. But they listened.

And then, light. A pinpoint before us and far below us, but a pinpoint that grew brighter and larger with every instant. As I saw it, the men on the deck began to point, and to shout. "A city! People!"

But by then, I had recognized the shape of the light. The lights. An illuminated dagger that blazed high above the ground and thrust deep into the belly of the sky.

We were closing in with incredible speed upon the Spire.

CHAPTER 18
RUMORS OF TROUBLE

They were still shouting "A city! People!" as we soared nearer.

I said, "Papa, that is the Spire. But Catri, Jagan, and I were the only three people there."

That might have been true when we left, but as we neared the landing, I could see things had changed.

The ship circled the Spire once, and I saw humans in clusters along the balcony, and humans in the vast open areas, and the immense doorway to the city through which Catri and I had first entered flung wide open.

I clutched the rail and stared harder. Was this some strange dream? Or madness?

It was neither.

In my head, a familiar voice said, *There were others who would not have survived the night. When I was sure you were safe, Sunrider, I sought them out through moonroads and forest and used every bit of magic I had to get them to the Spire in one piece. They have no idea how they got here, of course. The stories they tell should be interesting, once their hysteria dies down.*

The cat had come back.

We had slowed greatly in our circle around the Spire, and now, the ship roared at the people in the open spaces below us. They looked up, saw what must have appeared to be a monster emerging from darkness, and scattered. I heard screams.

I tried to imagine the ship I had seen descending at me with great speed, and I could understand their terror. Wings and legs and huge bird talons and bird-of-prey head and vast, glittering body — no creature known to our world would fit such a description.

Then we were down, and the men on the deck clapped Jagan on the back and praised him and raised another stomping cheer. I cheered with them.

I was not home — I could never go home again. But I was determined to make the Spire my home. I thought if I got to be Sunrider in the Spire, it might not be too hard. Or too dangerous. Easy and safe sounded like an excellent future to me.

The families in the cabins were coming out to investigate the noise, and I watched their faces. They huddled together, looking up and up and ever higher up at the lighted windows that rose in spirals before them.

Danrith joined me at the rail and said, "This is where you've been? With all these strangers?"

"No one was here when Catri and I arrived," I told him. "No lights burned. The outside was dark and looked like nothing but the black glass that forms this place."

"Who are the people, then?"

I gave him a look. "All of them? When I just told you I had never met them?"

He stuck out his tongue at me. "How did they get here, the ones who were not here when you left?"

I leaned in and whispered, "The *cat* went and got them."

My brother said, "Of course *he* would be in this."

I kept my voice low. "If he were not, the people who are here would likely be dead instead. He woke me to come after you, for that matter. I did not know what had happened."

Dan caught my caution and lowered his own voice. "I was not complaining that he is here. But you have to admit, wherever trouble comes, he's close behind."

I waited while the villagers and the strangers went down the stairs to the immense obsidian-and-marble balcony. I would exit the ship in the company of my family — and because my father was Hillrush's headman, even if Hillrush was no more, we would go last.

Catri and her parents and sibs were waiting in the group we'd saved when at last we reached them. The men I'd talked to were gathering people into groups, shouting instructions at them to follow Catri and me, that we would show them where to go. They stayed with their groups. The men who knew some of the sun wizard language — the few scholars — would handle speaking to doors and any other tasks that required knowledge of Tagasuko for each of the families under their care.

We were excited, Catri and I. The night had been terrible, costly to our families and friends and to us as well. We would not understand the full extent of what we had lost until later, I realized — until the dead and the missing were counted, and the injured recovered as best they could. Until we had made inventory in our minds and hearts of all those things that had not escaped — our sheep, our goats, our dogs and cats and cattle, our favorite toys and favorite books and simply being able to walk through our own front doors, or sit beneath our own favorite trees, or walk beside the stream that ran through the meadows.

We did not yet feel the loss.

All we felt at that moment was gratitude that we were with our families again, and that they were well away from Banris and his monsters.

We were alone in the Spire no more.

In this place where Banris could never reach, surely no neighbor could consider capturing one of my sibs to sell to that monster to be used as bait.

I had not forgotten that. I would never forget.

But that, at least, was all behind us.

You would think so, wouldn't you? the cat's voice whispered in my mind. *But trouble comes.*

I looked around, hoping to see him, but I could not. *Tell me what you know.*

He did not answer me. In that regard, he is a typical cat. He keeps his own counsel, and is only around when he wants to be and not when you might wish him to be.

Catri and I did all we could to gather our villagers, to lead them into our corridor, to keep everyone close, and show them to empty apartments that would fit their families. We made sure each one of our people had a place to sleep that night. The cat had vanished again, and I was too busy directing the multitude of strangers who were now wandering around, lost and helpless and bewildered, to chase after him.

Catri and I had looked that confused and frightened when we first arrived. Actually, I recalled that we had looked worse. I'd seen the pictures.

Catri and I both passed each other and our own dwelling several times on our way to help families get settled, but it was only once our own families had found places that she and I met in front of *our* door.

"I will be staying with my parents tonight," she told me as soon as she saw me heading down the corridor toward her.

"I was going to tell you the same thing," I said.

We smiled, a little sadly. "I do not know if I'll be permitted to stay here," she said. "Now. With Mama and Papa here and all."

"I know," I said. "You should stay with your family anyway. We'll still live close. I think I'm going to live with mine. We have the haw and our training to attend to. And . . ."

We would see each other every day. Those were the words on my lips, but a chill ran down my spine, and the pinch place on my right arm tingled. I did not say them. Something had changed again. Some shift in my future, I thought, had made everything sideways and wrong.

We might have managed to talk longer, but Catri's older brother shouted for her to come home.

"One left, one right, then straight," she said.

I nodded. My parents' directions were the same, just one door farther. Just for this one day, of course, and then there would be the Aglak for them, and lessons for Catri and Jagan and me.

Catri left.

I walked into what had been our dwelling. I had told my parents I would be back soon, and I was eager to see them. But that feeling of something gone wrong kept getting stronger, and I did not want to bring the wrongness to them.

The cat crouched on the table, his tail flicking back and forth in irritation, when I walked in.

What is the matter with you? I asked him.

He gave me that unblinking cat stare. *I've missed you, too, girl.*

I will be staying in my parents' quarters tonight, I told him. *And when they have finished the Aglak, I plan to move with them to wherever they go.*

And the last I heard, you were going to be a sun wizard and one of their Ag disciples.

That's right.

Things change, the cat said, and he stared off at nothing, and his ears went back. *I'll be listening for your call when they change again.*

I looked at him closely. *I feel something wrong,* I admitted. *Do you know something?*

The cat's ears flattened all the way. *No. I cannot find the one I need to ask. So I know nothing beyond the truth that Banris has brought the beginnings of war, and the humans whose side I favor are outnumbered a hundred to one by some counts, and a thousand to one by others. But the air smells like lightning though the sky is clear, and in the wind I hear whispers of words I don't know. And what moves in the forests below moves to no good. Trouble will come.*

The room was warm; the temperature perfect. The temperature was always perfect in the Spire. But my skin prickled, and I shivered.

I am going home to be with my parents, I told him.

I know where to find you, the cat said. He paused. *When I need you.*

Which made me feel no easier than I had.

I walked back the way I had come, suddenly aware of how bone-deep weary I was. The excitement had gone — finding my family, flying in the ship, bringing everyone to a new home, and worrying about what might yet come. I could barely put one foot in front of the other, and I stumbled more than once over obstacles that did not exist.

Everyone in my parents' dwelling slept already, except for Mama. She sat at the table, looking worried.

"I waited," she said when I walked in the door.

I smiled. At least I think I smiled.

"Without the noise, I can thank you properly for coming for us."

"You are my family," I said, thinking that should be obvious. What I had done was not the sort of thing that required thanks. It was a daughter's duty, and a daughter's privilege, to serve the people I loved. Any one of them would have done the same thing for me.

My mother did not smile in return. "You need to sleep. Trouble comes."

"I feel it," I admitted. "And a friend said the same thing. But he did not know what sort of trouble."

"Nor do I. The yihanni's magic is not in seeing the future but in the application of the practical. Still, there are . . . portents." She frowned. "Things that suggest the Sunrider's time approaches."

Things, in other words, that I did not want to hear. "Then at least I'm in the right place."

She might have read my worry from my face, she might have seen it in the set of my shoulders, or she might have felt it because she is my mama, and mothers know these things, but she rose and came over to me and hugged me fiercely. "Your brothers are sharing the bed in that room, your sisters are sharing the bed in that one, and your father and I have the back room." The dwelling they found was one of the very few we had located in the Warrens with more than two bedrooms, and with three privies. The beds would be an unimaginable luxury to my brothers Danrith, Morith, and Yorni in the one room, and my sisters Ebecka, Lilangi, and Marni in the other.

But I had become accustomed to a comfortable bed, not the cob-mattress cot in the attic, for which I had been grateful, too. I knew for a fact that Ebecka talked while she slept, and Lil flailed her arms like she was trying to catch lightning bugs. Marni was too small to be much of a problem, but she flopped on top of the person closest to her, I suspect, out of some sleeper's sense of self-preservation.

I told Mama, "I will sleep on the long couch. That way I will not wake anyone."

Mama hugged me a little tighter. "Yes. Well. And soon you will be ready to return to the dwelling you have been living in."

I pulled back and started to protest, but she said, "The wild bird once freed does not return a second time to the cage." She sighed. "Some part of you is still my little girl, Genna. But some part of you is already grown. You have done more in your few years than I have done in all of mine. Someday, if I am remembered at all, it will be only as Genna's mother . . . the mother of the Sunrider. And because of what you will do, Genna, that will be enough."

She kissed my forehead — I was almost her height, but she still did that. And then she sent me to the long padded bench, very like the one in the rooms Catri and I had chosen, but blue instead of pale green, with a gentle, "Shoo. Sleep."

Days passed, while the moon faded to darkness, and the pull of the moonroads ceased for a time.

But if I had some peace during the dark hours, I had none during the day.

The Aglak was the first thing that went wrong, and my family is the perfect example of *how* it went wrong.

They went to the Aglak the next day — my father, as headman, had to go first so everyone else could see it was safe. So he went through, and the *aglakari* made no mention of Sator Kizen Haw, and in spite of the fact that Papa already knew Tagasuko and was headman of our village, he received Segundus access and was directed to begin work as an Intermediary, teaching Tagasuko to barbarians. The barbarians, of course, being the people of my village and those that the cat brought in.

That would not have been bad — my father loves to teach people how to do things. However, my mother followed him at the Aglak, and we discovered that *she* was the descendant of that accursed Sator Kizen Haw, and more so, because of her work as a yihanni, she had magical skills that the Spire and the Ag decided they wanted. So Mama was given Ag access and placed in importance over Papa in front of many families from our village who were waiting in that corral behind them.

I was with them, of course, because I wanted to be able to tell them what to expect. But I could not have told them to expect that. The Aglak had no respect for what was, I realized. It did not care that Papa had led our people since he was seventeen, or that our people loved him. It did not care that Mama was horrified to be put in a position of authority over him and wanted no part of it. What it said was what was. I heard the murmurings of those behind us in the line, and watched some families squeezing past others to head back the way they had come. They would, I thought, stay in the Warrens. And I could not blame them.

But my parents gritted their teeth and kept going. My brother Danrith also went through, and he, like me, was given Ag access and a place in the sun wizardry.

It felt to me almost as if the Aglak were trying to humiliate my father.

My parents did not put my younger brothers or sisters through the Aglak, though they had brought them intending to.

The humiliation was not finished there, though. Jagan took my whole family to one of many vertical carriages hidden away behind brown doors — doors that would again only open when the palm the Aglak had stung was placed in the center of the sun — and started to put us all in the carriage to take us up to the Segundus floors, which would have to be where my family lived, since my father was not permitted on the Prime or Ag floors.

But the doors closed when my mother, carrying my youngest sister, started into the carriage. It closed again when my father, carrying my youngest brother, tried to pass through the doorway.

Jagan stood there, bewildered. "You have all been through Aglak, correct?" he said.

Which is when my parents and I discovered that in order to live above the Warrens, every man, woman, child, and infant had to go through the Aglak. According to Jagan, it was not so difficult for new babies, because there was a special Aglak for them that was done when they were born — he made it sound like a midwife might actually do it. It let babies pass until they were old enough to go through the true Aglak, at about six years of age. But barbarians — how I had begun to hate that word — had to all go through the Warrens' Aglaks, no matter what their age.

Most of the villagers, including most of those few who had braved the Aglaks, returned to the Warrens, where they set up a little community as close to what they had back in Hillrush, or the villages of Smeth and Little Sheepshank, as they could manage.

Everything was changing. The villagers were made to watch the history of the Spire and the world of the sun wizards before and during the Fall. They understood Tagasuko through the magic of the haws. According to the haws, they ought to be ready to become productive citizens.

But the villagers no longer had their crafts, their skills, or the work they knew and loved and had mastered. They could not tend their herds, or work with their dogs, or shape iron and silver. They could not weave or sew or knit or spin, they could not cook their meals, they could not work their fields, tend their crops, build their barns, walk through their pastures, or do any of the things they had done since they had been children. They had more food than they could ever eat, more clothes than they could ever wear, more things than they could ever have imagined that they might want when they lived in the village.

And they were miserable.

They no longer had purpose. Without purpose, they had no desire to work or do. Because Papa had been stripped of his authority, they had no one who could lead them or tell them how to set their lives right again. They had no idea what to do with themselves.

And so, one family at a time, they crept back to the Aglak, put all their family members through it, and then they slunk off to live where the Spire put them, and they did the work the Spire gave them. It was better than doing nothing. Being nothing.

They had already discovered that having . . . having *was* nothing. Then the Aglak scattered them, and they lost one another as much as they had lost the village, their work, their purpose.

Catri's family no longer saw mine. People we had known our whole lives ended up on different levels, in different sections, all according to some decision made by magic that cared nothing for people or their needs and everything for its own.

And Catri, Jagan, and I? We were no different. Catri and Jagan studied together. Dan had his own tutor, a woman named Rika Vao Haw, and he studied in a different room than Catri and Jagan. I ended up apart in an entirely different pinnacle, tutored by a haw ghost named Remmnor Mikav Haw, who had once — he never tired of telling me — been Master of the Ag. This was the position my mother was being pushed into, and that, he kept reminding me, I would someday be trained for. Because, he said, the blood of Sator Kizen Haw ran true, and it was our duty to serve the Spire as masters of the people.

I traveled by *okunaeso* each morning, alone, spent all day alone with Remmnor Mikav Haw, and sometimes returned to my family's apartment so late that only Mama would still be awake when I arrived. Because I was also required to leave early, I sometimes went days without seeing any of the rest of them.

Remmnor Mikav Haw never wearied of claiming that the Spire's system was best, that the Aglak magic put people where they might do the most good, and that, always, everyone would be taken care of. The Spire could find uses for them all. Not doing anything they might want. "Talent," he said, "is no respecter of desire, my girl. What you have talent for, that you do. I might wish to flap my arms and fly, but am I a bird? Of course not."

They lived to do what the Spire needed them to do.

As did I. And in the Spire, I was the descendant of Sator Kizen Haw. I was *not* the Sunrider. According to Remmnor Mikav Haw, the Sunrider was some ridiculous heresy cooked up by nightling slaves, and he would not tolerate any mention of it.

He had no interest in pursuing any history of prophecies of the Sunrider from his own time — he said any that might have existed came from disreputable sources — or of discovering what a Sunrider might be for in our time. He refused to consider that there was something else I was supposed to do besides serve the Spire, and he refused to help me figure out why I had been told I was the Sunrider.

I was a part of the Spire, and the Spire did not need a Sunrider. It needed sun wizards. It needed Ag. So I would become a sun wizard, and I would accept my eventual place as Master of the Ag. It was the way things were. It was the future for which the Aglak had marked me, and what I thought about it was of no importance to anyone.

My education, such as it was, went well. I was learning

what the Spire demanded I learn. Under Remmnor Mikav Haw, my Tagasuko was quickly becoming fluent. Under him, I grasped the fundamentals of sun wizardry and quickly learned the sun wizard way of writing basic spells, designing them to do only what I wanted them to do and no more, and then testing them in ways that would limit their damage if I made mistakes.

He spoke in glowing terms of my ability; according to him, I ranked among the better students he had ever taught, though according to him, the preconceived notions about magic taught to me by my mother — as well as my "unfortunate association with nightlings and their heresies," as he put it — were keeping me from being one of the best he'd taught.

I did not care to be his best student. I did not care to serve the Spire, to be a sun wizard, to become Ag.

The pinch place on my arm was always cold now, and I knew what I was learning would do nothing to help me destroy Banris. Or free human and nightling slaves. Or close the moonroads.

My world just got worse and worse.

CHAPTER 19
DRAGON IN CHAINS

The cold bit into the pinch place on my arm, and something heavy and pointy sat atop my chest.

I struggled up to wakefulness to discover the cat sitting on my chest, digging into my collarbone with his claws.

Oh. You.

Yes, me. I know the shape of our trouble now, and one way or another, it is desperate trouble.

I sat up, rubbing sleep from my eyes. The room was empty save for the cat, and, from the quiet in the place, I had to guess everyone still slept.

Desperate trouble. The cat had not referred to my family and the villagers hidden away in the sun wizard's lair as desperate trouble. So what sort of trouble was this?

Is my family in danger?

They're fine. They'll be waking shortly. Before they wake, you need to be gone.

I hated when he was cryptic, and he seemed to revel in being cryptic. Foul animal.

Why, then?

The cat said, *Follow.*

He led me into the white room, for even in my parents' grand new home, there was a white room with a sunken couch.

He jumped down to it, and I followed.

Instantly, the room came to life.

I saw a huge black dragon, bound by heavy ropes to the deck of a sailing ship. He was hurt. Bleeding.

"Why are they —"

DON'T SPEAK, the cat thought, so loud and so sudden in my skull that not only could I not speak, but I could not think, either.

I pressed my hands to my forehead, trying to stop the pain inside.

Is that . . . my dragon?

The cat put a paw on my leg and stared into my eyes. *Yes. Your dragon. The last dragon. He came a day earlier to deliver survivors to the Spire, but the Spire is awake now,* and it remembers the dragons and their role in the Fall. So it brought weapons to bear against him and attacked him. The humans he sought to rescue died. He was badly injured.

But how did he get to the sea?

Nightlings — an army of them. Not from Arrienda — these nightlings were from elsewhere, but somehow knew he would fall, and knew where to wait. They were aided by creatures of the Moonworld in dragging him to the sea. Banris could have a hand in this.

I closed my eyes tight and pressed my hands to my temples. *Why? Why would they do this, why would Banris work with them?*

As for Banris, he may be building alliances against Arrienda, and giving a dragon to the nightlings would help him do that. Why would the nightlings want a dragon, though? Because the dragons betrayed everyone in their desire to gain power, and they were betrayed in return. Now these nightlings are taking this dragon to a gathering place where he will be tried, and found guilty, and executed. But not before he has been forced to confess that he is the last dragon, a truth he has kept hidden until now.

I thought of standing on the Spire, watching the dragons spewing out monsters.

I thought of watching the sun wizards die.

I thought of seeing humans desperate to reach the Spire cut down as the forests grew in, as the monsters pursued, as the world they had known and trusted died.

And I looked at that dragon, wounded, bound, and knew I owed him my life and Catri's life.

I wavered.

He had been one of the creatures who had tried to destroy humanity.

He was the creature who had saved me and my best friend.

He was dangerous, mad, confused; he talked to himself and argued with himself, and I could not know if he would thank me for trying to help him or if he would kill me.

He had tried — with the rest of his kind — to destroy humanity. He had nearly succeeded, and because of what he and others like him had done, my people had been slaves for centuries.

He had saved my life, and he didn't have to.

He had been the cause of the massacre of hundreds, if not thousands, of humans, and I was in the Spire, a place where I was unlikely to ever become the Sunrider, because of what he had done . . . and it all could have been a clever trick, the way dragons carrying the injured to the Spires had been a clever trick, one that had diverted wizards from the walls, and that had made the Spire vulnerable. And that had released hidden monsters into the heart of the most important levels . . . .

Remember the picture you found in the scroll on your doorstep that second day you were here?

The one where Catri kissed Jagan?

That one.

I remembered it.

Do you remember what you thought about it? the cat asked.

I remembered being angry. That picture had not shown the magic that had compelled Catri to do what she did. It had not shown the way I had been drawn to the door, or the way she had been drawn to Jagan.

That picture had lied.

That's it, the cat said.

Pictures could lie. They could show the facts but not tell the truth.

Did the pictures of the dragons on the day of the Fall lie?

The cat moved off my chest, and I sat up.

Get dressed, he told me.

I went into my room, for our home in the Segundus level had enough rooms and enough beds for all of us, and pulled on my warm clothes. The red sweater my mother had made for me, my blue skirt, the socks I'd knitted myself, and my farm boots. These I chose in favor of the many sun wizard dresses I had. The chill running down my spine told me I needed to be ready for . . . something.

Trouble.

Danger.

While I dressed, the cat stared pointedly out the glass wall that led onto a balcony. Here, far above the commons below, my room did not face the setting moon.

It would be more than a quarter full, I realized. I could faintly feel the tug of it. But it did not reach for me in this place. And morning, I realized, looking east, was nearly upon us.

The cat told me, *Yes, what you saw about the dragons and the humans and the Fall had pieces of a lie in it. You do not know why the dragons chose to do what they did. They had good reasons. You do not know why the sun wizards chose to act as they did. They had both good and bad reasons. Nothing is as simple as it looks in a picture, and if you value what the dragon did for you and Catri, you would not be a criminal for helping him now.*

I thought about that. *And if I do nothing?*

You would not be a criminal then, either. And not help-
ing him would be the safer and the easier path.

If he had not said that, I might have struggled longer
with my decision. I might have decided differently.

But he did say that, and it made me remember what my
father and mother both said so often that after a while I
almost did not even hear it anymore.

The easy thing to do is almost never the right
thing to do.

I took a deep breath and looked at the cat.

He saved my life and Catri's life. And he tried to save
the lives of other humans. I want to do the right thing,
not the easy thing.

The cat trotted out of my bedroom in front of me. *Then*
get Danrith and find Catri. And the boy Jagan. You must
convince them to come with you, without saying anything
is wrong. The Spire is listening.

I did not want to involve Catri in anything that would
cause her problems. And I did not want to involve Jagan at
all. Sometimes he seemed like my friend, sometimes he
asked questions that made me wonder why he wanted to
know the answers, and every time I saw Danrith looking at
Catri and Jagan together — and I saw the frustration and

the disappointment on his face — I wanted to never see Jagan again.

Can't Dan and I do this alone?

No. You cannot fly a ship-of-the-air. Jagan can. And if Catri is with you, Jagan will come.

What, then, do I tell them?

That you can get them up to the ships-of-the-air level, and that you want to take a ship and go flying. You can, in fact, do this. With my help.

So I woke Danrith, and he did not ask questions. We have our own signals, he and I, and I let him know with a gesture that we had to move quietly and quickly.

Getting Catri meant traveling to another part of the Spire, but I used the *okunaeso*, which I had become good at, and used my Ag access to open her door without having to knock — no, I did not like doing that, but yes, I did it.

And then she took us to the family who had adopted Jagan, and I went in without knocking and woke him, too. I had to tell both Catri and Jagan the story about the ships-of-the-air, but both were eager.

Then we were in the *okunaeso*, and I pretended to be concentrating on getting us to the ships-of-the-air, but in fact the cat, sitting in the back of the *okunaeso*, and unnoticed by both Jagan and Catri, took us there.

When the door opened, we stood in a place filled with natural light, the radiant light of first dawn. We stepped out, and Catri, Dan, and I gasped. We had to be at the very top of the Spire's tallest peak or near it. I could see the other towers rising toward us but ending below us.

I could imagine myself at the top of the tallest mountain in the world, looking down at all the other mountaintops. If, of course, those mountains were tall and spindly and made of black glass that gleamed in sunlight. If they were punctured in uncountable places with carved doorways and lined with railed balconies.

First we saw out and down, because the *okunaeso* opened on a narrow walkway facing a window, with the whole of the world outside below us. As we stepped out and turned, though, we saw that we were, indeed, at the top of the Spire. For the first time, I could see the dome of the actual ceiling, though it still remained far above us. No more balconies waited overhead, though, no more half-seen doors, no more mysteries. This was the very top.

And inward, the ships waited, crouched like cats, still, their heads down and their eyes closed, their wings tucked tightly to their sides. Some of them were gemstone-covered — rubies and emeralds even I knew, but I saw ships covered in gems of yellow and purple, orange and blue, lighter and darker reds and greens and pinks, blacks that let light through, and blacks that did not, pearl-whites and whites that were, when the light hit them, every color instead of just one. The stones and finishes were in every shade and in every shape. Some were cut so the sunlight glittered off them, and some were domed so that they seemed to drink in the light and let only a little of it back out from deep inside. I liked those best.

But there were more ships, too. Some were smooth metal — copper, gold, silver, and metals in colors I had never seen before — green and blue and purple, red and black, and one in the most impossible pink I could ever have imagined. And some were carved of wood, and some were clad in leather, and several were mostly of clear glass, and I could see right through parts of them.

They ringed the whole top of the Spire, all of them facing outward, nestled close to each other, but not so close that people could not walk between or get aboard them. Each had a broad bay door of glass in front of it. Most of the doors were closed, but a few stood open, as if those ships were just waiting for someone to take them away.

I could not count the ships. I started and gave up when

I reached a hundred and hadn't reached the point where the great ship bay began to curve. At the same moment, I realized I was only counting big ships and not the little ones tucked in between. I'd missed even seeing most of those. There were so many ships, all beautiful, all wonderful to me.

A broad walkway ran behind them, lined with a tall rail. I walked to the rail and looked down. Far away, I could see the floor of what I understood was the great entryway.

Jagan stood staring at the ships. "It's been so long," he whispered. "To me, it only seems like one cycle of the moon, but they have been sitting here like this for . . . centuries. Waiting. I wonder if all of them still live. I wonder if Suka still lives."

"Suka," Catri whispered. Something about the silence of the place, about the stillness of the ships, made it seem like the inside of a chapel, though endlessly bigger.

Danrith started to speak, but I put a finger to my lips.

"Suka is my ship," Jagan said. "A gift from my parents when I turned sixteen. They designed her, and when she was built, they spelled her to life. I'd only had her for two months when — well . . ." His eyes turned glassy and he bit his lip and blinked back tears. He turned his face away from us for a moment. And then he turned to me. "You could pick any ship, but my Suka is a wonderful one, a racer —"

"I would not ask you to fly any ship but your own," I said softly. "I want to meet your Suka."

His grin made me like him again.

"Follow me." He moved at a trot past ships huge and ships small, until he stood at last before a small emerald ship.

"Suka, I, Jagan, summon and wake you." He put a hand on her head, and the ship opened her eyes and answered him eagerly.

"I have slept, but in my sleeping I dreamed of dark times," she told him. "All the other ships waited in the dream with me, but our people were gone. Now you are here again, and I see that it was just a dream." And she nuzzled her peregrine head against his chest. "I was so lonely."

"They get *lonely*?" Dan whispered to me.

"It looks like it," I said.

The cat glared at us, and we stopped talking.

Jagan hugged her neck, then ran to our side. Suka did not have elegant unfolding stairs that let us ascend easily, as the great ship we had flown in had. Instead, she poked out one of her knees so we could climb on that, and we had to climb up. Jagan went first, then leaned over and gave a hand to Catri, who went next, with Jagan holding out his hand to pull her aboard. Dan winced when he saw that, and I saw his cheeks flush dark red. Dan climbed in on his own, vaulting over the side. And then I did the same. The cat followed, jumping gracefully from ground to knee, knee to wing, and in.

Jagan looked at Catri and me, and said, "You can change in the cabins. They have working cabinets. Suka is designed to be sleek and fast, but my parents made sure she had the basics. Prime-access cabinets, a white room, good beds — though very narrow — self-navigation, those sorts of things." And he grinned at me again. "This was a wonderful idea, Genna. And I never would have dared it on my own. But with you being Ag —"

"An Ag apprentice," I corrected and inwardly felt like a terrible person for having lied to him about what we were really doing aboard his little ship-of-the-air.

"It's as good as Ag when we get home and have to face the haws. You have the right to say you wanted to go and that you told us to come with you. They won't argue with the descendant of Sator Kizen Haw."

I suspected they would. But at least I knew that neither Catri nor Jagan would be in trouble for their part in this. Danrith and I could claim we had commanded them to take us.

CHAPTER 20
LIES AND TRICKERY

Everything aboard the ship was simple and tiny. There were two cabins, which each had two bunks. That would work out well — one for the boys, and one for the girls. Behind the cabins were two tiny privies, so small they made me think of the outhouse behind my family home, save that they had washbasins built in, and splinters were no danger. Each also had a shower, as narrow as the privy. The main room at the front of the sheltered areas held seats and a table, a kitchen almost like the one in each of the Spire's dwellings, only so much smaller, and to the back, the white room. It would seat all four of us if our knees were touching.

Jagan caught up with Dan and Catri and me as we were exploring. "We should go now," he said. "Before the haws start looking for us and find us in the air-dome."

In my head, the cat said, *The sooner, the better.*

"Let's go," I said, managing a bright smile, and Jagan turned and hurried to the front of the ship.

The ship turned her head to speak to him, asking him where we should go. Jagan said, "For now, just out and away. And fast."

Suka stood up, walked to one of the open bay doors, spread emerald-green metal wings wide, and jumped.

And that was when I discovered the biggest difference between the grand ships and little ships.

Little ships did not shield passengers from ship movement.

The ship dropped like a rock and my stomach rose at the same speed. I shrieked and flopped to my belly on the deck and started crawling toward a metal rope-holder bolted to the decking.

I grabbed it and held on for dear life. The ship kept dropping, and I could hear wind screaming past, whistling through the ship's wings and causing wild ringing through the metal feathers. I had no weight. I was absolutely certain that if I let go of the rope-holder, I would float out of the ship, then plummet to my death.

Though it felt like I was plummeting to my death anyway, and it occurred to me that maybe letting go and floating away might be a good idea.

I did not, though.

And then the ship started turning and twisting in the air, as little birds do when they try to escape hawks.

I realized I'd had my eyes squeezed tight. This I realized at the same instant I became aware that I was screaming at the top of my lungs.

I could not feel my weight, I could hear the howling wind, I knew we were falling and twisting and turning, and yet . . .

I was not being banged around the way I had been when flying in the dragon's mouth.

I opened one eye. Just a little.

Jagan and the cat stood on the deck, side by side.

They just stood there.

Nothing had changed, but instantly I felt stupid.

I let go of the rope-holder. I did not float away. I raised up on my hands and knees. The ship leveled out, then suddenly began to rise, and suddenly I weighed twice, maybe three times as much as I had ever weighed in my life. But I could still crouch there.

I pushed against the unaccustomed weight and sat up.

I could see again. We were dodging from side to side and climbing in the air. The ship's neck was outstretched, its wings were a blur of motion, and the noise of them was incredible, as if my mother and all the other mothers in the village had decided to shake their spoon drawers all at once.

I looked behind us. Another ship followed, but it was falling behind. It was not climbing anywhere near as quickly as we were — its wings moved much more slowly. It was bigger. Big and broad and heavy compared to our ship. I tried to make out the faces of the men aboard it, but I could not.

"Ha-ha!" Jagan shouted. "Truant ship!" He was laughing, delighted, his body crouched close to the neck of the ship, directing her which way to fly next. My stomach went in all directions, my weight went from nothing to everything to nothing again, but through some magic of the ship, my feet never left the floor. And it was easier to know which way the ship would go next from watching Jagan as he commanded her.

"They go out automatically whenever someone our age leaves during hours of study!" He yelled over the fierce ringing of the wings. "Send it back with a command, Satimaja — I mean Genna."

"How do I do that?"

"Go into the white room. The ship will be demanding we stop. When you go into the couchpit, hold up your right hand and say, 'I am Ag, and we sail at my command.'" He glanced back at me and grinned again. "I've been on ships with Ag," he said. "The rules don't apply to you."

I considered that, did not like it, but said only, "Well enough. I shall tell them."

And he was right. I did as he said, and the ship stopped chasing us. Because I was Ag. Because light came out of nowhere, and spun itself around my raised right hand, and then went away again.

I walked out to tell Jagan. And Catri and Danrith. And realized I had been speaking in Osji, and Jagan had been speaking in Tagasuko. And we could still understand each other — which was supposed to only happen when we were in the Spire.

The Spire is still with us, the cat said in my head. *It knows where we are and what we're doing, because its magic and the ship's magic are connected.*

That's not good.

No. It isn't. Neither is it fixable. The ship was born in that Spire, of that Spire's magic. It will always be bound to that Spire and will always communicate with it. Right now, be assured that the ghost haws back in the Magics Department are watching everything you do and listening to everything you say. They have awarded you great power,

Genna, because you already have great power, and they want to gain it from you. But they do not trust you.

I looked for the cat as I stepped up onto the deck. He was sitting at the back of Suka's deck, his tail wrapped primly around his feet, looking for all the world like he was enjoying the ride.

I am, he told me. *I don't get up here at eye level with the birds all that often.*

I wanted to think to the cat, and suddenly aware of being watched, I did not wish to look like I was staring at nothing, lost in some fit of the mind. So I leaned against the side of the ship and looked down. Down was a very long way. Clouds raced beneath me, and far below them, the ground turned misty and pale, as if the sun had bleached most of the color out of it.

I was warm, and no wind blew past me. But the wings jangled cheerfully, and from time to time I'd hear the metallic voice of the ship speaking to Jagan.

I asked the cat, *Why are they watching me so closely now, when they did not at first?*

The Spire now knows how important you are. It did not know it when just you and Catri were there, because the Aglak had not told it. Remmnor Mikav Haw has been studying you, though, and now he knows the Sunrider myths are true. He knows you have magics he and his kind don't have and cannot yet understand. He has seen hints of magics you contain within you — some of which you have not even discovered yet. Through him, the Spire and the ghosts in the Ag who still mostly control it understand how critical you are to the survival of humanity. What they don't understand is that they cannot take what you have and use it themselves. They cannot replace you, though they think they can.

The Spires were designed to keep the things that can save humans — and the humans themselves — safe inside. Everything this Spire does, it does toward that goal.

I considered that. If the Spire had its way, then, I would have never left.

But Remmnor Mikav Haw is not letting me learn what I need to know. If he understands that the Sunrider is important, and that I have the magic to save my people, why won't he help me?

You're a young girl, and you have not been trained from earliest childhood to believe life in the Spire is the best life a human being can aspire to. You have questions, Genna, and you make observations that are not . . . favorable. The Ag cannot tolerate dissent. So the haw who has become your advisor is seeking to understand the magic that you wield so that he can teach it to someone who will use it the way he and the rest of the Ag want it to be used.

The cat sighed. *You have a lot of ideas about freedom and finding common ground with the nightlings and banding together with them for protection and greater strength that the Ag find . . . unfortunate. Jagan, for example, has no such ideas. If they could teach him how to do what you can do, they would be very happy to teach him to be Sunrider.*

I turned away from the beautiful scene below me and stared at the cat. *Nobody taught me how to become Sunrider.*

That's because it isn't a thing that can be taught, the cat told me. *It is a thing you are, earned through inner conviction, honorable character, and courage in the face of great fear. Jagan could be a boy who gained those qualities. But he will not gain them so long as the Spire shelters him and keeps him weak and content.*

I hated hearing what the cat was saying, but for the first time in a long time, the pinch place on my right arm was not cold or aching or twinging. I knew trouble was coming, but *this* trouble was where I was supposed to be, and dealing with it was what I was supposed to be doing.

I'd thought that to be the Sunrider, I needed to learn the language and magic of the sun wizards, that I needed to be able to study with Remmnor Mikav Haw and perhaps the other haws in the Spire so that I could understand what being the Sunrider meant. So that I could be powerful and have the sun wizard weapons in my hands. I'd been wrong, and I'd wasted so much time in the Spire. My true future lay . . . elsewhere. I did not know where, but I could not hide away in a tower. In a fortress.

The cat came over and sat beside me. *Your time there was not wasted.* He rubbed his head against my boot, and I crouched down and scratched under his chin and behind his ears before I had a chance to think about it — that he was not really a cat.

But he purred. So I scratched. It was soothing. I knew I was not going to like the news I got next, so I did not let myself think. I just sat there, petting the purring cat, while the ship and the boy took us out, through the sky, accompanied by ship chimes.

I did not learn what I needed, I told him at last.

You don't know what you need. So what you learned might be exactly what you needed. You simply don't have enough pieces to put them all together yet.

Every day I don't figure this out, people stay slaves, people die, and things go more wrong.

He flopped on his side, and I scratched his tummy, and

his purring became loud indeed. *People die every day, Genna. People are slaves every day. And the world will keep going wrong even once you are the Sunrider. You cannot, will not, be able to save everyone or fix everything. If you save some, you will have done more than most.*

I did not want to hear that.

By the way, he added, *if the Spire gets you back, it won't let you go again. It has hostages. If it thinks you are within its control, it will use them.*

I'd thought of that.

So what do I do? How do I keep Catri and Dan and Jagan from getting in trouble?

Worry first about the dragon. If you get yourselves killed rescuing him, we need not worry about what your best course of action afterward should be.

I did not need the cat's version of optimism.

CHAPTER 21
LOVE AND FRIENDSHIP

After Jagan assured me that Suka could and would fly her course without guidance if necessary, I, following the cat's instructions, told Jagan to take us over the Westerling Sea.

And then I called a meeting in the kitchen, which the cat called a galley. The meeting he called a war council. He had also instructed me in what to say.

The food was my idea. I did not know what would happen next, but I did know it would not involve me having anything else to eat for at least a while, so I had the cabinets spew out a nightling bag for me, of the same sort that Yarri had carried and had provided for Dan and me, full of the same useful equipment that that other bag had held.

Well, that had been my intent. The bag was nice enough, but nothing I could do would make it come with a magical heat-ball, a tent lighter than cobwebs, or nightling food. So

I satisfied myself with jerky, dried fruit, nuts, and a water flask. And I made — well, summoned — for the four of us the sort of first meal my mother made in winter. Hot pork, sourdough rolls, relish, mounds of scrambled eggs, smoked salmon, steamed cabbage, and apples.

And as we ate, I told Dan, Catri, and Jagan what the cat had told me, making it sound like it was information I had discovered on my own. The cat, still wishing to hide the truth that he was not really a cat from Jagan, the ship Suka, and the Spire, curled up on one of the galley benches, to all appearances asleep.

Appearances can be deceiving.

"Catri and I would be dead if it were not for the chance someone we met took to save our lives. We have not talked of this, either of us, but when we were in Arrienda, studying sun wizardry with Doyati and Yarri, there was a plot to kill us." I paused, veering a little in what I'd been told to say. "Well, mostly my life, but because Catri was always with me, she would have died, too."

The cat opened one eye and glared at me, and with a sigh, I decided not to add my own words anymore.

"The creature that saved us has been taken captive by nightlings and is to be killed."

Catri, who had been digging into the rolls and pork with dedication, stopped and looked up at me. "The . . ." She mouthed the word *dragon?*

I nodded.

And saw the same struggle cross her face that had crossed my heart. Was he good, was he bad, did he deserve to die for his past evils, did he deserve to live for our past rescue?

"I am Ag," I said, looking directly at Jagan, who would be the only one this comment truly meant anything to, and watched a sudden tension appear in his shoulders. He had good instincts. "I invoke my rights as Ag to command this ship to attend to the rescue of the creature who saved our lives."

The glowing happiness that had been in Jagan's face died. And the fact that I had been the one to make it go away broke my heart. But . . . he would not have to put up with me much longer.

He said, "As you command, Satimaja."

And there it was. I had used the power that being Ag gave me to mistreat a friend.

I said, "We need to go into the white room."

Everyone left their meals, although Catri brought her plate with her, and we sat, knee to knee, in the couchpit.

"Show me the dragon," I said.

And suddenly the screen showed us a nightling ship-of-the-sea, a wind-and-oar-powered watercraft manned by human slaves whipped to action by human slave drivers. Nightling officers, dressed in uniforms that completely covered their skin, and wearing enormous darkened spheres of glass that shielded their eyes from daylight, so that they looked like silk-swathed bugs, commanded the ship.

"The dragon?" Jagan said. "Satimaja, I do not question your command but only seek . . . understanding. Do you truly wish us to rescue a . . . dragon? Or is one of the human slaves on the ship the one who saved you?"

You are Ag, and as such may not be questioned except by other Ag, the cat said. *And Danrith, this is not the time to question her.* I glanced at my brother and saw his eyes widen. *If you answer his questions, Genna, your command is subject to doubt. Tell him to command Suka to proceed to the ship.*

"Command Suka to proceed to the ship," I said.

We looked at the dragon. I felt my hands clenching into fists. His blood was all over the deck. I could not tell if he was alive or dead.

He's still alive, the cat said in my head.

Why haven't they killed him? I asked. *If the dragons*

betrayed them, too, why is he still alive and bound to the deck?

Because the nightlings don't know he's the last one. He has let them believe hundreds upon hundreds of others are waiting to destroy groundlings — human and nightling — to finish the job they started a thousand years before. The cat raised his head and looked at the boy Jagan, then lowered his head and closed his eyes again. *And you must not say aloud — anywhere — that he is the last one. The Spire can hear you, even on this ship. What you say, the Spire knows as well. Better for everyone if it does not know that.*

I turned my attention to my brother and Catri. "Danrith will go down to the ship with me and help me cut the ropes to free the dragon. Catri will stay in the ship with Jagan."

Catri put her hand in Jagan's and turned to me, her face full of fear and worry. "You cannot make him do this, Genna. You know what the dragons did."

"You mustn't speak to her like that," I heard Jagan whisper in Catri's ear. "She is Ag, your superior and mine. We are Prime and may hope to ascend to Ag someday — but that will not be today."

Now you say, "I can, Mosanija, and I do." The cat. The ever-helpful cat, who was demanding I treat my friend like . . . like she was . . . well, whatever a Mosanija was. Whatever it was, it did not sound good.

If you ignore me, you make her a part of your conspiracy, Genna. Be harsh now, and save her life.

So I said it. I acted like I was the princess Catri had dreamed of being, and I hardened my heart, and I made my voice cold. "I can, Mosanija. And I do."

Jagan bowed his head at those words, and I saw his face turn red.

I blinked rapidly so the tears that swelled at the corners of my eyes would not fall and betray me.

Catri looked like I had slapped her. She did cry.

Stealth and duplicity, the cat said, *are the best weapons of the outnumbered. Do not forget that you are outnumbered. Do not forget that the Spire will see everything you do, and that the people in the Spire will see everything you have done that the Spire wants them to see, and that you cannot tell them why you do this. Even if you tried, the Spire controls the pictures and it will not let you speak against it.*

I felt sick. *The pictures will lie.*

The cabinets gave us such weapons as we understood. I could not get them to give me fire-throwers that I had seen wizards atop the Spire using in their battles, but they did give Danrith and me good short swords, well balanced for our height. And sturdy and light, if hot, chest armor to go over our clothes. But that did not change the fact that we were two children, and that the nightling officers and the human slave masters in the ship-of-the-sea below us were hardened sailors and soldiers, well armed and as dangerous as nightlings can be.

Jagan stood at the head of his ship, grim-faced and sullen. Catri had vanished while Danrith and I raided the cabinets for things we would need, and when she reappeared, she wore an identical twin of the blue dress Jagan had given her our first morning together, and matching slippers, and she had her hair done up in braids and wrapped with strings of pearls, just as images had shown us the female sun wizards had worn theirs before the Fall.

She went to stand beside Jagan.

I did not miss the symbolism in her actions or in the manner of her dress. She had chosen sides, and I was on the one that lost.

Be grateful, the cat said. *She will be held blameless for all that happens next.*

The ship-of-the-air circled high, high above the ship-of-the-sea that held the dragon. The sun beat down on the water and made the sea sparkle as if the sun wizards had tossed all their gemstones onto its surface. That ship cut through the water like a toy boat in a pond, the side oars rising and dipping in rhythm, the single sail bellied out, full of wind, red as blood. The ship and the men on it did not look real to me. The shoreline edged by taandu forest looked like moss on rocks. People were dots; rivers were scribbles from a mapmaker's pen.

But the sea was no toy. Even from high above the world, it awed me.

I had never seen so much water. Never imagined so much water. Land lay in one direction, but water was every-where else, spreading to the line at the end of sight, touching the sky. I stood on Suka's deck, staring down and out. I had wished to go stand beside Catri, to try to get her to under-stand, without saying anything that would cause her trouble, that I was still her best friend. That the way I acted was because I loved her and did not want harm to come to her.

But I could say nothing, and when I so much as looked in her direction, she turned her back to me.

So I watched the sea. The horizon, marked by a faint line of blue just darker than the sky, curved enough to make the world below look like part of a ball. Papa had said the world was round, the same way the moon was round.

Standing there, hands gripping the rail, I could believe he was right.

Danrith came to stand beside me. He held armor, sword, and supply bag, but like me, he had not yet put them on. He looked down at the endless water and said, "What is in there, do you suppose?"

I looked down at the waves, and at the big sailing ship, dwarfed by the amount of water around it, and all I could think to say was, "Fish and monsters."

"Monsters there, too," he mused.

"Monsters everywhere."

"It seems so."

We stared down.

"She likes Jagan," he said after a few moments.

"She likes you, too," I said.

"She won't after this."

I imagined he was right. She would see that we were villains being cruel to Jagan, making him use his ship to save another villain.

I looked at him sadly. What we were doing would not leave him much of a chance to catch Catri's heart. "She likes that he's going to be a sun wizard and important. That he may someday become Ag."

"I'm Ag already," Danrith said.

I nodded. "But you're twelve. He's sixteen."

"He's prettier than she is," Dan muttered. "I hate him."

Now is the best time, the cat said, interrupting our discussion. *The nightling officers have retired to their cabins to wait out the midday, and the slave masters are in charge. You'll have a little time.*

You are sure this plan of yours will work?

It has a chance of working.

Which means no, you are not sure.

Life is full of surprises. The cat came trotting around the corner, ears forward, tail up and curled into a little shepherd's crook at the tip, to all appearances an eager kitty enjoying a bit of fresh air. *Stealth and duplicity are the best weapons of the outnumbered,* he repeated.

Of course, stealth meant we had to get right into the middle of trouble, being quiet and careful, with nothing but the dragon to get us out again. And duplicity — that was lies. Deception. That meant if we got caught, we had to come up with some clever reason for a fourteen-year-old girl and a twelve-year-old boy to be aboard a sailing ship in the middle of the sea that we could not have gotten on. And we had to get away with our skin intact.

I am very sorry, but my idea of a best weapon was something I could point at the people on that sailing ship from the safety of our ship-of-the-air, and tell them if they did not let the dragon go, I was going to pull the lever and they would all suddenly burst into flames.

The cat had said that plan would not work anyway. But I had tried. Oh, how I had tried.

So stealth it was. Stealth and duplicity, and I did not think myself much qualified for either. I was not sure about Danrith. He had become quite good at surprising me.

The cat sat on the deck. *Tell Jagan to take the ship down. It's time.*

Now?

We had to go now?

But we have not come up with a distraction yet, I protested.

We have. That will be my job. You get down, get to the dragon, and cut the ropes away from him. And by Spirit and all your little gods, Genna, make sure he can fly.

CHAPTER 22

THE RIGHT THING

Hang on to the rope, the cat was telling Danrith and me, but that was foolish advice. Our hands had nearly grown into it, we were hanging on so hard. Below us was the ship, which suddenly looked very small, and the sea, which did not.

We dangled, knives in our pockets, swords in sheaths belted around our waists, packs on our backs and armor on our chests, wearing our village clothes, as the ship-of-the-air swooped closer.

And closer.

No nightlings remained outside beneath the brilliant midday sun. The light was too much even for their silk body coverings and thick, dark goggles. Only the humans — slave masters and slaves — were on deck. The slaves saw the ship-of-the-air, and stopped what they were doing, and pointed at the sky. The slave masters turned as well, and one dropped his whip, and the other just stood, mouth gaping.

Something streaked past us from the ship-of-the-air to thud onto the deck below.

Now! The cat's voice in my head was loud, but not so loud it made me lose my grip. The ship-of-the-sea's deck was close. And we were, for the moment, alongside the deckhouse, so mostly out of sight and very near the dragon. But everything was moving.

NOW! the cat yowled, and I let go. Dan let go.

We tumbled. I skinned my knees and skinned my hands, and my sword clanged like a summoning bell. Dan landed on his feet, but the momentum carried him into me as I was getting up, and we crashed to the deck together.

But no one came running to investigate. The ship-of-the-air, piloted by Jagan but acting for yet a little longer on my word, was circling as I had commanded it to. Any hope I'd had of patching the rift I'd caused between Catri and me, or Jagan and me, died when I used my Ag rank one final time and told his ship what to do.

In spite of screaming and shouting — and a certain amount of inexplicable cheering accompanied by indescribable animal noises — the nightlings did not leave their hiding place within the deckhouse. The sun was so bright in the cloudless sky it was a weapon against them and a good one.

On my second try, I got to my feet, and Dan got to his, and the cat said, *Do hurry. I can only be a distraction for so long.*

I realized the cat was on board the ship with us. I wished I could see what he was doing, for no one at all came to look behind the deckhouse to see what the dragon was doing, or what might have happened with those noisy thuds on deck.

The animal noises got louder.

The ship-of-the-air circled above us, and Dan and I ran the few steps to the dragon's side and began cutting ropes.

We were alone with him, and as he felt our hands on him, he opened one eye and rolled it, looking from Dan to me. Even his head was bound to the deck.

"We have come to rescue you," I told him.

"You're mad," he answered and closed the eye. "(They came,)" he said in a different voice. And, "(Don't trust them, just eat them,)" in a third.

Dan paused in his cutting. He had not met the dragon before. "Dan, you have to trust me," I whispered. "Keep cutting."

"(Trust,)" the dragon muttered in a crazy, high voice,

"(is the way to get a good dinner.) (Or be dinner.) Shut up, all of you," said the voice I thought of as the dragon's real voice — the deep, ground-shaking, scary one.

My dagger was sharp — I kept it so — and I sawed through ropes as quickly as I could.

Dan, on the other side of the dragon, was hurrying, too. There were a lot of ropes. Some bound the dragon to the deck of the ship and some simply bound him.

How are you coming? the cat asked, but he sounded frantic. Beleaguered. I could hear roaring now — deep, terrifying roaring, and screaming, and running feet.

Going as fast as we can.

Go faster. I'm having to make a mess I don't want to make.

We cut and cut, until at last the dragon said, "I think I can break the rest."

"Can you fly?"

"No. The wing beneath me was nearly burned off."

He can't fly, I told the cat.

Whatever it takes, make him fly. Or the bloodbath here will be beyond belief.

The dragon stretched, sending the last of the ropes that bound him slithering across the deck.

"Will you let me heal you?"

He laughed. The sound was soft and rumbling. "As if you could."

"Hold still," I told him and reached a hand up to touch the stump of his wing, from which ragged bone ends protruded. The skin was charred, and the smell was terrible. The blood poison had crept in, I realized. The wound, untended, was rotting and would surely kill him.

But I was good at fixing physical damage. I sank myself into his pain — and was so overwhelmed by the clamor of voices that erupted when I did that I almost lost my grip. Almost. I used the same trick of the mind I had used when I was younger to silence the fighting of my brothers and sisters. In my mind, I wrapped them in a blanket, and shoved the blanket far away, so far away I could not hear them anymore. Then I focused on what I was doing, what I needed to feel. The clamor died down to blessed silence.

The silence filled with incredible pain. The whole left side of my body ached, and I channeled the pain downward, through my feet, through the deck of the ship, into the sea. The sea was big enough to hold it.

I focused on feeling the things that were wrong in my own skin, on becoming the dragon with the wing stump. I could sense the healthy wing on the right side of my body.

I concentrated on making the left side match the right. On making the bones stretch long. On making the skin stretch wide. On making the blood filter through, and through, and through, deeper and deeper, and . . .

"Ahhhhh," the dragon said in his deep voice. "Ah, it is magnificent."

I released my hold and opened my eyes. He stretched the wing high, up over the deckhouse, and pulled it back.

"Remarkable." He tipped his head to one side to look at me. It was hard not to back up. "That was very cleverly done. And, for a little while, you have silenced the yammering voices. I will weary before long, and they will come back, but to be alone in my head is a wondrous thing. So, little human. Little *Sunrider*. How goes your quest to save the world?" And he chuckled.

From the other side of the deckhouse, swearing, and scrabbling, and screaming, and a roar that was also words: "If you try to sneak by me again, you caviling, belly-crawling humans, you'll follow your slave masters into the deeps. You have been given a *gift*, you fools, if you have but the belly to take it. Come after me and die, or go after your nightling owners and live!"

The words sounded like the cat, the voice sounded like — I did not know what the voice sounded like. Like the horrors that live under your bed when you're very small and night is the monster that devours the world.

I told the dragon, "It goes rather shakily right now, in truth." And I told the cat, *He can fly again.*

About time. Let's go.

He came padding around the corner of the deckhouse, and for a moment I did not understand what I saw.

He was unmistakably the cat — or, at least, he bore the cat's markings. White chin and belly, four white feet, swirling black stripes on a gray-and-rust body. But he was as long as a good horse, and as high at the shoulder as my chin, and he had two fangs nearly as long as my forearm that jutted from the top of his mouth and ended below his chin. He was covered in blood, but I could see not a single cut on his hide.

He saw Dan and me, then glanced up. "Well, about time."

The dragon was staring at him. "You!"

"Me," the cat — the monster cat — agreed. "We need a ride out of here."

I looked up where the cat was looking and saw the ship-of-the-air sailing away at impossible speed, heading straight toward the sun, and then arcing back the way we had come, in an instant a tiny pinpoint and, an instant after that, gone.

Gone.

I knew it would happen. That it had to happen. But knowing that Jagan and Catri had abandoned us on the ship still hurt. She was my best friend. She had always been my best friend.

Then I heard nightlings. Back on the deck, commanding people to do things, to act, to come after us. I heard swords, too, and screaming.

The dragon smiled, and the cat chuckled. And then the cat said, "No. No, no. Much as I'd fancy ripping them to pieces, we need to leave something for the humans to do. And we need to leave. Trouble is not done coming for us."

He started to shrink. He didn't do it all evenly. Parts of him shrank fast, and parts of him shrank slow, and he kept pacing in circles, shaking his feet or his head, or whipping his tail back and forth, and yowling the whole time, as if he hurt.

It does hurt, he said. *A lot.*

Men were shouting. Whips cracked. Swords clanged.

The dragon raised his head and looked over the top of the deckhouse to see what was going on.

And everyone started screaming, "Dragon! Dragon! The dragon's gotten loose!"

The cat muttered, "I hate dragons. Hate them. They haven't the sense Spirit gave rocks."

This time, the sounds of running feet were coming toward us.

The dragon whipped his head around to us and roared, "Get in!"

Dan stared at me.

"In," I screamed. "Cheek pouch! There!"

The cat jumped in.

And I dove after him. Into the dragon's mouth. Having been there before did not make the experience any more pleasant the second time.

We were flung downward, tossed side to side, and then tossed up and down, up and down, as his wings thundered. I did not lose my last meal. But we were not done yet, either. I hated flying dragon-style.

We haven't a lot of time, the cat said.

Time for what? That sailing ship is slow, it's without its slave drivers, and the slaves and the officers were at one another. It's likely they won't make friends with one another so they can come after us.

They won't, the cat agreed. *But the Ag has surely already sent out ships to search. For the dragon, for you, for your brother . . . And with them, searching is not a matter of if they find you. It's only a matter of when.*

That ended *that* conversation.

We careened up and down, up and down, in a horrible rhythm, and all I could do was concentrate on not throwing up. Not. Not.

When I heard Dan in the other cheek pouch lose his meal, I barely hung on to mine.

The cat, bouncing up and down with me, scrabbling for purchase, reached for everything with claws out, and snagged me more than once. It hurt; I yelped; he didn't apologize.

I could do nothing but wait for it to be over.

Whatever came next would have to be better.

Wouldn't it?

CHAPTER 23
HIDE AND SEEK

We lay beneath the blazing heat, with sand and gravel and bare rock. Neither heat nor burning sun bothered the dragon. His skin had changed color from its normal iridescent black to a bleached gray almost as light as the sand. And he had burrowed himself in, and flipped sand across his back as well. He did not talk, but he did not seem unhappy. He just crouched there, wings tucked tight, tail buried in sand, and he watched the sky.

The cat, too, seemed to at least tolerate the heat and the light, though I saw him slink around the dragon as the sun moved across the sky, keeping to the shadows cast by the great beast.

Dan and I, though, suffered. We were children of cold and shady places, places where the sun was gentle and long-angled and weak, and where we appreciated the days when we saw much sun at all. We had never experienced the sort of baking, burning, blinding light and heat that cooked us where we sat.

I had shed armor and sweater and boots and socks, and rolled up my blouse sleeves, but my head throbbed from the heat, and my tongue swelled in my mouth from thirst. I sipped at the water from my flask, wishing I had brought only water and no food.

My nose started to bleed. I pinched it.

Everything was glare. White and burning, reflecting off white sand and bleached white sky.

We had no breeze, and to start with, only two hands' breadths of shade at the dragon's side. Dan and I had started to tie our sweaters together to crawl under them, but the cat said, "They'll see that from the sky," and made us take our shelter apart.

The dragon stretched out his wings — the way birds do when they yawn — and for a moment the shadow of one wing shielded me. I cannot describe the relief.

"Could you stay that way?" I asked him.

"No," he said.

"No?" I wiped at the blood dripping from my nose, using one of my socks to dab at it.

Dan said, "We are burning. My skin has blisters on it."

That had been hours ago.

We sat still, but now in the shade cast by the dragon's bulky form and by the setting sun.

Dan said, "Can't we get up and move around? I hurt everywhere, and I want to stand in the water to cool my skin."

"There are things in that water that will eat you if you try," the cat said. "That's the ocean, not your little stream."

The dragon turned his head. "You cannot move. You have human eyes, and you cannot see what I can see. I am watching ships-of-the-air quartering the sky, searching for us. They are going over an area some distance from here, and when the moon comes up, you or the cat may hide under my wing while you call a moonroad, if you have the skill to do that. But the ships will know my form, even if the men who search for us do not, and if I spread out my wings so that they cast shadows, changing my color to blend with sand and hiding my outline with dirt and rocks will not save us. The men who hunt us watch, but the ships watch, too. And the ships' eyes are as good as mine."

Dan and I huddled closer to the dragon and studied the cloudless, empty sky. Ships-of-the-air?

"I cannot see anything," Dan whispered to me.

"Nor can I. They are close enough the dragon can see them?"

"Even closer," the dragon said. "I have little hope that they will change from their present search path. If they don't, they'll reach us before twilight and the coming of the easy moonroads. And if they reach us and we cannot escape, then they'll kill me."

"You could fly away," I told him.

Dragons can smile. They should not, though. All it does is remind you how many teeth they have.

The dragon smiled at me. "If I fly, they will see me. The Spire is awake now, and men who know the history of the dragons are inside it, so it once again remembers that I am the enemy. I have no place in this world where I can hide — none I know of, anyway. I could hide from the nightlings; for all their cleverness, they have not managed to fill the earth and the sky with eyes and ears. It was humans who did that, and while, in the thousand years that have passed, some of those eyes and ears have surely broken, I cannot know which. Or where. I cannot know when I am safe, and when they can see me."

He was no longer smiling. "If you can call the moon-roads before they find us, hold on to my wing as you step through and take me with you."

The cat said, "You think you'll fare better with the

taandu monsters and the moonroaders and the denizens of the twilight worlds?"

"If I fare at all, cat, it will be better. The ships-of-the-air draw closer, and with them, the last breath I or my kind will ever take."

I was listening to the dragon and the cat, but I was looking out at the sea, trying to make out a speck on the horizon. It zigged and zagged a little and faded in and out of what looked like a fog bank.

I thought it probably shouldn't concern us. After all, the dragon was watching the ships-of-the-air, which nothing I tried would bring into view. Surely he also saw the dot on the horizon and had already decided it was no problem.

But still . . . better to ask and know than keep silent and worry.

"What is that?" I asked him and pointed.

He looked, and frills of bone and skin around his face went wide with alarm.

"It's the Bone Ship." He narrowed his eyes to slits and hissed. "*She's* not dead yet?"

"Who?" I asked.

"A woman — creature really — that has been a plague in the world for time out of mind. Her name is Agara —"

"The huntress!" Dan and I interrupted at the same time.

The dragon stopped looking at the sea and turned his attention to us. "You know her?"

"She and her hounds are hunting us. She caught me once," I said. "Her dogs are horrible."

"The hounds are nothing compared to her," the dragon said. "She finds them useful, but don't think she cannot hunt without them. Or that she would be hindered to lose them. She destroyed uncounted numbers of my kind, back when the nightlings took her into their pay."

I shivered at the thought of her. Silver skin, a cold smile, and a pack of enormous blind hounds that were to dogs what the dragon before me was to the little lizards that sunned themselves on our rock wall in Hillrush.

I closed my eyes. There was no willing that would fool the huntress or send her away. Stillness would not do the trick. Hiding — well, the dragon was the only one among us who had the ability to fade into the ground and look mostly like a rock. The cat — the huntress's dogs probably already smelled him, and, if I thought about it, Dan and me, too.

Would that the dragon could fly us someplace safe. Would that we could go back to the time before the dragon was caught, before the Moonworlders overran our world, before the kai-lords and their magic set the trees to overgrowing the human lands, such as they had been.

"Moon's up," Dan whispered.

Whispering seemed the thing to do. If the Spire had ways of finding us through the eyes of the ships-of-the-air, then that was frightening enough. But at the thought of the huntress coming as well — she with her drooling, blind, mind-reading hounds — what little the heat had left of my voice dried up so that all I could do was whisper.

I turned to see where Dan pointed. Yes. The horizon cut the rising half-moon into halves. I did not yet have enough moonlight to call a moonroad. But the light was coming.

And then Dan whispered, "I see the ships-of-the-air, Genna," and I saw them, too.

They sparkled in the sky, so beautiful, so wonderful, so human. And they were now as much enemies to the dragon, the cat, Dan, and me as any nightling kai-lord or any taandu monster. Or Banris.

We were to be captured. The dragon, killed. I could not guess my fate or Dan's, but I could guess it would not be a happy thing.

Dig a hole, the cat said inside my head. *You and Dan. Hurry. They haven't seen us yet. Not yet.*

Dig a hole? I knelt on the sand and began scooping it behind me with both hands. Dan crouched on the other side and did the same. My skin felt like it was going to peel from my body with every move I made, but I dug, and sand flew.

Suddenly, the dragon erupted from the sand and spread his wings over us. "The hole will be too slow," he bellowed. "Use the shade from my wings! The ships-of-the-air have seen us. They're coming straight on."

I crouched under his wings, in the shade, and for the first time, felt the little tug of the moon. That tug might be enough to reach a road and bring it to me. Certainly it was enough to start calling one.

I let the hunger in me build. Anyplace safe, I told myself. I did not want the roads that wanted me to walk them. Down that path lay disaster. I wanted the roads that would give the four of us safe harbor.

The tug within me grew stronger as the moon slipped upward. It did not pull on me with its full power, but it pulled hard enough that I felt the yearning. I felt myself slip into the place where I wanted . . . something. The something that only the roads could give me.

I smelled fresh water first and almost rejoiced, but the dragon hissed, "The huntress sends her fog, girl. If it reaches us before you bring the moonroad, it will block the moon and she will have us."

Overhead, someone said, "Ready fire!" and someone else screamed, "No, no! Not the fire. The Sunrider is down there!"

And someone else shouted, "She's a traitor. Ready FIRE!"

The fog. The first ship-of-the-air. My fear. The hunger. The moon.

A bell, tinkling at my feet.

"Cat," I whispered.

"Go," the cat said. "I'll follow."

I grabbed the dragon's wing, and Dan grabbed me, and something screamed down from the sky at us, and the huntress howled, "Don't kill her! She's worth a *fortune* to Banris!"

And we were falling.

Falling.

The light around us ran with yellow and green and blue, like part of a rainbow being washed from the sky. Like dyes poured onto the ground. Bells tinkled everywhere, uncountable, happy. The road watched us. I had never felt watched by a road before, but this one seemed awake. Curious.

I was alone as I fell, even though I knew I still held the dragon's wing, even though I knew Dan still held me.

I always felt alone on the moonroads.

Without warning, everything felt like it tipped, and we began falling up.

I scrambled to get my bearings. This road was only sight and sound, lacking smells, tastes, or the company of spirits or other creatures that had become trapped there. It felt . . . new. New.

It occurred to me that a new road might not be a good road, but my road skills were still poor. The cat talks of finding exits along the sides of a road, of walking them with control. I cannot do that.

So we fell up into darkness, and fell graceless and flat onto soft, cool grass. The air smelled of night flowers, and in the air above us I could hear what sounded like the wings of a sky full of bats.

I hate bats.

I squinted, for this world had no moon, but it did have stars. Brilliant, gleaming. Under starlight, an army of monsters shambled forward, not in ranks such as men at war practice but in a mob. They were very near us, but below us. We had landed on a grassy ledge, one very nearly too narrow for the dragon, who clung sideways to it and stared down, hissing softly.

The cat murmured, "Dear Aganapa preserve us!"

Neither Dan nor I said anything.

The creatures wore armor that covered their chests and arms and heads, armor that looked like it had been carved from trees with the bark still on. They hunched, eyes glowing dim and green — but glowing. They carried weapons that seemed a world away from their pathetic armor; master armorers had crafted their swords and shields. They moved forward, some loping, some dragging along, and men — human men — men with whips, spurred some of them forward.

They were marching up to a spiraling oval of light held between two enormous stone pillars, and they were jumping in. And vanishing.

Some of them screamed as they reached the light. Some leapt in eagerly. All disappeared, though.

Moonroad, I realized. Someone had caught a moonroad and done some sort of magic to pin it in place. I could not imagine the magic that would make something so slippery and tricksy stand still.

Whatever had captured the moonroad and given the weapons to the creatures of this world and was causing them to be herded where they did not wish to go, that was a creature I did not wish to meet. I had once again failed to find a safe place for us — but at least it was safer than the one we had just left. No one was dropping fire on us, anyway.

From the other end of the ravine, I heard something roar, "Faster, you fools! Get them in there."

The masters with the whips whipped harder and screamed threats. The creatures they herded ran faster.

I looked down the way they had come and thought I might just die from terror. And disbelief.

None of us up on that ledge breathed as a towering horror twice as big as any of them, dressed in armor that gleamed black beneath the stars, came into view at the end of the narrow pass.

I knew him.

Worse, he knew me.

Worst of all, he wanted to catch me and kill me in order to become an immortal. He was, I knew, nearly immortal already. I was the final ingredient he lacked, and he would be walking right below me — below the four of us — in just a moment.

But he was not alone. At his side strode a human man, one who had been bent and shrill-voiced and wizened when last I had seen him. Now his back was straight, his shoulders were broad, and he wore the robes and cloak of a sun wizard.

Doyati, Yarri, Catri, Dan, and I had known him as Master Navan, doddering old fraud.

But he was no fraud. When some of the shambling creatures balked before the pinned-down moonroad, he raised a hand, and lightning — blue-white and crackling — ripped from his fingertips straight into them. Those creatures the lightning struck exploded in bits of fur and flesh and bone. The rest fled into the pinned moonroad as if it were their salvation.

"We have them trapped on a small island, pinned down by sun wizard ships. They won't escape this time," Master Navan said.

"You hope," Banris growled.

I felt myself starting to shake. I shivered and my knees buckled and I collapsed onto the shelf, landing facedown, banging and scraping my already-scraped knees and palms, and smashing my nose on the ground.

At some point earlier, my nose had stopped bleeding. It started again, and it throbbed, and I yelped. The noise in the ravine seemed to cover my cry of pain, but I did not know if Banris, the taandu monster who had once been my father's best friend and my honorary uncle, heard me. Or Master Navan, real and powerful sun wizard.

No one said anything. No one dared even think anything. Banris had proven able to speak into my mind and to haunt my dreams. And somehow, out of all the worlds I could have brought us to, I had brought us to the one where he was pushing an army into a moonroad. Navan had fooled us all — even the cat and Doyati — into thinking he was harmless.

If they found us within their reach, even with the dragon at our side, I did not think we would survive long.

Dan sat beside me and handed me my sweater, which he had somehow had the presence of mind to bring. I held it to my nose to stanch the bleeding and tried not to whimper from the pain. I would have to heal myself, if we lived long enough for me to get the chance. I had broken my nose. I could feel it crunching as I tried to find a way to hold the sweater to it that did not hurt.

But to use magic with Banris and Navan so close? No. Never that. I knew Banris could feel magic, and using it would be better than throwing myself at his feet to get his attention. I had no idea what Navan could do.

The ragged, ugly army poured forward. We held fast, with darkness, the ledge, and the noise below our only allies.

Everything hunted us. Everything hated us.

The men with the whips were below us, and then beyond us. And then Banris and Navan stalked beneath. I could have reached out and touched the horns on the top of Banris's head.

I did not allow myself to breathe, or to think, or to make

any sound or any movement. I did not look at him, at them, at anything around them. I noticed that the cat and dragon both had their eyes closed, and that Dan was staring fixedly at a red star overhead. I turned my eyes to the grass beneath my knees and counted blades, slowly and with great care.

Banris and Navan passed. They did not look up, they did not look back, and when they reached the moonroad, after what seemed a dozen lifetimes, they stepped into it and disappeared.

"I held a sword, and Banris was close, and I did not kill him," I murmured. I knew in the future I would regret that I had not.

"Your sword would not have killed him. But it would have killed us. We live," the cat said. "For the moment, be thankful for that. This is no time for regret or wishing. We will all wish him dead until he is dead. Don't waste your energy on such an obvious thing."

CHAPTER 24
UNEXPECTED MEETINGS

I looked at the dragon, who with the last of the army and Banris all gone, had straightened up. He was watching the monstrous clouds of bats that still dipped and swirled around us. I looked down at the cat, who was staring around him. And the dragon watched the bats, while his tongue darted in and out, tasting the air.

"What now?" I finally asked, for the cat did nothing but stare from the sky to the pillars where the moonroad had been until Banris went through it, to the ground, and back again.

The cat said, "This world is empty now of thinking creatures. Only animals and plants remain. This world lacks makers of magic. It lacks . . . finishing."

"Its lacks are an improvement, if you ask me," the dragon said. "No huntress. No ships-of-the-air. No eyes watching."

But that was not true. I had felt something watching us as we fell through the moonroad that brought us where we were, and I still felt watched. Something remained after all the thinking creatures, as the cat had called them, were gone.

"We aren't alone," I said.

The cat glanced at me. "Why do you say that?"

"We're being watched."

Dan said, "You feel that? I feel it, too."

The dragon jumped off the ledge, smacking one of his wings against the cliff behind us as he did. He snarled something and flapped wildly to get his balance and get himself back up in the air. The cat said, "Let's go the way he's going," and trotted away from the pillars that had held the moonroad. Dan and I followed.

The feeling of being watched stayed with me. We did not have to struggle, and the path we trod was easy enough — it had only been too narrow for the dragon, but that left a world of room for humans. The cool air and the darkness felt wonderful against my burned and blistered skin. Nothing made my nose feel better, though, and my head throbbed.

And I had to breathe through my mouth, which I hate. When we got off the ledge and to someplace where we would not be trapped if Banris came back, I would take the time to sit down and heal it. And while I was at it, the sunburns Dan and I had. I had never in my life imagined that the sun could be so . . . terrible.

I heard the bat wings flapping again, in droves and hordes, and then Dan pointed at the sky. "Look."

I looked. The dragon blasted through a cloud of huge bats with his mouth open. He scooped them out of the air, laughing.

At least one of us was having fun.

The ledge curved around the edge of the cliff, then started upward. Travel became harder then. It curved still more and became carved steps, awkwardly shallow and uncomfortably short, made for shorter feet and legs than mine.

The stairs narrowed. Looking down became terrifying, so I stopped doing it.

The cat kept going, and I could see that the dragon was circling above. I did not like climbing on a road built by hands and intent toward something I could not see. Built roads implied builders, not just meandering beasts, and builders built toward destinations. We had found nothing but grief in either humankind or the rest of the thinking universe lately, and I wanted nothing more than to hide away from builders of every sort for a while.

As we climbed, the feeling of being watched grew stronger. I wanted badly to turn back, but the dragon could see what was up there, and the cat had better ears than mine, and both of them were still going.

We reached the top, without warning. A little turn out of sight, three steps up, and suddenly the carved stairs became a place of delicate birch trees, bark white as snow, leaves the pale green that promised spring, and beneath them, the greenest, most even grass I had ever seen, dotted through with wildflowers. A broad path led beneath the trees, straight as truth, and at the end sat a fieldstone house with a tall, thatched roof. Waiting.

Watching.

The dragon waited until we were a ways up the path before he came swooshing in behind us.

"No room for me to take off here," he said. "No room to spread my wings."

"But you think this place is safe?" I asked. "Because I swear I feel it watching me. What if it is Banris's house? What if he has left someone behind?"

"Not to worry," the dragon said. "Neither the trees nor the path nor the house were here when Banris left. They weren't here until the three of you came around that last little curve on the stairway."

Which stopped me and Dan and the cat.

"And you don't think that's a problem?" the cat said to the dragon in a voice that dripped sarcasm.

The dragon said, "No one's here."

In front of the door, a woman who had not been there before said, "How rude. I'm someone."

Dan jumped and I covered my mouth with my hand, hitting my swollen nose in the process.

I knew her. Unlike Banris, I liked her. But I didn't trust her. She had snow-white hair, a bright and cheerful face, and the warmest smile anyone has ever seen. Her plump hands rested on round hips. She wore a green dress the color of the leaves on the birch trees, and she laughed out loud at our surprise.

When I first met her, she had been a filthy, wretched, twisted little woman in the smallest house in the world. Back then, she had been the audiomaerist. Through magic and luck — and with a little help from me — she had survived the attacks of Banris's cronies.

For my help, she had pinched me and said it was a gift.

"I thought," she said, "that you lot would never get here. The dragon won't fit in the house, but the rest of you will." She studied the cat. "*You,*" she said. "I can't believe you're still alive."

I forgot to mention that she had sent the cat with my brother and Yarri and me, back when we were trying to appease a kai-lord. That fact by itself would have been enough to keep me from completely trusting her.

"And *you*." She smiled at my brother. "You have been doing remarkable work."

He slid his hands behind his back and twisted them, and stared at his shoes. "You know what I've been doing?"

"People talk, and the roads listen," she said. "Don't be embarrassed, Danrith. I am saddened that the burden you and your sister face sits on the shoulders of children. But I have found in my very long life that sometimes the only people with the courage to act against the wrongs of the world are children — and that when children act, sometimes they win. You account yourselves well, you and Genna."

She glanced at the trees all around us, seeming to me to be lost in thought. Or memory. With a little start, she said, "But you are hungry and tired and hurting. And I have the cures for all of those things. And news. And . . . other things."

We followed her into the house. In my case, it was not without some misgivings.

The fieldstone house could not have been more different

from the hovel she had inhabited when I met her in the little village of Peevish.

The walls were of wood, whitewashed, with flowers and garlands painted along the borders. The floor, also wood, had been stone-rubbed, then painted, too. More flowers, right up along the baseboards. The windows in her house let in light and air — they were large, paned-glass affairs that would have left me speechless had I not spent time living in the Spire, where sheets of glass were big as walls, and walls of glass came in rainbow colors interlaced with metalwork. I still admired her windows, though. Being from a place where the few windows people had were either covered by oiled sheepskin or built with pieces of thick, lumpy glass no bigger than the palm of your hand, I am impressed by glass you can actually see through.

The house seemed to have many rooms — and in fact, seemed bigger on the inside than it had been on the outside. Not a new trick to me.

The audiomaerist led us back to a broad kitchen with beautiful glassed doors that led out onto a sort of porch-with-no-roof. We could see birch trees and part of the dragon, who seemed to have wrapped himself around a good portion of the outside of the house. He was stretched out like a big dog, lying mostly on his back with all four feet sticking up in the air, and the one eye we could see watching us.

In the center of the kitchen sat a sturdy round table and eight chairs. Evidently, in this world, the audiomaerist expected more company than she'd had in ours. A lacy white tablecloth covered it, and fresh flowers in a silver bowl sat in the center. On one of her counters, I saw an enormous glass jar full of what looked to me like the little sweet biscuits my mother sometimes made as a treat.

"Sit," she said. "Sit. I'll bring you food."

More than food, I wanted sleep. And an end to the pain in my head and nose and on my skin. I thought I had the energy to heal myself, and probably Dan, before I fell over from exhaustion.

But as she walked behind me, the audiomaerist touched me. The sunburn, the blisters, the swollen, broken nose, the skinned palms of my hands, the skinned knees — all were gone. And with them, my weariness was gone, too. I might have just woken on a perfect morning in my own bed back in Hillrush, with the tiny window open and sunlight streaming in.

I felt wonderful. I felt new.

She touched Dan, and for the quickest of blinks, he glowed. And then he was fine. Clear-eyed and awake, unburned and smiling.

"Thank you," he said.

I echoed his thanks.

"It was a small thing." She brought out pans and started cooking for us. Big chops of pork, eggs scrambled with bits of meat and vegetables in them, what we call hard bread, which is deep brown and very coarse, and steamed greens with diced fruit. Some of it was the sort of thing my mother made. I was not at all sure about the greens with fruit. Greens are bitter and I do not like them, though my mother always made me eat them.

The audiomaerist was making too much, though — enough for many more people than the three of us. The cat would eat a little. She could not even hope to make enough to feed the dragon.

Then I heard footsteps on stairs.

"There are others in the house?" I asked. My first thought was that Banris had returned and found a way past the dragon and into the house.

But Yarri came around the corner right after that, and I screamed, "Yarri!" and she screamed "Genna!" and while we were shrieking and hugging each other and dancing in circles in the kitchen — and while my brother sat looking thoughtfully at Yarri, I could not help but notice — I did not think of anything at all.

"You are alive!" I shouted.

"You as well!" she shouted back. Even at high volume, her voice was all bells and choirs. Just louder.

I did not realize I had grown until I hugged her, and her head was just at my chin. She was so thin I feared I would break her, but her squeeze was as hard as mine. She pulled back and studied me with those odd, all-green eyes, looking suddenly serious. Her yellow dandelion-puff hair waved around her face, a little longer than the last time I had seen her. I had forgotten how very not-human she was — when we spent time together, we were just friends and companions. But seeing her again — the pale yellow of her skin, the points of her ears, and the impossible delicacy of her face and bones — made her new to me and strange. I felt almost embarrassed by my reaction, as if I were some coarse, bumbling creature facing my better. But then, she had acted the fool greeting me, too.

"When your note came, I feared you had come to harm."

"I never sent you a note," she said.

"I know that now. Then Banris attacked the villages

around the Spire, and Papa said you and Doyati had vanished just after we did. I was sure you were dead." I was babbling. I knew it.

She hugged me again, hard, and then I did not care.

Yarri grabbed my hand and dragged me to the table, and we both sat down. I noticed that she took the seat beside Danrith, though there were many others open. And she grinned a little. "No. Not dead. Nearly. *She* found me when we were trapped." Yarri nodded at the audiomaerist.

"Master Navan found Doyati and told him you and Catri had been kidnapped. He sent Doyati to find me, telling him to get one vial of refined night taandu essence and the Staff of the Kai as ransom for your lives. He said he would meet Doyati and me at the ransom place — just outside a cave on the Fallowhalls level."

"I've been there," I said.

Yarri said, "It was where we were told you would be fed to the dragon if your kidnappers were not given their ransom."

Dan and I waited. Neither of us had heard any of this.

"Doyati found me, then gathered up the ransom — the Staff of the Kai is a mere symbol, with no official power and no magic, though it is very pretty and made of expensive materials. The refined night taandu essence was harder to come by. But he found that as well. And then we went to Fallowhalls, and to the cave mouth, and we were told by a mob there that an old human man had raced in at the sound of the screams of two human girls who had been dragged in and had not come back out.

"We heard the screams as well, so we ran in. Following the sounds of screaming, we fell into a trap. A mob of taandu monsters awaited us. They took the essence and the staff, and Doyati fought them with magic. But we were badly outnumbered, and they had magic of their own. Then *she* came and got us."

I heard more footsteps on the unseen stairs, and before I could ask Yarri anything, or she could say another word, Doyati ambled into the room, rubbing his eyes, yawning, his face and hair damp from his having just washed them. "I smelled food —" he started to say, and then he saw us.

"Oh, Spirit and little gods," he whispered.

And my heart went *thud, thud, thunk*.

No, he was not, would never be, as handsome as Jagan, the blue-eyed golden boy. Yes, though he looked my age, he was in truth a century older than me — or thereabouts. No, nothing could ever come of what I felt at that moment. Nothing.

But my cheeks burned and my hands hung on to each other for dear life, and I could not think of a word to say or even remember my name. I could barely breathe, my heart had risen so high in my throat. If I had forgotten how not-human Yarri was, I had also forgotten how . . . how . . . oh, there are no words for what Doyati was.

He was looking at me, staring, his eyes huge, and he said, "You're *here*." In the same voice a poor man would use if he fell into a field of gold and found out it was all his. *You're here*. I will never as long as I live ever, *ever* forget the sound of his voice as he said those two words.

"I am here," I agreed, and he ran over to me and picked me up out of the chair and spun me around as if I were as light as Yarri, hugging me and laughing.

And I hugged him back. I did. And I did not even feel sorry for doing it.

Such moments cannot last. He put me down, suddenly shy and awkward, and straightened his clothes to look presentable, and said to my brother, "We thought for sure she was dead when the dragon ate her. I cannot imagine how she could have survived."

And then he looked out the back and saw the dragon, and the expression of shock on his face was so comical that

Dan and I laughed, and Yarri laughed, and even the audiomaerist laughed.

He turned to her and said, "There are some things your roads did not tell you. Why could you not find where she was?"

The audiomaerist grinned. "Little Genna's feet never touched a road. But there are some things I did not tell you, either. She and Dan were in far more danger than either of them knows, and I could not go where they were to rescue them. A traitor with them could also hear what the roads said — if I told you what I knew, the roads would carry my words straight back to their enemy. Their enemy *could* go where they were. And I could not be sure they would survive."

"You did survive," Doyati said, looking at me and smiling.

I smiled back, feeling warm and fluttery inside. But that feeling passed. "The one who could hear the roads, the one who could reach us . . . was that Master Navan?" I asked her.

"Very good, Genna," she said.

"We saw him. He was here."

The audiomaerist nodded. "He has joined forces with Banris."

Doyati looked stunned. "That old fraud?"

The audiomaerist said, "He's a sun wizard, an ancient and tremendously powerful one — as dangerous as Banris, and with his own allies. But he is not an issue for today. He has taken a wrong turn, and he and Banris are not happy with each other. For now, we may celebrate."

I straightened my dirty blouse and skirt and sat down again knowing I still looked like something the cat would have turned up his nose at.

Yarri winked at me. And grinned.

Doyati leaned his head close to mine and whispered, "I intend to celebrate that you're alive and here."

With my heart doing little dances — for, oh, he had worried about me — I basked in my happiness. My mind ran in silly little circles. He had been so glad to see me. Me. Not because I was the Sunrider, but because I was me.

And he was safe. Yarri was safe. Dan and I were together, and free of the Spire. We had the cat, and the dragon, and the audiomaerist, and at that moment, all those seemed to me *good* things.

I returned Yarri's happy grin.

CHAPTER 25
ALL THAT REMAINS

The audiomaerist put food in front of all of us, and made a place for herself, and opened the doors so that the dragon could roll over and rest his head on her big wooden not-quite-a-porch.

She told him, "Food for you in a bit. We have bison and elk in plenty here, and you may have your fill. Once we've talked. "

The dragon said, "I'll be well enough. I ate a flock of your fat bats. I can wait a bit. (You need not wait. These are lesser creatures.) (Fly away and free yourself from her.)"

Ah. His voices were back.

"They're still with you, I see," she said. "Keep them in line, or I will." She returned her attention to those of us at the table. "I had not meant to tangle myself so thoroughly in your affairs. Truly, I had thought I would avoid all contact

356

with any of you, since the roads all whisper hideous strife and danger wherever your feet have tread or will tread. But the roads do speak, and they told me I could not abandon you. So, for a little while at least, you will be safe with me."

"Thank you," I said, and the other five — cat and dragon included — started to thank her, too.

She held up a hand to stop them. "This is not kindness. I am not kind. I am . . . expedient. Do you know what I mean by that?"

Doyati shrugged, but Yarri, Dan, and I shook our heads.

"I will explain. It does not fit my plans or my needs that humankind be destroyed. It does not fit my plans or my needs that nightlings, taandu monsters, and Moonworlders overrun the whole of the Sunworld, or that humans and nightlings and taandu monsters and Moonworlders remain slaves to the monsters that own them."

I must have made a little sound, for she turned her attention to me. "You think you will only unite humans and nightlings, my little Genna? The others act of their own free will in small things, as your people did when the nightlings owned them. In big things, they serve a multitude of lesser masters and a greater master they do not know.

"In any case, it does not fit my plans or my needs that this greater master of theirs owns the Sunworld."

"Banris," I whispered.

"Banris is a flea," she said. "Another unwitting slave."

"Oh." I tried to see him as a flea and a slave, but he still scared the socks off me.

The audiomaerist turned her attention to me. "You were in the Spire, and you succeeded in finding the silver door. And in getting inside, and in discovering what was there. What did you learn?"

"How did you know about the silver door?"

"Floors speak, too, and you have walked across my floor. So. What did you learn in the Spire, my Sunrider?"

I hung my head. "Not very much. A bit of language, a bit of magic, but not language I needed, and not magic I needed. I didn't learn to close moonroads, or to bring humans and nightlings together, or —"

She cut me off. "No. That's what you didn't learn. And frankly, I don't think these things were what you needed to learn from the Spire. Regardless of what you might have been told." And here she gave the cat a hard look.

I stood up. "Wait a minute. The dragon gave me a rhyme, and told me 'she' had told him to tell me to look for the silver door. And I'd had dreams about that exact door even in Arrienda. And the dragon came straight to you."

"Happenstance," she said, looking at the sweet biscuit in her hand.

The cat and Yarri and Dan and Doyati all looked from me to her, and back to me.

"I don't think so," I said.

"Happenstance," she repeated.

"Dragon," I said, turning to face him. "Did the audiomaerist tell you I would be coming? Did she have anything to do with you taking me to the Spire?"

"I have nothing I wish to talk about."

"I risked my life to free you, and I fixed your wing."

"And I am in your debt. Do you wish me to repay you with a single word and be forever after free of the considerable debt I owe?" The ridge of spines over his right eye rose up, then lowered again.

I considered it. "No."

"Wise," the dragon said.

And the audiomaerist told me, "If you're finished with your speculation, I asked you a question. What *did* you learn? What did you learn about the sun wizards, about humanity before the Fall, about the Spire, about the world as it once was?"

I sat there and thought. I thought carefully, because

there is no child alive who has not been tested by an adult over something or other, and the problem with these tests is, you always know adults want something, but you never know quite what.

"Do you mean the history? About the dragons and all?"

"No. What did you learn about the humans?"

"Oh." I took a deep breath. "It was all very pretty at first," I said. "Well, it was all very pretty even at the last. On the outside. But I . . ." I winced a little. "I did not like the Spire. It was always . . . watching. And the more I found out about it, the more I knew how much it watched. It was everywhere. And it took things about me that I did not want anyone to see and put them in its sheets — when I was afraid, when I was tired and dirty, when Catri did something she should not have. It did not ask, and she would have been horribly punished if her parents had found out about her kissing Jagan to wake him."

My brother, for just an instant, looked like he might cry. Then his face went stony.

I had forgotten that he had not known about that kiss.

The audiomaerist nodded. "Go on."

"The Spire kept everyone fed and clothed. And safe, I suppose, though the dragons figured out a way around that right before the Fall. But there is only one dragon left, so I do not suppose that will happen again." I stared down at my plate, covered with good food that someone had cooked for me, and I realized that it had tasted better than anything I had eaten in the Spire. "I loved the ships-of-the-air — they were so beautiful, and flying in them was wonderful. I loved the beds — they were soft and warm. And the water that was always just the right temperature. I loved that. And when humans owned the world, the roads and the open fields and the beautiful, colorful cities full of people off in the distance were . . . wonderful."

She was watching me. "But . . ."

"But humans lost. They had all of that and they had their sun wizards and their sun wizard magic and their ships-of-the-air. They had everything. They ruled everything." I wanted to stop. I did not want to say the next thing that came to my lips, for it was questioning adults and adult wisdom, and for all that my village had made me an adult, at that moment I did not feel like one. I felt fourteen and certain I was about to get myself in trouble.

But she sat there. Silent. Waiting.

And I blurted out, "And what I keep wondering is, they had everything — power and magic and so many people — and if all of that could not save humanity from the Fall, how can you hope it will save them now?"

"I don't," she said simply. "Let me tell you, my little Sunrider, the full scope of the task that awaits you — and these, your friends and allies, without whom all the voices I hear say you cannot survive. I have sought long and hard for the answer. We knew at the end you would have to battle the enemy of humanity. *We*," she added, "being me and those few like me who are left, and who are not actively working to bring chaos."

"Like Agara? The huntress," my brother asked.

"Very good," the audiomaerist said.

I ate my food in silence. I wondered again what, exactly, the audiomaerist and the huntress were, but perhaps she would tell me.

"You have a task I do not envy. The nightlings built the magic that made roads between places in your world — the real world, the Sunworld — and all the realms of What If possible. These are the moonroads. But What If is a twilight state that burns away in the full sun, so nightlings used the power of the moon to fuel these roads and to keep them always in twilight."

"Oh," I said. That answered one question I had — why the nightworld was always dark.

"Their spelling seemed to have no consequences at first,

and the nightlings were able to travel by day for the first time, so long as they had a shadowed place where moonlight could fall.

"But the magic was twisting things, changing things. Beyond the veil of the Sunworld, there were . . . possibilities. Worlds that had not been born but could have been. And the nightling magic reached through the veil with its roads and woke the possibilities into being. Worlds that might have been became worlds that are — but they are unfinished, trapped in perpetual dark.

"The creatures that live in them, the beings that think and hope and dream within them, fade closer to real, and then farther from it, with each phase of the moon. They are vulnerable to the whims of those, like you, who are fully real, who can withstand the light of the sun. They can be changed by the will and power of those who can walk the roads and who wish to change them — and almost always, those who wish to change them do not mean well."

"Banris," I said.

"You saw the creatures he herded out of here — the army he built from unthinking beasts that he stretched into barely thinking creatures with his magic."

Dan and I nodded.

"I hid us away while he was here. This world has been a hiding place of mine from time to time, and I like it. I did not want to abandon it, and I knew he would do what he had come to do, and then he would leave. He has gone to many of the twilight worlds to create his armies."

I shivered.

"You," she said, "*all* of you, hold the fate of these almost-worlds and everything in them in your hands." She sat with her head bowed for a moment. "You could, of course, simply find a way to close the moonroads. That would end the damage the taandu monsters and the twisted Moonworlders could do to the Sunworld, and would greatly weaken the nightlings. That would be the easiest course of action, though it will not be easy."

"But . . ." I said. "The easy way is almost never the right way."

"Exactly." She laughed just a little and raised her head to look at me. "But if you can find a way to meld the magic you know, the magic the sun wizards knew, and the magic the nightlings use, and if you can defeat the enemy who seeks to own the whole of the sun and its power for itself, then you can bring the sun to these worlds. The roads you walk will change in nature, and the worlds will become fully real. And those who live and love and think in those worlds — and everything around them — will cease to be vulnerable to the walkers of the moonroads. They will become fully real, they will become what they *can* be, and what they *choose* to be. They will not perish."

Choice again. My destiny was choice, and my destiny was to give choice to others.

"Who is the enemy we have to fight?" I asked.

"There are too many to name, but they all serve one. That one you cannot know."

I closed my eyes. "But everything else depends on that."

"No. Everything else depends on you staying blissfully ignorant of that one truth until you have paved the path for the sun to shine through."

I nodded, but I closed my eyes. It was no small task she asked of me — to trick an unknown enemy, to beat Banris. It was no small task — to find a way to unite enemies and save a city, or a country, or a world.

She told me that what I had to do was nothing short of the impossible. I and the friends and companions who were with me had to bring the sun itself to uncounted worlds.

She patted me on the arm.

"Look at the happy side," she said. "Banris will never

return here, and you have your friends with you. And until you're ready to move on, I'll cook for you."

And she winked.

At that moment, I had two choices. I could have cried. Or I could have laughed.

I laughed.

ACKNOWLEDGMENTS

Heartfelt thanks to my editor, Lisa Sandell, whose incredible support and encouragement made writing this book such fun.

To my agent, Robin Rue, who found these books such a wonderful home.

To Joshua Middleton, my cover artist, who has twice now blown me away with his vision of my world.

To Phil Falco, my book designer, who made the books beautiful in uncountable ways.

To my beta readers, Lyn Ratliff, Heather Clow, Pamela Templin, and Don Poort, whose suggestions and comments made revision a clear sky instead of a twisting path.

And to my readers, those who have been with me for more than seventeen years now, those who have just found me, and all of you in between. Thank you especially for giving me the chance to tell you stories.

AUTHOR'S NOTE

I never intended to be a writer when I was a kid. I was pretty sure I was going to be a famous artist. And when I got my first guitar at the age of fifteen, I decided I'd also be a famous musician.

I actually gave both a shot, in between working at a newspaper and working at McDonald's and eventually becoming an RN. I discovered that, though I liked to draw, I didn't like to draw for money. And though I loved to sing and play guitar, I simply wasn't good enough.

Some dreams change, and some fade away when you actually try them and discover they aren't what you thought they would be, or could be.

But new dreams wait. For me, writing was a new dream. I didn't go looking for it. It found me, and it's a dream — and a reality — that has only gotten better with time.

For Genna, the narrator of the Moon & Sun stories, the lifelong dream she had of becoming a yihanni like her mother got lost when men and monsters alike told her she was the Sunrider. Now she's trying to understand her new path, and to discover if anywhere in the life of a Sunrider there's a dream that she can catch and hold . . . and make come true.

Dare to dream. Dare to chase the dreams you love.

— Holly Lisle, Thursday, September 4, 2008

ABOUT
THE AUTHOR

Holly Lisle is a native of Salem, Ohio, but she's also lived in Alaska, Costa Rica, and Guatemala. She is the author of many bestselling adult suspense and fantasy novels, as well as the children's novel Moon & Sun Book I: *The Ruby Key,* also published by Orchard Books. She has three children, a handful of cats, and believes writing is the best job a person can have. She currently resides in the Deep South, with her family.